April's gaze lingered on the word *brother,* then flickered
to her real name. She was an only child, and she'd gone
by one alias or another forever. So what was the story?
And more important, how dangerous would it be to try
to find out?

All she really knew was that the "212" area code meant
that whoever had placed the ad was right here in
New York. And given the "collect," he likely had no idea
where she was.

How many people would read the ad and recognize her
name? Would wonder why someone wanted to get hold
of her badly enough to put an ad in the *Times?* And if
someone from the FBI noticed it and decided it was
worth following up on...

Or maybe it was the feds who'd placed it.

She'd have to phone to make sure.

ABOUT THE AUTHOR

With sixteen Superromance novels under her belt, Dawn Stewardson is a longtime contributor to the line. Writing everything from madcap comedies to romantic suspense, she adds special touches to each and every one of her stories. Sometimes it's her love of animals; sometimes it's the research from a recent trip. But it's always interesting!

Dawn and her husband live in Toronto, Ontario.

Books by Dawn Stewardson

HARLEQUIN SUPERROMANCE

HARLEQUIN INTRIGUE

THE WANT AD
Dawn Stewardson

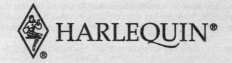

HARLEQUIN®

TORONTO • NEW YORK • LONDON
AMSTERDAM • PARIS • SYDNEY • HAMBURG
STOCKHOLM • ATHENS • TOKYO • MILAN • MADRID
PRAGUE • WARSAW • BUDAPEST • AUCKLAND

ISBN 0-373-70795-9

THE WANT AD

THE WANT AD

CHAPTER ONE

THE WANT AD WAS too disquieting for April to ignore, yet each time she read it, a creepy-crawly feeling slithered up her spine.

Deep down, she knew she should simply bury the entire classifieds section in the center of the recycling pile. But her curiosity wouldn't let her. What harm could it do to just call the number and find out who'd placed the ad? And what he was after?

Curiosity killed the cat, she reminded herself. When she'd been growing up, her mother must have told her that a million times. Still, she couldn't keep her eyes from straying to those four lines again. *Anyone knowing the whereabouts of Jillian Birmingham, born St. Vincent's Hospital, June 22, 1968, please call her brother collect 212-555-1427.*

Her gaze lingered on the word *brother*, then flickered to her real name. She was an only child, and she'd gone by one alias or another forever. So what was the story? And more important, how dangerous would it be to try to find out?

She glanced at the ad yet again, wishing she was one of those people who did the crossword with her Sunday morning coffee. But she preferred reading the Personals because, usually, some of the ads made her smile. Not this morning, though.

Wandering into her tiny galley kitchen, she poured the last of the coffee and considered phoning her parents to see what they thought—then quickly rejected the idea. Even after all these years, every contact with them carried a risk. Besides, she was a pro at being careful. If she did call that number, she wouldn't make any mistakes. She only wished the ad told her more than it did.

All she knew was that the "212" area code meant that whoever had placed it was right here in New York City. And given the "collect," he likely had no idea where she was. Considering the distribution of the *New York Sunday Times,* though, he was casting a nation-wide net—a most unsettling thought. How many people would read the ad and recognize her name? Would wonder why someone wanted to get hold of her badly enough to put an ad in the *Times?* And if someone from the FBI noticed it and decided it was worth following up on...

Or maybe it was the feds who'd *placed* it. Maybe, for some reason or another, they'd decided to take a fresh stab at finding her parents and were trying to use her to do it.

That was a possibility she couldn't rule out. Even so, by the time she finished the dishes, her curiosity was overcoming her caution.

But she'd have to go out to phone. She'd barely plugged her cell phone in to recharge, so it was out of commission. And she couldn't use her apartment's line in case whoever she was phoning had Caller ID. If he got her number, locating her would be a piece of cake.

Her heart racing just a little, she ripped the ad from

the paper and headed out of her apartment, down the old brownstone's three flights of stairs and along West Seventy-fifth to Bennie's Deli. As she opened the door, she told herself that if the pay phone was in use, she'd take it as an omen. When she saw it was free, her pulse skipped a beat.

"Yo, April," Bennie called from behind the counter.

"Hey, Bennie." She manufactured a smile and continued toward the back, half hoping there'd be an out-of-order sign on the phone. She'd take that as an omen, too.

But there was no sign, and when she picked up the receiver she heard a dial tone.

Trying to convince herself she was only sweating because it was a hot July day, she fished a quarter from the pocket of her shorts.

Then, praying she wasn't doing something irreparably foolish, she dropped it into the slot and punched in the number.

It rang once…twice…three times. She was just deciding that if no one answered she wouldn't call again, when a man picked up.

"Paul Gardiner," he said.

He had a deep, mellow voice and sounded somewhere in his thirties. Fighting the urge to hang up without saying a word, she took a deep breath and said, "Hello. I'm calling about your ad."

There was a heartbeat's silence before he said, "Jillian?"

"Yes, but if you're really looking for your sister, I'm not the right Jillian. I don't have a brother."

"And I don't have a sister. But I needed something to make you call, and I hoped the 'brother' bit would make you curious.''

She exhaled slowly, awarding the first point to him. ''All right, I've called. What do you want?''

''To talk to you. In person.''

She realized her hands were trembling and told herself to relax. She didn't have to talk to him ''in person'' if she didn't want to, and nothing terrible was going to come from just this phone call.

''Who are you?'' she said.

''My name's Paul Gardiner, and I'm a writer.''

Alarm bells began going off in her head. ''I see. Well, I don't have anything to say to a writer, so—''

''Wait. Please. Wherever you're living, I can fly there to see you. It's essential we meet.''

''It's not essential to me.''

''Yes, it is. This is about your parents.''

That came as no surprise, and it almost made her hang up. But before she could, he was saying, ''We can get together wherever you want. Whenever's convenient for you. I don't have to know exactly where you live or what name you go by. I—''

''No. I'm sorry, but—''

''I have evidence that your father's not guilty. That he was set up.''

Her heart stopped for an instant, then began to pound. There couldn't be evidence. Not after so much time had passed. But what if there was? ''What sort of evidence?''

''I can't discuss that over the phone. I can't risk anyone finding out about it. No one except you and your parents.''

''Look, if you think you can get to them through

me, forget it. I'm not in contact with them. I haven't been for years." Lies, of course, but he wouldn't know that. She'd been taught to lie as soon as she'd learned to speak; she was very good at it.

"Whether you're in touch with them or not, it's critical we get together. What I've learned could give them back their freedom."

She closed her eyes, hearing her father's voice. *Never trust a stranger, darling. Our lives depend on that.*

"Jillian?" Paul Gardiner said quietly. "Just meet me and hear what I have to say. Half an hour, that's all I'm asking for."

"I'll think about it," she said at last. "And if I decide to see you, I'll call back."

EITHER THE COFFEE at La Guardia was among the city's worst or it was April's nerves that had her stomach upset. Probably a combination, she decided.

Taking a final sip from the cardboard cup, she dropped it into a waste container and uneasily glanced around once more, telling herself there was no reason to be this nervous.

She'd given herself a few days to think things through, hadn't called Gardiner back until yesterday. Then she'd told him she'd do the flying, that all he had to do was meet her at the airport. And she'd gotten here two hours ago, so there wasn't a chance he'd realize she'd arrived by taxi from the Upper West Side, not by plane from another part of the country.

She checked her watch, then looked over at the

Budget car rental counter again. This time, he was standing next to it.

Her mouth suddenly dry, she stood gazing at him. Not even a close inspection would tell her whether she could trust him, but it never hurt to size people up before meeting them.

He was a little over six feet tall, with dark hair and eyes—just as he'd described himself—and was wearing the jeans and blue T-shirt he'd told her to watch for. His features were even, yet rugged. His eyebrows were pronounced, his hair just long enough that it curled a little at the ends, and he had a five o'clock shadow that emphasized his strong jaw line.

Objectively speaking, he was a very attractive man. Subjectively speaking, just looking at him was scaring the devil out of her.

While she was gathering the courage to approach him, he glanced over and saw her watching him. The way he held her gaze made her even more anxious. Forcing herself to start moving, she walked toward the rental counter.

"Jillian?" he said when she stopped in front of him.

She nodded.

"Thanks for coming. I wasn't sure you would."

"I wasn't, either."

He smiled at that. It was a warm smile, but it made her no less uneasy.

"Where would you like to talk?" he asked. "My car's in the lot, if you want to get out of the airport."

"No, here's fine. I noticed a coffee shop that'll do."

When she turned and started down the concourse,

Paul followed along, warning himself that if he came on too strong he'd scare her off for sure. She had no reason to trust him, and she was clearly nervous as hell.

They reached their destination and found a relatively quiet table. A waitress with a coffeepot materialized the moment they sat down, and while she filled two mugs, he surreptitiously eyed Jillian.

He knew virtually nothing about her, not where she lived or what she did or even what name she went by. The lack of a ring suggested she wasn't married, but it wasn't a surefire indicator.

None of that mattered, though. The important thing was who her parents were, and just looking at her left no doubt about that—about who her mother was, at least. He'd viewed a lot of film with Colin and Mary Birmingham in it—every bit the network's archives contained—and Jillian looked a lot like her mother.

Oh, her dark hair was short, while Mary's, in those 1960s shots, hung down well past her shoulders. But Jillian had her mother's tall, slender build, as well as the same enormous dark eyes, high cheekbones and full mouth that he'd seen in the old news footage.

"So," she said, wrapping her hands around her mug. "You have evidence that my father's not guilty."

"Right." It might not precisely qualify as evidence, but she'd never have met with him if he'd told her it was only hearsay. And with any luck, by the time she realized that's all it was, she'd have already decided to cooperate.

"And the details are…?"

"It might be a good idea to tell you a couple of other things first."

He took a sip of coffee, buying himself a few seconds and wishing he could think of a way of easing into this without spooking her even more. He couldn't, though, so he'd just have to hope that she didn't bolt before he had a chance to explain everything.

"On the phone, I said I was a writer," he began. "But I want to tell you exactly what I do. It'll probably raise your anxiety level, but I don't want you to think I'm trying to hold anything back, okay?"

She nodded.

"All right." He dug his wallet from his jeans and flipped it open to his staff ID. "I'm an investigative journalist with NBS. Primarily, I put together stories for 'Today's World.'"

For a moment she simply gazed at the card, then she pushed back her chair. "I've heard enough."

"No, wait. This has nothing to do with the show. I just wanted to be up front about my job. But I'm writing a book. On my own time. And it was while I was doing research for it that I learned your father was set up."

"I see. And your book's about... Let me take a wild guess. The war in Vietnam? With emphasis on the antiwar movement?"

"No."

"Oh? Then why did your research have anything to do with my father?"

Taking another sip of coffee, he tried to decide if telling her the entire truth would be a really dumb move.

"Look," he said at last. "Almost nobody knows I'm even working on a book, and absolutely nobody knows what it's about. So can I assume you'll keep it a secret if I tell you?"

She gave him a sardonic look. "I have a lifetime's experience in keeping secrets."

"Yes…I imagine you have." He felt a sudden pang of sympathy. She'd been barely two years old when her parents had gone underground, so she must have had one hell of a weird upbringing.

"I just didn't want to take any chances," he explained, "because the FBI's not going to like my book. And since friendly contacts are helpful in my job, the longer I can go without anyone at the bureau getting wind of it, the better."

"Why won't they like it?"

"Because it's about major crimes they've never solved. And known criminals they've never captured."

April gazed across the table, anger spreading like dry heat through her body.

"I see," she said, barely able to keep her voice low. "So you're interested in my father because of his 'known but never captured' status. Well, let me tell you something. He isn't a known criminal. He's a man the feds charged with a crime he didn't commit. Both my parents were totally against violent protests.

"But that's not what you wanted to hear me say, is it. And I'll bet you don't have any evidence of my father's innocence at all. You were just hoping I'd give you a few juicy tidbits for your book. Well, you can—"

"No, listen. I assume you know all the details about the bombing, but—"

"Yes, I do," she interrupted, cutting off the rest of his words. The last thing she wanted was a rehash of the bombing.

Her parents had told her the entire gruesome story as soon as she'd been old enough to understand it. And later, as a teenager, she'd read and reread every painful article written about it—so often that it took no effort at all to see them in her mind's eye.

The earliest headlines screamed things like: Anti-war Radicals Bomb Napalm Factory! Protestors Murder Seven Innocent People!

The texts of those articles detailed how AWV— Americans for Withdrawal from Vietnam—was responsible for bombing the Unique Technologies factory in an attempt to halt production of napalm that was allegedly being dropped on Vietnamese civilians.

Follow-up articles quoted various AWV members—all of whom told a different story. Some denied the bombing was an AWV protest at all. Others claimed it had gone wrong. That the bomb was intended to go off at night, when the factory was empty. That its exploding while workers were there was an unfortunate accident.

Still later articles refuted this claim, stating that the FBI's investigation showed the incident hadn't "gone wrong," that the timer had been set to go off when it did. And while those stories were front-page news, her father was warned that two other AWV members had named him as the bomber.

It was a lie, of course. But true or not, their testimonies would have sent him to prison for the rest of his life. So, despite his innocence, the Birminghams had disappeared.

After that, the press had gone to town printing lies about him, fueled by the theory that an innocent man would have stayed to defend himself, that only the guilty ran. They'd convicted him in print to sell their papers, when all he'd been guilty of was not believing that justice would prevail if he was arrested.

"Jillian?" Paul said, bringing her back to the moment. "Look, I'm sorry I upset you. I really am. And I'm not after juicy details for my book. I honestly did learn something that says your father's innocent. Do you want me to tell you about it?"

She exhaled slowly. Possibly this man was sincere. Just as possibly, he was trying to con her. But until she figured out which it was, she had to listen.

"SO WHEN I TRACKED DOWN the men who pointed the finger at your father," Paul continued, "they—"

"Who are they?" April asked. Finally, she was going to get the answer to that question—unless Paul refused to tell her.

If he did, she'd be out of here. If he wasn't going to trust her, there was no way in the world she'd even consider trusting him.

"Their names were never mentioned in the paper," she added when he looked at her curiously. "I read all the coverage I could find about the bombing. Years and years ago."

He nodded. "The feds can usually keep the names of their sources from the press, unless too many people know who they are."

"Well, at least a few people must have known who those two were, because somebody told my parents. They never really talked to me about them, though."

"No?"

She shook her head. "They told me what they had to, enough to explain why we were underground. But all I know about those two men is that they couldn't have been directly involved in the bombing themselves—that they both had alibis. And that they probably weren't even in on the planning, because they were followers, not leaders."

"Do you know why your parents didn't tell you more?"

"Not for sure. But I think they were worried that I might try playing V. I. Warshawski someday and get us all in trouble."

He smiled—another warm smile that bracketed his eyes with laugh lines. "Well, their names are Tom Walker and Ken Gutteridge."

"And where are they now?"

That made him hesitate, but she couldn't tell if it was because he was deciding how much he should confide in her or if he was about to lie.

"Walker's in Connecticut," he said at last. "In Bridgeport. Gutteridge fled to Canada to avoid the draft and he's still there—a place called Port Credit, which is more or less a suburb of Toronto."

"And you talked to them by phone or in person?"

"I went to see both of them."

"And exactly how did you track them down?"

"You know, if you'd lived back in fifteenth-century Spain, they'd have offered you a job with the Inquisition.''

Forcing herself to smile, she gave him credit for having a sense of humor. But putting people at ease probably got him a lot of information, and she wanted to be the one getting answers right now.

''I'll try not to ask too many more questions,'' she promised. ''But was it hard to locate them?''

''Not really. These days, once you have a name you can usually do the tracking part electronically.''

She didn't comment on that, but she knew he was right. The Internet had turned information retrieval into a whole new ball game. ''And you initially got their names by…?''

''Well, the files on the bombing are stored at the bureau's New York field office.''

She nodded. That made sense, since the factory hadn't been far from New York City.

''And I know one of the agents there fairly well. He gave me their names.''

A chill ran down her spine. ''You told a special agent you were interested in the case? But didn't he wonder why? What if it made him think—''

''Hey, not a month goes by that I don't ask him about one case or another. It wouldn't have raised any flags.''

She sincerely hoped that was true, because she doubted it would take much to make the feds start actively searching for her father again.

The bureau was like a bulldog. Once it sank its teeth into something major, it never let go. And she was certain her father was still something major. After all, the Napalm Bomber, as they'd dubbed him, had spent years on their Most Wanted list. And even though they'd eventually taken his name off, as far as they were concerned, he'd murdered seven people.

Turning her thoughts back to Walker and Gutteridge, she said, "So you talked to these men who claimed my father was the bomber and…?"

"Well, things went pretty much the same with both of them. I said I was doing research for 'Today's World'—for a retrospective segment on the antiwar movement. And we talked about AWV for a while, then we got specifically onto the Unique bombing.

"When I asked how they'd known that Colin Birmingham was the bomber, neither of them wanted to talk about it at first. They were both pretty upset that I knew they were the ones who'd told the feds. But after I assured them 'Today's World' wouldn't reveal their names, they came around."

"And how did they say they knew it was my father?"

"They gave me the same story they'd given the FBI back in 1970—claimed they'd been drinking with him the night before and he'd told them what he was planning."

"But that's absurd! You're saying the feds actually believed that someone planning a bombing would be stupid enough to talk about it? Did *you* believe it?"

"Well," he said slowly, "it wouldn't have been the first time a guy said things he shouldn't when he'd been drinking. And Walker and Gutteridge were pretty convincing. I didn't get the sense that either of them was lying."

"But the feds must have talked to other AWV people."

Paul nodded. "According to my contact, special agents questioned every member of the group they could identify."

"And did anyone else claim my father was the bomber?"

"No, nobody else said they had any idea who it was."

"So, convincing or not, Walker and Gutteridge were lying."

"Actually, Walker eventually told me they were."

For a moment, she simply looked across the table at him in stunned silence. "I thought they both told you my father was the bomber," she said at last.

"They did the first time around, which was months ago. But a couple of weeks back, Walker called and said he wanted to talk to me again. And when we got together the second time, he'd changed his story—claimed he and Gutteridge had only said your father was responsible to protect the man who actually was."

"Oh, my Lord," she whispered. This was the sort of information she'd been praying would surface for as long as she could remember. "And who *was* responsible?"

"Unfortunately, Walker wouldn't go so far as telling me that. And when I flew up and talked to Gutteridge a second time, he stuck to his original story— said he didn't know what Walker was up to, but that your father definitely was the bomber."

She hadn't realized how high her hopes had soared until those words brought them crashing down.

"Jillian...look, I know Walker's admission isn't rock-solid evidence, but it's a starting point."

"A starting point?" she repeated numbly. "When you told me you had evidence, I thought you meant... But why did he even talk to you a second time? Why tell anyone the truth after almost thirty years?"

"Because he discovered he has inoperable cancer. And apparently he's always felt guilty about destroying your parents' lives. He didn't want to go to his grave with that on his conscience."

She merely shook her head. He *had* destroyed their lives, so what good was confessing at this late date?

"Did he talk to the FBI?" she asked at last. "Or only to you?"

"Only to me. But he let me tape our conversation on the understanding I wouldn't contact the authorities until after he was dead. I also convinced him to sign a written statement."

"But that's not enough, is it? Especially not with Gutteridge sticking to his story."

"No. It's not enough."

"Then what earthly good is it?"

"Well, as I said, it's a starting point."

"For trying to learn who the bomber really was?"

He nodded.

"You think that might be possible? After all this time?"

"It might be. That's why I had to meet with you. Because if you could help me get something more..."

"How?"

He was silent for a long moment, then said, "My

contact tells me the list of AWV members in the bureau's files is enormous. Even if he gave me the names, it would be impossible for one person to follow up on all of them. But your father must have some idea who the real bomber might have been. And if I could talk with him, if he gave me a solid place to start..."

If he could talk with her father. She'd been almost certain that's what he was after. "I told you over the phone that I'm not in contact with my parents."

"I know. But I figured if you really had to reach them you could."

"Even if I could, I can't imagine my father would actually talk to you. A list of names might be a possibility, but nothing more."

"If you'd at least ask him about a phone call, Jillian... I'm an investigative journalist. Sometimes by asking questions, I learn things that nobody would have thought to mention."

She let that pass. The idea of her father talking to someone who made his living by ferreting out information made her blood run cold. And she hadn't forgotten, not for a second, that Paul Gardiner could easily be a special agent. Even if he'd officially worked at NBS for years, it might only be a cover. She simply couldn't risk trusting him. Not when he might actually be trying to set a trap.

But what if he was telling the truth?

"What do you think?" he pressed.

She thought she was in an impossible situation, one she simply didn't know how to handle. Staring down at the table, she decided the only thing to do was keep him talking and try to trip him up.

That probably wouldn't be easy, but she'd developed her personal "lie detector" to the point that few people could fool her for long. And she had to try something. If he really was what he claimed to be, and if she rejected his suggestion, she might be rejecting the only chance she'd ever had to—as he'd put it—give her parents back their freedom.

"Tell me about yourself," she said, looking over at him.

The question clearly surprised him. "What do you want to know?"

Whether I can trust you, she silently replied.

"There's a chance I could contact my parents," she said aloud, "although it would take time. But before I even think of trying, I need to know more about you."

He gave her a self-conscious smile. "All right. I'm thirty-three. I studied journalism at Columbia and started working at NBS right after I graduated. I've never been married. I came close once, but we both realized it would be a mistake. I have an apartment in Tribeca.... You know New York?"

The question was slipped in so casually that she couldn't tell if he was trolling for information.

"I've only been here a couple of times," she lied.

"Well, Tribeca's toward the south end of Manhattan—basically south of Greenwich Village and SoHo. At any rate, have you heard enough details, or should I go on?"

"Keep talking." Thus far, neither his words nor his body language had told her much.

"Okay, my father died when I was a little kid."

He hesitated, only for an instant, but long enough that the statement was probably true.

"My mother remarried when I was eleven, and she and my stepfather live in Queens with my two half brothers. I play squash, go white-water rafting whenever I get the chance.... And I guess that's it—unless there's something you were specifically wondering about."

"Actually, there is. The book you're writing. What made you choose my father as one of your 'known criminals'?"

When he suddenly looked uneasy, she went on red alert.

"I'm not really sure," he said. "I was just curious about the bombing. And I figured it would be interesting to look into."

She didn't buy that for a second. "I think there's more to it than that." She caught his gaze and didn't let it go.

"All right...I didn't mention this before because it's still only a possibility. But after what Walker told me, I started thinking that maybe your father's story is too important to be merely a chapter in the FBI book. I mean, if I could learn who was actually responsible for that bombing—prove your father was wrongly accused, after he's spent more than half his life in hiding...

"I know it's a big if, but if I could uncover the real facts, the story should be written as a stand-alone true crime book." He paused, then shrugged. "I figure it's worth my spending some time on, because if I could learn the truth, your father would be looking at his freedom, and according to my agent, I'd be looking at a bestseller. Everyone would win. Except the real bomber.''

''And the feds. They'd hardly be happy if an exposé about one of their mistakes ended up on the *Times*' bestseller list.''

''Right. Which gets us back to why I don't want them learning what I'm up to just yet.''

April considered everything for a minute, then said, ''You didn't exactly answer my question. I can see how your thinking about the book would change after Walker told you my father wasn't guilty. But you still haven't explained why you chose him as one of your subjects in the first place.''

A silence stretched between them.

''You're asking me to take a big risk,'' she pressed. ''And there's no way I'll even consider that if I figure you're not being totally honest with me.''

''All right,'' he said slowly. ''I'll tell you why I was initially interested. But you're not going to like it.''

''Try me.''

He eyed her for a few seconds, then shrugged again. ''My father was a manager at Unique Technologies. He was one of the seven people that bomb killed.''

CHAPTER TWO

PAUL'S WORDS ECHOED in April's mind, giving her an eerie sense of the past reaching ghostly fingers into the present.

When she looked at him again, he was watching her, his dark eyes unreadable.

"I'm sorry," she murmured.

"It was a long time ago."

She forced her gaze from his and stared at the table once more. This added yet another complicating wrinkle to the picture. At first she'd only been worried that Paul Gardiner might be an undercover agent. Now she also had to worry that he might be exactly who he claimed he was—but with a hidden agenda.

What if his real interest lay in avenging his father's death? And what if, regardless of everything he'd told her, he was certain her father was the bomber? For all she knew, Tom Walker hadn't made any near-deathbed confession. Maybe Paul had never even talked to Walker or Gutteridge. And the story about writing a book could be a total fabrication, nothing but a creative ploy to get to her father.

As if reading her mind, he said, "I didn't mention revenge, but I guess there's no denying it's a factor. I've always wanted to see my father's killer brought

to justice. And if your father wasn't the one responsible... Well, if you help me learn who actually was,
you'll be helping clear his name.''

"Did you tell Walker and Gutteridge your father
was one of the victims?"

"No. I played things as cool as I could. I suppose
that if either of them recalled the names, they'd have
realized one of them was Gardiner. But neither of
them said anything, so I doubt they remembered.''

Exhaling slowly, she tried to organize her
thoughts. She simply had no way of knowing
whether it was safe to trust this man. And that being
the case, she wasn't sure she should even tell her
parents about him. What if she did and her father
decided he'd talk to him? And then it turned out Paul
was a fed? And he managed to figure out where her
parents were living from something her father said?
Lord, she didn't even want to consider that possibility.

And even if he wasn't after anything but the truth,
so many years had passed that there'd be only the
slimmest chance of establishing the real bomber's
identity.

Weighing the pros and cons, she realized she
should probably just walk away. But as long as there
was a possibility that Paul was telling the truth, she
didn't see how she could.

"I'm having some problems with this," she said
at last. "After all these years of believing my father
was the bomber, you suddenly decided he wasn't?
Based on nothing more than Walker's say-so?"

"No, there's more. What he said started me digging, but after I'd looked into things a little... Well,
aside from the statements that he and Gutteridge gave

the feds, the bureau actually didn't have much evidence. There's a bit of circumstantial stuff, but it's about as solid as cheesecloth. And the only other thing is that your parents took off—which the feds and the press jumped on as an admission of guilt."

"It wasn't. It was pure self-preservation."

He nodded. "I can see how it could have been. And no matter which way I looked at things, I kept coming back to the fact that what Walker said rang true. That he decided to tell the truth to assuage his guilt."

"But Ken Gutteridge says it's not the truth."

"Well, we know one of them's got to be lying. And my gut feeling is that it's Gutteridge."

Maybe that was his gut feeling, but maybe it wasn't.

Thinking she'd give just about anything to be certain what he really believed and what he was really after, she said, "I'd like to hear the tape of Walker's confession. And see the statement he signed."

"Of course. I figured you would, so I've got copies of them in my car."

"Good." But were they copies of the genuine items or were they fakes?

"How much longer before your flight leaves?" he asked, glancing at his watch.

"I left the return open."

He dug some ones from his pocket, put them on the table and pushed back his chair.

April followed him out of the coffee shop and they started through the terminal. They'd walked about fifty yards when someone called, "April?"

She didn't miss a step, but her stomach began to

churn. In a city the size of New York, you almost never ran into anyone you knew. So why today, of all days?

"April?" he called again. "April Kelly?"

She kept on walking. But Brett Carlson did the legal work for her company, and unless she was very lucky, he wasn't going to decide he had the wrong person.

A moment later, he was right beside her and impossible to ignore.

"I thought it was you," he said. "How have you been?"

"Fine. Just fine, thanks. And you?"

Her gaze flickered to Paul. So much for her thorough planning and her out-of-towner cover. Now that he'd learned what name she was using, he could find out practically anything he wanted to about her.

"Terrific," Brett was saying. "I was made junior partner a month or so back."

"Well, congratulations."

He glanced at Paul, leaving her little option but to introduce them.

"And what about you?" Brett asked, turning back to her after he and Paul had shaken hands. "Your business doing well?"

"Oh, the summer's a little slow, but things always pick up in September."

"Right, that's pretty common. Well, look, I've got to run, but the firm's toying with the idea of moving into new office space. So if we seem to be getting beyond the talking stage, I'll call you. You're still living on West Seventy-fifth? Didn't move without letting your lawyer know?"

"No, I didn't move." She managed a smile, despite the fact that her stomach was churning even harder now.

"Well, nice meeting you, Paul. Be talking to you, April."

As Brett walked away, Paul quietly said, "It doesn't matter."

She simply looked at him.

"It doesn't matter that I know the name you're going by or where you live. I realized you'd be suspicious of me, and I don't blame you for not wanting me to know anything about you. But I'm not trying to put something over on you. I'm who I told you I am, and I want what I told you I want."

When she remained silent, he held up two fingers and said, "Scout's honor."

She nodded then. But she knew that not all Scouts were honorable.

ONCE APRIL AND PAUL reached his Cherokee, he dug a tape out of the glove compartment and stuck it into the player.

April could feel her heartbeat accelerating in anticipation, but instead of playing the tape, he started the engine and said, "I'll turn that on when we get out of the lot. You can listen while I drive."

"Thanks, but you don't really have to drive me."

"West Seventy-fifth is practically on my way."

She doubted that was true, regardless of where he was going, but she let it pass. The longer she spent with him, the more chance she'd pick up on something that would help her determine if he was for real.

Once he'd paid for the parking and they started off, he glanced over at her. "I guess I shouldn't have just assumed you'd want to go home. Would you rather I drop you at your office or someplace?"

"I work out of my apartment," she told him. There was little point in playing Mata Hari at this stage of the game.

"Oh? Doing?"

"I manage moves for companies."

"Ah, that's why your lawyer mentioned his firm might be moving."

She nodded, telling herself to keep in mind that Paul didn't miss a thing.

"And what does managing a move involve?" he asked, turning onto the parkway.

"It varies. Sometimes I start at square one, locating new space and negotiating the lease. Other times, the clients do that part themselves and just hire me to look after the physical move."

"Making arrangements with moving companies, you mean? And making sure everything ends up where it's supposed to?"

"Well, yes, but it's usually more complicated than that. Especially if the client is customer-oriented or high tech. Then it's important there's no interruption of telecommunications or computer systems. And that can get tricky."

When April lapsed into silence, Paul could see she was dying to hear the tape, so he reached toward the player. As he leaned those few inches closer to her, he could smell the faint scent of her perfume. It was soft and sultry, making him think of languid summer nights and slow sex.

Telling himself that sex was the last thing he should be thinking about, he pressed the play button.

She sat forward as his voice came on, beginning the interview by noting the date the tape was being made and identifying the speakers. Then she focused on the tape deck while he asked Walker an initial question, as if looking at it would help her hear better.

He kept glancing over while she listened to Walker talk about the bombing, thinking she was even better looking than her mother had been as a young woman. And every bit as intense. She'd barely smiled since they'd met.

Of course, given the position he was putting her in, that was hardly surprising. When your father was wanted for murder, you had to be awfully leery about arranging to have him talk to a stranger. Hell, maybe he was dreaming to figure there was even a chance she'd set something up for him.

"So," Walker was saying on the tape, "Ken and I decided we'd go along with it. Protect...Mr. X by laying the blame on Colin."

"You're referring to Ken Gutteridge and Colin Birmingham," Paul's own voice said for the record.

"Right."

"And Mr. X is the man who actually placed the bomb and set the timer."

"Yes."

"What made you decide to lie and name Colin Birmingham? Were you paid to?"

There was a pause, then Walker said, "I told you, I'm not prepared to say who Mr. X was. And you might be able to figure that out if I explain why we agreed to the plan.''

"But the bottom line is that the bomber definitely wasn't Colin Birmingham, despite what you told the FBI at the time. And despite what you told me during our previous meeting on March 4.''

"Right. Colin had nothing to do with the bombing. Nothing at all.''

"And why have you changed your story after all these years?''

"I told you.''

"I know. But tell me again now that we're recording.''

"Because I'm dying,'' Walker said, his words barely audible. "Because I'm dying, and it's time I told the truth.''

"Thank you,'' Paul said, almost as quietly.

When it became clear that was it, April looked at him. "How do I know that was really Tom Walker?''

"You only have my word on it. But as I said, that tape's a copy. So take it with you. And if you decide to contact your parents, play it for them. Even after all these years, they might recognize his voice.''

April pushed the eject button and tucked the tape into her purse, thinking it was unlikely they'd recognize a voice that had aged almost thirty years since they'd last heard it. Still, the content of what Walker had said—if it *was* Walker—might tell them more than it had told her.

"Take the copy of the statement, too,'' Paul added. "It's in that folder on the back seat.''

She reached for it and skimmed the two pages of print inside. They were more or less a written version

of the tape and bore the signature Thomas Walker—
in a slightly shaky script that might well belong to a
dying man. Or might be one more finely crafted detail in a plot to get to her parents.

As she tucked the statement back into the folder,
Paul said, "The contact I mentioned having at the
bureau?"

"Yes?"

"If you do decide to talk to your parents about
this, and if your father is willing to try to help me…
Well, if I can learn who the real bomber was, I think
I could help smooth the way for them."

"Meaning?"

"Meaning that if I can find proof your father
wasn't the bomber, then obviously the murder
charges will be dropped. But there'd still be other
outstanding charges."

"Unlawful flight to avoid prosecution or giving
testimony—that's against both of them," she said.
"And aiding and abetting against my mother. Along
with a few lesser charges." She knew only too well
what the legalities of their case were.

"Right. But there's a good chance I could help
broker a deal for them with the feds. Assuming, as I
said, I got proof your father's innocent."

"That's an awfully big assumption."

"The point," he said quietly, "is that if things did
come together, I think I could help them walk away
free."

They'd reached the Queensboro Bridge, and when
they started across it she gazed down at the gray
water of the East River, wishing she had some way

of knowing whether Paul was even half as sincere as he sounded.

When she glanced across at him again, he was looking into the rearview mirror. The tight set of his jaw sent a shiver through her.

"What?" she said. "Is someone following us?"

"I'm not sure."

She turned and looked out the back window at the stream of traffic behind them.

"Don't let them see you looking," he said, his tone so sharp that she immediately faced forward again, her anxiety level rising.

"There is someone, isn't there?"

"There could be. I noticed a green Taurus just after we left the airport, and it's been a couple of cars back ever since. We'll see if it tries to stick with us when we get off the bridge."

She resisted the urge to look around again, but she'd like to see that green Taurus for herself. Otherwise, how could she know he wasn't simply saying he thought someone was tailing them? To convince her he wasn't one of the bad guys. And if he was one of them...

"Hold on," he said. A moment later, they were barreling down the off ramp and wheeling into the Manhattan traffic, cutting off a cabbie, who leaned on his horn and gave them the finger.

Zigging and zagging their way west, with Paul glancing into the rearview mirror every few seconds, they ran a yellow light at Park Avenue and narrowly missed a pedestrian. Then he headed north on Madison and cut over to Fifth and into Central Park at the Sixty-sixth Street entrance.

"If he was on our tail, we lost him," he announced, checking the rearview mirror once more and slowing to only a few miles over the speed limit.

April released her death grip on the armrest. "You must have taken driving lessons from Michael Andretti."

Paul glanced across at her and grinned. "I scared you?"

She managed to smile. "A little. But not as much as the thought that someone was following us."

His grin faded.

"Look, I'll admit I'm a bit paranoid," she said, "but in my family, that's an essential for survival. And I'd really like to figure out if we *were* being followed. Did anyone know you were meeting me today?"

"No. Not a soul."

"Then maybe the want ad..."

"What about it?"

"Well, when I saw it I wondered who else might notice it and recognize my real name. And be curious about who was trying to contact me."

They'd reached the far side of the park, and Paul pulled to a stop at the lights. "I thought about that, so I placed it in person—paid cash and used a phony name."

"But you put your phone number in it. So it wouldn't be hard for someone to find out whose ad it was."

"Actually, that was my cellular number. It would be tougher to trace to me."

"But far from impossible. And tuning into a cell phone's frequency is hardly rocket science. If the feds were monitoring the area around your apartment, they'd have heard us arranging to meet."

He made the turn onto Central Park West, his jaw tight again.

"Or if they figured it was worth putting you under surveillance," she pressed, "if they followed you to the airport and saw you meet me, they'd know who I was. And if you hadn't noticed them, they'd have tailed us all the way to my apartment and blown my cover right out of the water."

"I'm not certain we were being followed," Paul said slowly.

"You thought we were."

"Well, if we were, we lost them."

This time, she said silently. But if the FBI discovered that April Kelly was actually Jillian Birmingham, she'd never know when they might be watching her. Waiting for her to lead them to her parents.

PAUL BEGAN PRINTING OUT the information he'd downloaded from the databases, then glanced at his watch. Seeing that he had a good ten minutes before the late-night news, he started reshelving the stack of books that had been multiplying on his desk.

As he slid the last one into place, his glance flickered to the row of framed photographs his mother had given him a few years back. Among them was a wedding picture of his parents. And one of him, when he was three or four, sitting on his father's shoulders. He gazed at it for a moment, recalling the anxious expression on April's face when he'd told her he'd always wanted to see his father's killer brought to justice.

It had probably been the wrong thing to say, but it was the truth. He'd never considered his father's death anything except cold-blooded murder.

Oh, he knew some people thought otherwise, felt that the factory's napalm production somehow put the bombing into a different light. But, in general, that thinking had come with the knowledge of hindsight. At the time, most people—including his father—had believed what the government told them, that the chemical was only being used to destroy jungle gathering areas of the Viet Cong guerrillas.

Paul shook his head, telling himself his thoughts were drifting. The point was that, for as long as he could remember, he'd imagined himself tracking down his innocent father's killer. Which, of course, was what had made him start digging around— searching for some clue that would tell him where Colin Birmingham was.

But after his second talk with Walker, he'd no longer been so certain that Birmingham was guilty. As he'd told April, his gut feeling was that Walker had told him the truth—that it was Gutteridge who was lying.

Still, he was keeping in mind that his gut feelings weren't one hundred percent reliable. And while April might believe that her parents had been against violent protests, that didn't jibe with what Walker had said.

It wasn't on the tape or in the statement, but he'd mentioned that Colin Birmingham had frequently talked about the end results justifying any sort of protest. And Gutteridge had said basically the same thing.

So, despite the feds' flimsy case against him, it could be that Birmingham was guilty and that Tom Walker hadn't been trying to assuage his guilt at all. He might have had some other reason for changing his tune. Hell, maybe he'd concocted the story because he'd wanted a little attention. After all, a lonely guy, dying on his own…

Paul shook his head. He didn't have anywhere near enough facts to draw conclusions. But if Walker had fabricated his story, if Colin Birmingham really was the bomber, how would he react to hearing that Walker was now claiming someone else had planted that bomb?

Well, first off, he'd wonder what the hell kind of game Walker was playing. And after that…? Maybe he'd do nothing beyond wondering. Or maybe he'd decide there just might be a way to help an investigative journalist find ''evidence'' pointing to a different suspect.

Which meant that even if Birmingham did cooperate with him, Paul would have to be suspicious about every shred of ''information'' the man provided.

Reminding himself that he didn't even know whether April was going to tell her parents what he wanted, let alone whether Birmingham would talk to him if she did, he shut off his computer.

Then, taking the pages from the printer, he wandered into the living room, sank onto the couch and began glancing through the material.

Even though he took the electronic age pretty much for granted, he was sometimes still amazed by how easy it had become to collect supposedly confidential data about people. Even people who were careful not to reveal anything more about themselves than they absolutely had to. People like Jillian Birmingham, alias April Kelly. Of course, most of the information he'd just printed out had come from documents on file about her company. Smooth Moves. Its name made him smile.

What little personal information he'd turned up told him that she lived alone, belonged to a fitness club a few blocks from her apartment, and had a driver's license but didn't own a car.

Reaching for the remote, he flicked on the television just as a makeup commercial filled the screen. The model in it looked a little like April—flawless skin, large dark eyes and a full mouth. As his gaze lingered on the woman's face, he began to wonder if he'd really only done a background check on April because of his interest in her father. Then he reminded himself that he routinely put together profiles on the principals in stories he was working on.

Not that April was exactly a principal. But it never hurt to cover all the bases. Besides which, he was a naturally curious guy.

But there's something about her that's making you more curious than usual, an imaginary voice whispered.

Well…yeah, he'd admit that. Almost from the moment they'd met, he'd realized he was attracted to her. But he also realized that was far from good, considering the circumstances.

Which meant that since he couldn't deny feeling a tug of interest, he'd simply have to do the next best thing and ignore it. Anything else would be downright stupid.

After all, if she decided not to put him in contact

with her father, she'd avoid him like the plague if he ever tried to get in touch with her again. And even if she did set something up for him, keeping things strictly business between them would still be the only way to go.

The last thing he needed was to get involved with a woman whose father might well have murdered his.

THE DAY AFTER APRIL had met Paul Gardiner was hot and sunny, perfect weather for enjoying a drive in the country. Unfortunately, she was too anxious to be enjoying anything.

She'd finally decided she had to tell her parents about him. After all, it was their future that might be changed if her father talked to him. But the decision had left her feeling very uneasy, which was probably why she hadn't called to let them know she was coming. That way, she could change her mind right up to the last minute.

Glancing at the odometer of her rental car, she saw she'd traveled almost two hundred of the roughly two hundred and thirty miles to her destination. And the good news was that there hadn't been the slightest sign of a car trailing hers.

Of course, that was hardly surprising. A lot of fathers probably taught their kids defensive driving, but her father had also included lessons on evasion tactics. And since she routinely used them when she was going to visit her parents, anyone who tried to follow her would probably have no idea where she'd disappeared to after the first few minutes.

Still, she was keeping an extra careful eye out today. Ever since Brett Carlson had popped up in the airport and blown her cover, she'd been as nervous as a mouse smelling Eau de Cat in the air. She didn't like the idea of anybody knowing who she actually was, never mind an uncertain quantity like Paul.

She smiled wryly to herself, unable to help thinking that most women would never dream of considering him an "uncertain quantity." He was the sort of man they'd find both easy to like and easy to trust—attractive and intelligent, with that warm smile, a relaxed sense of humor and reassuring manner.

But even if the situation were different, she wasn't a woman who could easily let herself like or trust anyone. She'd learned as a child to keep an emotional distance from people, so it wouldn't hurt as much when she had to leave them behind. Even now, not one of her friends knew her inside out. And when it came to men... Well, she'd had a few close relationships, but she'd never fallen deeply in love.

She suspected she never would. She didn't need a shrink to tell her that her upbringing had left her afraid to commit herself to anyone.

But why on earth was she thinking about that? More to the point, how had it begun with thoughts of Paul Gardiner? A man who was potentially dangerous?

Spotting her turn, she left the highway behind and began making her way along the secondary roads, absently looking at the houses she was passing and trying to recall exactly how many different places she and her parents had lived while she'd been growing up. If the total wasn't over twenty, it was awfully close. They'd never owned, always rented—moving on whenever they'd suspected, or the underground support network had learned, that the feds were closing in.

A couple of times it had been in the dead of night. To this day she had nightmares about being wakened in the darkness and hustled out to the car without even having time to get dressed.

Then, after each move, they'd had to go through the process of reinventing their identities and reestablishing their lives. Publically, her parents hadn't been Colin and Mary Birmingham since they'd gone under. They'd used so many different names over the years that April doubted she'd be able to remember them all if she tried. It hadn't been easy and it hadn't been fun. But keeping on the move had kept them out of prison.

She was still lost in thoughts of the past when she reached the narrow road that led to Ludlow Pond, a place her mother called ''the middle of nowhere, New York.'' The little lake was a bit of a commute from Ithaca, where her parents had jobs, but the winterized cottage provided the dual advantages of isolation and affordability.

Its driveway was well hidden by trees, so she drove slowly, watching for it and wondering if they'd be home from work yet. If not, they'd get a start when they arrived to find a strange car in their yard.

But when she turned into the drive, their old Ford was parked beside the cottage. And she hadn't even stopped the car before her father appeared in the kitchen doorway to see who was arriving.

''Mouse!'' he called, his face breaking into a grin. ''Mary?'' He glanced back into the cottage. ''Mouse is here.''

She cut the ignition, smiling at him. Mouse was

such a silly nickname, but it was what they'd always called her. In the beginning, she'd been too young to cope with answering to a different name after every move, and the nickname had solved that problem. Later, it had just stuck.

"Is everything all right?" he asked, walking quickly toward the car as she got out.

"Everything's fine." She stepped into the circle of his arms and hugged him. A moment later her mother was beside them, waiting for a hug of her own.

"What are you doing here?" she asked, wrapping her arms around her daughter. "Not that we aren't thrilled to see you, but—"

"Darling, give her time to catch her breath," April's father interrupted. "Come on. We'll sit on the front porch and have some iced tea. Your mother was just making it."

Following them around to the lake side of the cottage, April unobtrusively checked them out the way she always did when she hadn't seen them for a while—looking for signs of aging, signs of illness. But her father was the same tall, fit man he'd always been. And her mother, aside from the ever-increasing gray in her dark hair, looked the same, too.

Having satisfied herself of that, she breathed a tiny sigh of relief. Given the circumstances, she wasn't able to see them nearly as often as she'd like. And since she'd left them to live her own life, they really only had each other. If anything happened to either of them...

She ordered herself to stop thinking along those lines. They were barely into their fifties and nothing was going to happen to them. Not unless they decided to trust Paul Gardiner when they shouldn't.

That thought sent a chill through her. Trying to ignore it, she said, "Mom, I'll help you get the tea."

"Oh, thanks, but there's nothing to help with. You just sit and talk to your father."

"So," he said as her mother headed into the cottage. "Work's slow? You've got a weekday off?"

That almost made her smile. Her father worried about her being out in the big bad world on her own, but he'd never come right out and say so. Instead, he asked subtle questions like that one, when he really meant, Your business is doing all right, isn't it? You've got enough money to pay the rent?

"Actually, I did some work for a client this morning before I headed up here. But not many companies move in July or August, so all I have going are a couple of jobs in the planning stages. I'll get busy again come September."

"Ah. Well, it's nice to have some free time in the summer."

He sat watching her after he said that, clearly waiting for her to explain why she was here. But there wasn't much sense in beginning the story until her mother reappeared with the tea.

Once she had, she sat down and eyed April as expectantly as her father had been doing.

"Cheers," she said, raising her glass to delay the moment of truth.

"Cheers," her parents repeated.

She took a sip, then dug the want ad from her purse. "This was in last Sunday's *Times*," she said.

CHAPTER THREE

APRIL'S PARENTS SPENT forever reading the ad before her father looked up. "Have you done anything about this?"

"Yes. I met with him yesterday."

"Him being…?"

"His name's Paul Gardiner and he's a writer—an investigative journalist, actually—who's looking into the Unique Technologies bombing."

"Why?"

"In the beginning, because his father died in it."

"Oh, my," her mother murmured.

"So he's after revenge," her father said.

"I…yes, he admitted that's part of it. But the thing is, he interviewed Tom Walker and Ken Gutteridge." She paused, waiting for a reaction to the fact that she'd learned the names of the two men.

Her mother sat up just a little straighter and her father cleared his throat. That was it.

"And he claims," she continued, "Walker admitted they lied when they said you were responsible for the bombing. He has Walker's signed statement to that effect, as well as an audiotape, but I have no way of knowing if they're genuine. These are copies." She removed the statement and her tape recorder from her bag. "The tape's ready to play."

Heads close together, her parents read the statement while her stomach did a series of nervous flip-flops. At last she said, "Do you know what Walker's signature looked like? Could that be it?"

Her father glanced at her. "Whether it's his or faked, it would look like the real thing."

"Yes, of course. I just hoped that maybe..."

"What would have made Tom admit to this? What explanation did this Paul Gardiner give you?"

"Dad, it's going to take me a while to tell you the whole story. So maybe you should listen to the tape first. See if you recognize the voice. See if anything he says tells you whether it's really Walker or not."

Forcing herself to sit back in the chair, she waited while he pressed Play, then held her breath as Paul asked his first question. When the other man began speaking, her parents gave no clue as to whether they thought the slightly raspy voice was Walker's. After so many years of practice, they were experts at concealing their emotions.

By the time the tape finished playing, every nerve in April's body was on edge.

"Well?" she asked as her father switched off the recorder.

He exchanged a glance with her mother, then said, "I don't know. It could have been Walker. He used to sound something like that. But a lot of people would have known enough to say what's on that tape."

"Especially someone who's been looking into the bombing," her mother added.

"So you don't think it's for real," April concluded, uncertain how she felt about that.

On the one hand, her childhood fantasy had been that someday a mysterious stranger would come along with proof of her father's innocence. And if her parents had believed that was Walker's voice, if they'd decided to risk taking things further...

On the other hand, if Paul hadn't been straight with her, she didn't want them having anything to do with him.

"I didn't say it wasn't for real," her father objected. "I said I don't know. But let's hear the story right from the start. You saw the want ad and...?"

She took a deep breath, then began at the beginning. When she got to the part about Paul wanting to talk to her father, he said, "He has a point, you know. A list of names would give him something to go on, but if I actually talked to him, it would be more helpful."

"Colin, you wouldn't seriously do that, would you?" her mother said.

"Well, we'd have to give it some thought first. But let's hear the rest of April's story."

Neither of them interrupted after that, and she didn't stop until she'd told them every last remaining detail.

"But the feds haven't established that you're living as April Kelly," her father said when she finished. "Not if Gardiner lost the car that was following you."

"Dad, as I said, I'm not certain there *was* anyone following us. And even if there was, it could just have been part of a plot to convince me Paul isn't an agent. But if he is, then the feds have learned what my cover's been."

"It was safe for you to come here today, though?" her mother asked.

"Yes. I was super careful. But I wouldn't want to risk it again until we know exactly what's going on."

"Okay," her father said. "We'll get someone in the Network to see what they can learn about Gardiner."

She nodded, although she wouldn't count on them learning much. After so many years, the support network for the few people still underground was neither as extensive nor as enthusiastic as it had once been.

"I already did a little checking this morning," she said. "I made sure Paul actually does work on 'Today's World.' And I established that there is a Tom Walker in Bridgeport and a Ken Gutteridge in Port Credit, Ontario, which is where he said they lived. But he said a whole lot of things that I can't check."

"Well, you made a good start," her father said. "And at least you didn't catch him in any lies. That's a promising sign."

Or, she thought, it was a sign that he was a liar who was good at not getting tripped up.

"Now, when it comes to the idea of talking to him," her father continued, "I—"

"I think April should just tell him she couldn't contact us," her mother interrupted. "I don't think we should get into this at all."

"But if he *is* after the truth…"

"Colin, the idea of taking a chance on that makes me very nervous."

"It makes me nervous, too. But if he's an investigative journalist, he earns his living by learning things other people haven't been able to.''

''If he's only an investigative journalist and not an undercover agent.''

Her father rose, walked across the porch and stood staring out over the lake.

''Look,'' her mother added after a minute, ''if things were really bad, then maybe I'd be more inclined to consider this. But I'm sure we've always had a better time of it than most, so I think we should just leave well enough alone.''

April exhaled slowly, once again recalling those terrifying middle-of-the-night moves. But despite them, she knew her mother was right. They had been better off than a lot of people who'd gone under. Her grandfather had been a builder, so her father had learned a lot about construction while he was growing up. Because of that, he'd always been able to find work. And her mother had usually managed to get something, too.

It was a different life than the one they'd mapped out as university students, when her father had intended to be a lawyer and her mother a teacher, but at least they'd always gotten by. And they'd had each other.

Finally, her father turned away from the porch railing and looked at them.

''I guess what I'm thinking is that we have to consider everything,'' he said, ''including the fact that the feds could still catch up with us someday. There'll always be that risk unless someone can prove I wasn't the bomber.''

"But it's incredibly unlikely anyone could," her mother said.

"I know. But still…"

"Colin, if this fellow's a fed, we could end up in prison. You, for the rest of your life. I don't want to risk that."

Her mother had spoken so calmly that a stranger would have no idea how deep her feelings ran. But after thirty-plus years of marriage she still adored her husband. She'd rather die than have something awful happen to him.

Fleetingly, April wondered how it would feel to love a man that much. Then she forced the thought away and tried to ignore the lump that had formed in her throat.

"I understand why you're worried, darling," her father was saying. "But I think I should talk to him, and the sooner the better."

"Colin, at least don't rush into it. At least wait to see what the Network finds out."

"No, that's not a good idea. If he's for real, then we shouldn't be wasting any time, because Gutteridge is likely to let the real bomber know that Gardiner's nosing around. And if there is any proof, they'll both want to do whatever they can to keep him from getting his hands on it."

"But—"

"Look, Mary, even if Gardiner did turn out to be an agent—hell, even if he turned out to be the best agent in the whole damn bureau—we're only talking about a phone call. And it would be completely on my terms, so…"

"But, dammit, maybe you're right. Maybe we

would be better off to leave well enough alone. What do you think, Mouse?'' he asked, looking at her. ''What's your gut feeling? Can we trust this guy or not?''

Her heart skipped an anxious beat. She simply didn't know.

''You're putting her in a difficult position,'' her mother said.

April shot her a grateful glance. It was more than difficult. It was impossible.

''But she's the one who's been face-to-face with him,'' her father said. ''And you know what?'' he added, looking at her again. ''Maybe you don't consciously realize it, but if you figured we couldn't trust him, you wouldn't be here.''

''That means you're definitely going to talk to him, doesn't it?'' her mother said. ''Despite what I think.''

''Yes, I guess it does.''

April's heart skipped another beat. It might have been her father who'd made the decision, but she knew that if it was the wrong one, she'd hold herself responsible. Forever.

''THIS IS POSITIVELY insane,'' Mary Birmingham said.

''It isn't,'' April told her. The idea might be making her nervous, but it definitely wasn't insane.

''Colin, we cannot let her do this.''

Resisting the urge to point out that she was no longer a child, she said, ''Mom, when you're not sure if you can trust someone, it only makes sense to keep an eye on him. And if Dad talks to Paul, how are we

going to know what he does after that unless someone's right there with him?''

"No, it's just too dangerous. What did your father
say not an hour ago? He said Ken Gutteridge will
probably let the real bomber know that Gardiner's
nosing around. And the thought of what a cold-
blooded killer might do to keep his secret from sur-
facing…''

"Mouse, your mother's right,'' her father put in.
"The idea of your tagging along with this Gardiner
sounded okay when you first suggested it, but now
that I've had time to think… Well, I really appreciate
your wanting to help, but it could turn into something
dangerous. And I'm not going to take any chances
where you're concerned.''

"Dad, if it weren't for me, you wouldn't even
know Paul Gardiner existed. How do you think I'd
feel if it turned out he's trouble? And how are we
going to know whether he is or not if we don't know
what he does after he talks to you?''

"Maybe,'' her mother said, "someone in the Network could look into that for us.''

"Mom, nobody cares about how this turns out
anywhere near as much as I do. And nothing awful's
going to happen to me. I just want to make sure that
nothing awful happens to either of you.''

Before they could reply, the phone began to ring.
Her mother went inside to answer it and a minute
later called to her father that it was for him.

For a few moments April sat by herself, gazing
out over the lake. Then, feeling the chill of early
evening seeping into her bones, she headed across
the porch. As she neared the screen door, she could

see that they'd already hung up the phone. Her mother was speaking quietly but urgently to her father. She hesitated, her intuition telling her to stay where she was and listen.

"Do you want that, Colin?" her mother was saying. "Aside from it being potentially dangerous for her, do you want her to find out?"

Find out what? She stood stock-still, not even breathing.

"Maybe nobody will say anything," her father said.

"Right. And maybe the sun will rise in the west."

"Fine," her father muttered. "So it's possible she'd find out."

"Then if we can't convince her not to get involved, we'd better tell her about it ourselves."

"No. It's also possible it won't come up, so let's just leave well enough alone."

"But what if she's determined to go ahead with the idea? And it does come up?"

"Then... Well, dammit, Mary, if it does, she'll understand. You're underestimating her if you think otherwise."

April began silently inching her way backward. When she reached the porch railing, she turned and stood gazing out over the lake once more, wondering what on earth they hadn't told her about. She was still wondering a couple of minutes later when they reappeared on the porch.

"Look, Mouse," her father said. "The more I think about this idea, the more strongly I'm against it. So—"

"Dad, listen to me. I'm going to do it. One way

or another, I am. And it would be a lot easier for me if Paul believes you're the one insisting I keep tabs on him.''

"Dammit, Mouse, I don't know where on earth you got such a stubborn streak.''

"Don't you?'' her mother murmured. She eyed April's father for a moment, then removed the big silver locket from around her neck.

"Here,'' she said, holding it out to April. "I want you to have this.''

"But…I can't. It was Grandma's. And you always wear it.''

"And you know when she gave it to me.''

"Of course. Right before we went under.'' She'd heard the story a thousand times. "When you went to see her and Grandpa, to tell them we were disappearing, she gave it to you because she believed it brought the wearer good luck.''

Her mother nodded. "And I have been lucky. I've had you, and your father, and we've always been fine. So if you're going to insist on getting involved with this Paul Gardiner, I want you to have it.''

WHILE THE TAXI SLOWLY made its way up Eighth Avenue, Paul was thinking that talking to an alleged bomber would make this one of the more unusual Saturday nights of his life. In his line of work, though, he was used to gleaning information when and where he could get it.

He jotted down another question to ask Colin Birmingham as the cabbie drove along West Twenty-second to Seventh Avenue. Then he paid the fare and climbed out into the heat.

By seven o'clock in the evening, the city had normally begun to cool down, even on the hottest days. But that hadn't happened tonight, and the streets of Chelsea were crowded with people. Many of them simply stood leaning against buildings, likely choosing the hot air at ground level over an unair-conditioned apartment, which would be even hotter.

It was just as well, he thought, that April had specified he should wear shorts and a T-shirt.

Of course he'd found it pretty strange that she'd told him how to dress. But when she'd added that he shouldn't do anything foolish like trying to conceal a transmitter, he'd realized she was reasoning that the fewer clothes he wore, the harder it would be to hide anything.

He had no way of knowing which of the "conditions" for this conversation she'd come up with and which were her father's. But between them, they'd planned thoroughly. To set up the meeting, she'd phoned him on his work line, then had him call her back from a pay phone, giving him only part of the instructions each time in case anyone was listening in on either call. Among her other conditions, she'd told him to bring nothing except a notebook and pen. No phone, no laptop, nothing else. And she'd warned him that— just in case he did try to pull a fast one— she intended to frisk him.

Thinking back to her words made him grin. Over the phone, he hadn't been able to tell whether she was joking. But if she hadn't been...

Well, it would be tough to think of anyone he'd rather have frisk him.

Reminding himself he shouldn't be entertaining

those kinds of thoughts about her, he checked his watch and saw that she was late. He looked along the street, feeling a twinge of concern that her father might have changed his mind. Then she appeared from behind a truck on West Twenty-second.

Spotting her made him feel better—and not entirely because he was relieved that the conversation must still be on. Like it or not, it simply felt good to see her again.

She was wearing a pale yellow dress, and she struck him as even more appealing than she had the first time around. She looked...delectably cool, he decided. Like icy lemonade or lemon sherbet.

Good enough to eat, that annoying imaginary voice whispered.

He was still silently telling the voice he could do without its help when she reached him and said, "Hi."

"Hi." He smiled, but the smile she gave him in return seemed forced.

"Nice locket," he said, trying to put her at ease.

"It was my grandmother's. She claimed that wearing it brings good luck."

"So you never take it off?"

She smiled again—more naturally this time.

"Actually, my mother only gave it to me yesterday. But I was thinking I'd better not tempt the fates, that maybe I'll only take it off to sleep and shower. It has pictures of my grandparents inside, so I wouldn't want to get it wet."

He nodded. The other day she'd barely said a word about anything personal, which probably meant she was chattering because she was nervous—worried about his talking to her father. It made him wonder just how much of her life she'd spent worrying about her parents.

"I'm parked down the street," she said, turning and starting back the way she'd come.

"Oh?" He fell into step beside her. She'd told him to leave his car at home but hadn't mentioned they'd be going anywhere from here. And his research had told him she didn't own a car.

When she didn't pick up on his "Oh," he tried again. "Most single women in Manhattan don't have a car."

"It's a rental. But I don't recall mentioning that I was single."

Her tone said she suspected he'd done some checking on her, so he gave her his best casual shrug. "I just assumed, because you don't wear a ring. Was I right?"

"Yes, but I didn't think investigative journalists were allowed to assume. This is it," she added, stopping beside a blue Cavalier.

Nonchalantly, he took a backward step, pretending to appraise the car while he memorized the license.

"I told you, it's a rental. Running the plates wouldn't get you anything useful."

For half a second he considered playing innocent, then decided she'd never buy it. "Sorry, just habit," he offered. "But can I ask where we're going?"

"Nowhere, really. I'll simply drive around. We decided it would be best for my father to call while we're in a moving car."

He nodded, thinking again that they'd planned thoroughly. A phone in a moving car didn't use a stationary frequency, so the call would be almost impossible to monitor. And he'd bet they weren't using his Cherokee because she figured he might stick a transponder on it—so somebody could track them from way back and pick up his side of the conversation with a long-range microphone.

"Before we get going," she said, "could I have a look at your pen?"

It was clipped to his notebook, so he handed that to her.

She flipped through it, then unscrewed the pen and made sure it wasn't concealing a tiny camera or microphone. Next she opened the passenger's door and said, "Would you mind emptying your pockets onto the front seat?"

He dug his wallet and keys out of his cutoffs and tossed them down.

"That's it?"

"I travel light. But if you really do want to frisk me..." He placed his hands on the roof of the car, thinking it might make her laugh.

It didn't. She simply stepped right in behind him, so close that he could smell her sultry perfume and feel the softness of her breasts against his back.

As she began gingerly sliding her hands across his chest he stopped breathing. He didn't start again until she'd finished patting him down to the bottom of his cutoffs. But even not breathing couldn't prevent his blood from running hot and his groin from tightening. Or keep him from imagining her touching him under entirely different circumstances.

"Yo, mama," called a punk who'd been gawking

at them from across the street. "You wanna do me next?"

Ignoring him, Paul turned away from the car. April looked embarrassed.

"I just had to be sure," she said. "I know they're making awfully small transmitters these days."

While she headed around to the driver's side, he picked up his wallet and keys, then got into the car, wondering why he was annoyed that she was suspicious of him. He was used to people not trusting him. It came with his job. And, logically, he knew that April would be foolish if she did trust him. But for some illogical reason, it bothered him that she doubted he was playing straight.

"Look," he said, once she'd started the engine. "I realize how careful you've got to be, but I want you to know I haven't breathed a word about any of this. And I sure as hell wouldn't have come prepared to transmit signals or anything."

"Not unless you were one of the bad guys."

She smiled after she said that, but he knew she wasn't kidding.

What did it matter? he asked himself. Maybe he *was* attracted to her, but that was entirely the result of chemistry—hormones and pheromones and whatever other "mones" there were involved. He didn't know her well enough for it to be anything more. And he had no interest in getting to know her any better. At least not unless he became convinced that Colin Birmingham wasn't the Napalm Bomber.

Unless that happened, he had to view her merely as the woman who could put him in contact with the man he wanted to talk to. And since she was doing exactly that, why did he care whether she trusted him?

He didn't know why. But he did know it was irritating the hell out of him that she didn't.

APRIL TURNED THE CAR'S air conditioner to what she'd decided was the arctic setting and pulled away from the curb, her anxiety level sky high.

She'd had a long, leisurely lunch with a friend today, but the entire time she'd had trouble keeping her mind off the fact that her father would be talking to Paul tonight. And now the moment of truth was only minutes away.

"When you saw your parents," he said, "did they finally confide in you?"

She glanced at him, not certain of his meaning but thinking it was an ironic question. When she'd seen them, she'd learned there was apparently something they'd never confided to her and she was still wondering what it was.

"About who they think could have actually been behind the bombing?" he elaborated.

She decided he suspected that her father might not call, so he was trying to learn what he could from her, just in case.

"No," she told him. "We only discussed whether my dad should talk to you or not. And the conversation was pretty brief."

He didn't look as if he believed her, but it wasn't exactly a lie. "Pretty brief" was a relative term. And since she'd had to head back to the city, there hadn't been time to talk about everything. In any event, her father would tell Paul whom he suspected and Paul would fill her in. If they got past square one, that was.

Glancing at him once more, she wondered for the millionth time whether he really was only after the truth. If that wasn't the case...

She checked the rearview mirror, just to be on the safe side, turned into the heavy traffic on Eighth Avenue, then glanced at him yet again, as if by looking she could see any deep, dark secrets he had buried inside.

But all she could see were his rugged good looks, the sexy way his hair curled onto his neck, and his broad shoulders. Of course, she could hardly miss his bare legs, either. Or the solid definition of muscles beneath his T-shirt. She recalled how hard those muscles had felt when she'd frisked him, and the recollection started a funny little fluttering in her chest. Ordering the fluttering to get lost, she focused every bit of her attention on the traffic.

This man beside her might well be the enemy, which meant her thoughts had just been drifting in a dangerous direction. She'd have to avoid that in future encounters. Assuming there'd be any future encounters. Assuming he agreed to her father's terms and didn't say anything that started warning signals flashing.

That disturbing possibility front and center, she reached down into her bag, dug out her cellular and reluctantly handed it over.

Paul could feel his tension growing as he took the phone. "What should I call him?" he asked. "What name's he going by now?"

April shook her head. "Don't worry about that.

For your purpose, he's Colin Birmingham, so I imagine that's what he'll expect you to call him.''

"Right," he said, then told himself to relax, that this was merely another story he was after. But it wasn't. He was after his father's killer. And if Colin Birmingham wasn't the bomber, he must have some pretty good ideas about who was. Otherwise, why would he have agreed to this conversation?

You already thought of a possible answer to that, he reminded himself. Maybe Birmingham was guilty but saw this as a chance to get out from under by setting up someone else to take the rap.

After all, proving the bureau had spent almost thirty years chasing the wrong man would be a real coup for an investigative journalist—the sort of thing that would make a guy's reputation. And some journalists would be very willing to slant the facts of a story to benefit themselves.

Hell, if there was a chance it could win them a Pulitzer, they'd be prepared to downright invent evidence. Maybe Birmingham was hoping that Paul Gardiner was just that type.

Glancing over at April, he wondered if she'd ever considered her father might be guilty. He didn't think so. She'd probably never had a doubt in the world that Birmingham's version of the story was true.

He looked away from her and out of the car, absently noting that they were almost at Columbus Circle. Just as they reached it, the phone rang.

CHAPTER FOUR

"YOU'RE ON," APRIL SAID.

Paul glanced over at her, then pushed the send button. "Paul Gardiner."

There was a moment's silence before a man replied, "This is Colin Birmingham."

Paul's stomach muscles tightened. Until he'd heard those words, he hadn't been entirely certain this was going to happen. "Thank you for agreeing to talk to me."

"And thank you for wanting to learn who really bombed that factory. But let's get down to business."

Which translated, Paul knew, into, Let's not drag things out in case you've got any tricks up your sleeve.

"Okay," he said, opening his notebook. "Where would you like to begin? By getting straight to who you suspect could have been the bomber?"

"We'll get to that in a second. There's something you'll have to agree to before I tell you anything."

"Oh?"

"I want my daughter working on your investigation with you. I want her to go along when you talk to people and—"

"That's not a good idea, Mr. Birmingham. I—"

"You can introduce her as your research assistant."

"No, it just wouldn't work. I sometimes have to see people on short notice or at odd hours and—"

"I'll make my time as flexible as it needs to be," April interrupted.

When he looked at her, she added, "I don't have anything major on the go at the moment. I can be available whenever."

So this idea was something else the two of them had come up with beforehand. But agreeing to their "conditions" for tonight's conversation had been one thing. The prospect of April working with him was a completely different story, and one he had no intention of going along with.

Still looking at her, he said into the phone, "Will you both just listen for a minute. We're talking about trying to track down someone who murdered seven people, which means there's a chance things could get more than a little exciting. Surely you don't want your daughter exposed to any danger."

"My daughter's very good at taking care of herself. And I assume you are, too, so you won't be doing anything too risky."

"But—"

"Take it or leave it, Mr. Gardiner. I want her to know exactly what you're doing every step of the way. And everything you learn."

You mean, he said to himself, *you want her spying on me.*

"Decide," Birmingham told him. "Either she's in or we're done talking."

He glanced at her again. He didn't want her tagging along with him for a dozen different reasons. Aside from the potential danger, the most obvious one was that her father might be guilty.

What if that was true and April was there when proof surfaced? Hell, if they turned up something she didn't like, how did he know she wouldn't pull out a gun and kill him? No, her tagging along was definitely a bad idea. But he had a feeling Birmingham wasn't bluffing.

"What's your decision?" the man pressed.

Paul hesitated for a moment, but he'd come too far to back away now. "All right, she's in."

There wasn't the slightest change in her expression. At least, he consoled himself, he wouldn't have to worry about her giving anything away.

"Good," Birmingham said. "Then let's get down to the nitty-gritty. April said she told you that I've never really thought Walker and Gutteridge were the brains behind the bombing."

"Yes, she did."

"Still, since it would have given them one hell of a good reason to accuse me, I've never been absolutely certain. But you've already talked to them, so I'll just tell you about the fellows Mary and I think would have been more likely. We might be wrong, of course, but they're the ones I'd check out if I was in your shoes."

"Great. That's what I was hoping for. Some places to start."

"Okay, the first name is John Bellavia."

Paul scribbled it down as Birmingham spelled it.

"I have no idea where he is today, although a mental institution wouldn't surprise me. But during the Vietnam era he was in New York and was a member of AWV. And he had this thing for Mary. I mean, it started before I met her. John was on the scene before I knew her.

"He was a pretty crazy guy. Intelligent as hell, but… I don't really know whether he was a psychopath or just had a bizarre way of thinking, but he was definitely a misfit. The movement attracted a lot of the lunatic fringe.

"At any rate, Mary felt sorry for people like him. So she'd go for coffee with him and to the occasional rally, just to be kind. But he misread things and figured she was as interested in him as he was in her. She was trying to straighten out that assumption when she and I met. And then…well, I'd never really believed in love at first sight, but that's what happened with us."

Paul's glance involuntarily flickered to April. Thinking that he'd never believed in love at first sight, either, he forced his eyes back to his notebook.

"John didn't take well to my appearing on the scene," Birmingham continued. "He kept calling Mary and showing up whenever he knew where we'd be. He was…obsessed with her. That really isn't too strong a way of putting it. These days, he'd be labeled as a stalker and she'd have a restraining order against him. But back then, we just dealt with him as best we could.

"Anyway, he hated me. Blamed me for taking her away from him. But he was convinced she'd eventually see the light and come back to him. And when I say eventually, I mean this obsession lasted a long time. Even after Mary and I were married and our daughter was born, he was still hanging around. We've always wondered whether he could have deluded himself into believing she'd turn to him if I was out of the picture."

"You mean, if you were convicted of the bombing," Paul said, writing rapidly.

"Exactly."

"And he had the technical knowledge to have been the bomber?"

"Well, as I said, he was intelligent as hell. And good with his hands, too, so I'm sure he could have made a bomb with his eyes closed. Especially when the kind we made back then were pretty straightforward."

We. The word jumped out at Paul. It was more in line with "the ends justify the means" theory than with April's claim that her parents had only been involved in peaceful protests.

But there was no time to give that any thought because Birmingham had begun explaining about the bombs.

"Every self-respecting anarchist," he was saying, "knew that all you needed was a little nitric and sulfuric acid to make guncotton. Then you took some paraffin and a few other things, and presto, you had plastique.

"So, yes, I'd say there's no doubt John could have done it. I realize his motivation would have been insane, that any rational man would have given up on Mary after she'd married me. But as I said, John Bellavia was pretty crazy."

Paul didn't figure it was likely that someone would actually try to land a man in prison in the hope of winning his wife. Still, if Birmingham thought Bellavia was a viable suspect, he had to be worth checking out.

"Did he have any tie-in with Walker and Gutteridge?"

"Sure, he knew them."

"But would they have had a reason for saying you were the bomber? To keep Bellavia off the hook?"

"Well, they weren't friends. I mean, Walker and Gutteridge were friends, but John was a loner. He could have paid them to lie, though. His family was filthy rich."

"So he had both motive and means. But you said you've got no idea where he is today?"

"No. I've really told you all I can about him, though I know it's not much."

"Then what about your other possibilities?"

"Well, the second one's a fellow named Wayne Resdoe."

Paul's hand, poised to write, froze.

"What?" April said.

He glanced at her. She was eyeing him intently, and he realized she'd been watching all along for the slightest reaction.

"What?" she repeated.

He wasn't sure it was the smart thing to do, but he had a gut feeling he'd better go with the truth. Covering the speaker, he said, "I know one of the people your father suspects."

"Tell him."

Nodding, he said, "Mr. Birmingham?"

"Why don't we go with Colin."

"Colin, then...I know Wayne Resdoe."

There was a moment's silence before Colin said, "He isn't your contact at the bureau, is he?"

"No. I know him only slightly."

"Ah. Mouse mentioned you knew a few people there, but I figured the odds that one of them was Resdoe had to be awfully small."

"Mouse?" he repeated, looking at April.

She shrugged.

"My daughter."

"Yes, it just took me a second." But Mouse? She was one of the unmousiest looking women he'd ever seen.

"What do you think of him?" Colin demanded.

"Of Resdoe?" he said, forcing his eyes from April. "I don't know him very well, but... I guess the first words that come to mind are *self-serving bastard.*"

Colin laughed. "That tells me you're a good judge of character. And that Resdoe hasn't changed over the years. When I knew him... But maybe you already know that he infiltrated AWV for the feds."

"No, I didn't."

"Well, he did, and that's how I knew him. The bureau established a counterintelligence program against the protest movement, and they used a lot of their youngest agents—ones who could pass for university students."

"Cointelpro," Paul said, recalling the program's name from his research.

"Right. And Resdoe was part of it. Of course, at the time, we thought he was one of us. We didn't hear the truth until ten or fifteen years later, after someone in the Network learned he was an agent.

Then, when they checked into it, they discovered he'd been with the bureau while he was a member of AWV.

"At any rate, after the bombing there was buzz that it was Resdoe's caper. That was right afterward, before Walker and Gutteridge said I'd been responsible. I guess, after that, people forgot about Resdoe."

"But until then they figured he'd planted the bomb?" *And killed my father?*

"Not planted it. There were only a few hours when it could have been placed. You probably know the details about that, though."

"Yes. I do." The bomb had been set inside one of the worker's lockers. It hadn't been there when he'd gone off shift, but it had exploded four hours later.

"Well," Colin continued, "Resdoe had an alibi for the time, but he could have planned things and arranged for someone else to put it in the locker."

"Then...if the grapevine was right, the FBI was responsible?" Paul could feel his heart hammering against his ribs.

"Well, now we're getting into speculation. A lot of what I'm telling you is fact, like John Bellavia being a head case and Wayne Resdoe being an infiltrator. But when it comes to drawing conclusions, all I can do is guess."

"And what's your guess about the bureau's role in the bombing?"

"I think that if Resdoe was responsible, he wasn't acting on orders. Not that the bureau hasn't done things that go way beyond questionable, but I had

Resdoe pegged as an ambitious guy. And, as you put it, a self-serving bastard. So if he was the one, I think he had his own personal agenda.''

''Which involved?''

''Well, the way I see it, this would have been his thinking. He intentionally arranges for the bomb to go off while there are workers in the factory. That way the incident attracts maximum attention.''

''And he wants that because...?''

''Because he might have been a loose cannon, but he was still a fed. And the bureau loved incidents they could use against the protestors. You see, public sentiment was divided over the antiwar movement, and the feds milked the Unique bombing for all it was worth. They made sure there was a lot of press about how AWV members were violent subversives, murdering fellow Americans.

''But getting back to Resdoe's plan, before the bomb was set he'd have bribed Watson and Gutteridge to say I did it. And he'd have told them to be sure they had alibis for their whereabouts.''

He might have bribed them, Paul thought, using the ''discretionary'' funds that special agents had access to under some circumstances. He was about to ask why Resdoe would have chosen Colin to blame, but the man was already going on with his story.

''Then, the final step would have been revealing my whereabouts to whoever he reported to, so agents who weren't working undercover could nail me. Being instrumental in my arrest would have earned him a ton of points with his superiors.

''But that's where the wheels fell off his plan. Either he didn't get the information out fast enough or it wasn't acted on in time. At any rate, when the feds got to where I was supposed to be, Mary and Mouse and I were already gone.''

Paul slowly circled Resdoe's name in his notebook, wondering if his father and those six other people had really died because a renegade agent had made up his own game and been playing by his own rules. Died simply because Resdoe had wanted to earn himself points with the bureau.

He tried to force that possibility to the back of his mind. The fact that his father's life might have been sacrificed for such a trifling reason was something he'd need time to deal with. For the moment, he'd focus on the broader picture.

If an FBI agent had intentionally caused the death of innocent Americans... If that was what had happened, the story had to be told.

"You think that's an interesting possibility, huh?" Colin said.

"Yes. Extremely interesting."

"Well, just wait until you hear the other name I've got for you. How does Nelson Harmidarrow strike you?"

"State Senator Nelson Harmidarrow?"

"Bingo," Colin said.

APRIL DROVE ALONG Central Park North, still desperately wishing the cellular had an extension so she could be listening to both sides of the conversation. But she'd heard enough to know that her parents' list of names was awfully interesting.

When Paul had asked if her father thought the FBI was responsible, she'd almost driven into the car in

front of her. And when it came to Nelson Harmidarrow... She knew from what she'd read that he was
the New York counterpart of Tom Hayden—an outspoken student leader who'd later gone into politics.
And if he was on the list...

She wasn't sure exactly what sort of "suspects"
she'd been anticipating, but she'd never dreamed
they'd include the FBI and a senator. And the fact
they did was unsettling, to put it mildly.

By the time she'd reached the far side of the park
and was starting down Fifth Avenue, the conversation had moved from specifics to generalities. Paul
was asking questions about AWV, then jotting down
notes while her father talked.

Just as she was turning into the park at the Ninety-
seventh Street entrance, he said, "Well, that's all I
can think of right now, Colin, but it gives me a lot
to go on. I really appreciate your talking to me. I just
hope this ends up benefiting both of us.

"Sure," he added after a moment. "He wants to
speak to you." He handed April the cellular.

"What do you think?" her father asked the instant
she greeted him. "Was there anything in his reactions you didn't like?"

"No." She'd like to point out that she could easily
have missed something; trying to observe reactions
while driving in New York traffic was decidedly
tricky. But she could hardly do that with Paul sitting
right beside her.

"Good. And you're still okay about the rest of the
plan?"

"Of course."

"Then just be careful, Mouse. If anything happened to you because of this…"

"Nothing will," she said, with more conviction than she was feeling. If a senator wanted to keep Paul from learning anything more, she had little doubt he'd know people who could help him do it—in any number of ways. And she didn't even want to think about what the FBI was capable of arranging.

"Well, just be careful," her father said again. "And you know how anxious I'll be to hear what's happening, so keep me up to date."

"I will. Bye, Dad."

"Bye, darling."

She clicked off, then pulled over, stopped the car and said, "Okay, fill me in."

Paul smiled. "You don't believe in wasting time, do you."

"No. And hearing only one side of a conversation can be very frustrating."

When he smiled again, his dark eyes caught her gaze. She felt her pulse quicken and a warmth began curling deep within her. There was something just too appealing about that smile of his. And in the confines of the car she was very aware of his masculine, woodsy scent. It was subtle enough to be almost unnoticeable, so the fact that she could practically feel it seeping into her pores was most disconcerting.

Telling herself this was neither the time nor the place—and definitely not the man—for anything but the subject at hand, she forced her eyes from his.

"Okay," he said. "What we've got on your father's list is a guy from a wealthy family who was obsessed with your mother, a special agent who might have been marching to his own drummer, and Nelson Harmidarrow. Where do you want me to start?''

A special agent. So at least they weren't looking at the entire bureau. But she was most curious about Harmidarrow. "Let's start with the senator.''

"All right. He was one of the real biggies in AWV. Arguably the most influential of them. And at the time of the bombing, your parents had the sense that he had something to do with it.''

"Why?''

"Just things they knew and heard. No solid proof, but they felt he had to be involved one way or another.''

"Because?''

"That was a little vague, but I gathered it was mostly because not much happened in AWV that Harmidarrow didn't know about beforehand. Plus, Walker and Gutteridge figured he was the second coming. Your father thinks that if Harmidarrow had asked for their help, they'd have fallen all over themselves giving it to him.''

"They'd have said an innocent man was guilty just because Harmidarrow asked them to?''

Paul nodded. "And Harmidarrow might have had a motive for wanting to put the blame on your father. The two of them had knocked heads a few times.''

"Over?''

"He didn't really say. But if the senator wanted to protect his own hide by having someone else take the heat, who better than someone he didn't get along with? Oh, and he left AWV not long after the bombing. That's hardly an admission of guilt, but your father seemed to think it was significant."

"And who are his other suspects?"

Rapidly, Paul told her about them. By the time he finished, her head was reeling. This was the first she'd ever heard about someone being obsessed with her mother. And as for the possibility that a special agent had been the bomber...

Glancing across the car, she suddenly remembered that whoever the bomber was, he'd murdered Paul's father.

"Is this hard for you?" she said quietly, the words slipping out before she had time to consider if she really wanted to ask. "I mean, hearing my father talk about the bombing and who might have been responsible? Even though it was a long time ago, when you have a...personal involvement..."

She hesitated, aware her face was growing warm. She almost never asked personal questions because she didn't want anyone asking them of her, and she was already wishing she hadn't made an exception.

"It's a little hard," he said at last. "But it's something I've always known I had to do."

Fleetingly, she tried to imagine him as a child, determined that someday he was going to find the man who'd killed his father.

"What?" he said.

The mental image vanished.

"You looked lost in thought," he said.

"No. I mean..." She scrambled for a plausible explanation. "I guess it hadn't really occurred to me before, but how are you going to free up enough time to talk to everyone?"

He shrugged. "I've got some vacation days backed up, and a pretty good relationship with my producer. One way or another, I'll work it out."

"Then which of them do we start with?"

"Well, I already know where to find Wayne Resdoe. He works out of the Manhattan field office. Why don't I start by setting up an appointment with him?"

She anxiously caught her lower lip between her teeth.

"You don't like that idea?"

"I just wondered…well, an FBI agent…"

"You're having second thoughts? Look, you already know I don't think your being involved in this is a good idea. So I'm quite content to go it alone if you want out."

"I don't want out. I just wondered if Resdoe might not be the most dangerous of the three."

"April, the most dangerous is whoever's guilty. And we don't know who that is yet."

As APRIL HEADED OUT of the park, Paul said, "Are you returning the car tonight?"

She nodded. "I'll just take you home and—"

"No, don't bother. I'll go to the rental place with you. Is it near your apartment?"

"Uh-huh, over on Amsterdam. But driving you really isn't any bother. I—"

"Look, if you do that, it'll be getting dark before you make it home."

"Well…" She hesitated, not entirely sure why. New York might not be the safest city, and she was cautious enough to carry a can of pepper spray in her purse. But she didn't really worry a lot about being on her own at night.

"I could buy you a coffee or something after we drop off the car," Paul suggested.

If another man had said that, she'd have taken it as an indication of interest. She glanced over at Paul—and her pulse skipped a beat. His expression wasn't giving away a thing, but something in his eyes made her suspect he felt the same chemistry between them that she did.

"We should talk about how we're going to handle things," he added.

Things? She sincerely hoped he didn't mean they should talk about how they were going to handle the chemistry. She intended to pretend it didn't exist, so the less said the better.

He looked at her uncertainly for a moment, then elaborated. "You know. We've got to figure out the best way to approach our suspects."

"Oh, yes, of course," she said quickly. "Well, I think we should approach them very carefully."

For a split second longer, he continued to look at her. And then he laughed.

She'd never heard his laugh before, and it was so deep and easy that it did something funny to her insides. It also made her smile at him, despite herself.

"You're definitely right," he told her. "We do want to approach them carefully. So we should probably go with what your father suggested and introduce you as my research assistant. We could use the same approach I used with Walker and Gutteridge— give them the impression that 'Today's World' is doing a retrospective segment on the antiwar movement and kind of ease into the bombing.''

She turned onto West Seventy-seventh, then said, ''What if the senator or Wayne Resdoe finds out the show isn't actually doing anything on the movement? Wouldn't you be in trouble?''

''Not really. I'd just say he must have misunderstood—that I was only trying to see if there was the potential for an interesting segment. Anyway, I'll set up an appointment with Resdoe. And I'll start trying to track down John Bellavia and find out where Harmidarrow is. The senate won't be in session in July, so with any luck he'll be right here in town.''

They reached Amsterdam and drove the last block in silence. When she pulled up outside the rental place, Paul glanced at his watch, then at her. ''Would you mind if I used your phone? You asked me not to bring mine, remember? And I have to check for messages.''

She dug it out of her bag and handed it to him before they got out of the car. Then she went inside with the keys.

While the clerk did his paperwork, she absently looked out into the gathering twilight—and saw that Paul was talking on the phone, not listening to messages.   It made her wonder if he'd actually had enough time to check in with his machine and then make a call.

''There you are, Ms. Kelly,'' the clerk said.

''Thanks.'' She stuck the receipt into her bag and headed back outside, just as Paul was ending his conversation.

''I've still got time to walk you home,'' he said,

handing her the phone, "but I'm afraid we have to forget about the coffee. That was my producer I was talking to. He's got me booked on a midnight flight to Bogotá."

CHAPTER FIVE

"BOGOTÁ," APRIL REPEATED.

Her first thought was that Bogotá was a dangerous city. Her second was that Paul might not really be going there at all.

It would be quite the coincidence if he was suddenly being sent out of the country after he'd barely finished speaking to her father. Far more likely, now that he'd gotten those names he was trying to pull a double-cross. He wanted to talk to the suspects without her because...

Rats. She wasn't sure exactly what he was up to, but whatever it was, she didn't intend to let him get away with it.

"I've been working on a segment about some Colombian drug lords," he offered as they headed along Amsterdam. "And we got a tip that something important's going down in the next day or two."

"So you have to be there."

"Uh-huh. Me and a photographer."

"Do you get hit with this sort of thing often? I mean, here it is, Saturday night, and one minute you're going for coffee, the next you're heading for the airport instead?"

When he smiled, she realized she was almost getting used to the tiny rush of warmth his smile sent through her. Then she reminded herself that he was probably trying to double-cross her and the warmth vanished.

"Well, news events don't get scheduled around weekends, so I've learned to keep a bag packed. The last time I got a rush call like this, I ended up in California, covering a cult suicide. When there's something you know your competitors are going to be crawling all over, you want to get there fast to see if you can come up with a unique angle."

He began elaborating on that as they turned down West Seventy-fifth, but she was only half listening. Mostly, she was trying to figure out why he wanted to see those suspects on his own.

Or maybe that wasn't it at all. He might have something in mind that hadn't even occurred to her.

And of course, if he was a fed, everything was part of an elaborate plan to trap her father.

While she was telling herself she couldn't forget that for a second, he said, "I won't be gone long, and as soon as I'm back we'll start digging around about the bombing. And, hey, after they've had me working forty-eight hours or more straight, it'll be even easier to get off whatever time I need."

"Yes…but this delay isn't good, is it."

"What do you mean?"

"Well, my father figures that after you told Gutteridge about Walker's statement, he probably contacted the real bomber."

"Talking to him the second time was a calculated risk," Paul said slowly. "I realized that, but I was hoping I could make him admit the truth. Hell, I figured there was even a chance he'd tell me who the real bomber was.''

"He didn't, though.''

"No. But if he had... Well, regardless of that, he hasn't necessarily told anyone anything. I tried my darnedest to convince him I wouldn't be following up any further.''

"And he bought that?''

"I'm not sure. But when he said there wasn't a grain of truth to Walker's story, I acted as if I'd never seriously thought there could be—that I'd just been curious about why he'd have concocted it and was hoping Gutteridge might have some idea.''

"But if he didn't believe you... Paul, if there's anyone else who knows Walker's telling the truth—anyone who could back up what he said—then the longer they have to get to that person, to convince him he should keep quiet if you contact him...''

She paused, uneasily reflecting on the way that 'anyone' might be "convinced.''

"At any rate, now we've got this delay,'' she said, getting back to her point. "And if Gutteridge *has* talked to the real bomber...''

They'd reached her building and she stopped at the bottom of the steps. "In case he has, we shouldn't be wasting any time. Which means that maybe I'd better go and talk to Resdoe while you're gone. And the senator as well, if he does turn out to be right here in the city.''

"What? By yourself? Without me?''

She nodded, not letting herself react to the look of horror that crossed his face.

"I could say exactly what you were going to,''

she continued, watching him for more reactions. "That I'm your research assistant, and 'Today's World' is doing a retrospective on the antiwar movement. I certainly know enough about it—and the bombing—to ask intelligent questions."

"No, that's a really bad idea. I mean, I'm not doubting that you could handle it, but you'd be screwing things up for us. It's..."

She could practically see his mind scrambling for words that would sound convincing.

"It's the politics of the thing," he continued. "The status aspect. We're talking about a state senator and a senior special agent. I'd never send a research assistant on her own to see them. Not initially, at least. Hell, that would be a real slap in the face. And they both know it, so even if they gave you appointments, they'd realize something wasn't kosher."

"Oh. Yes...I guess that makes sense."

He nodded, looking relieved. "As you said, we should approach them very carefully. And if you went alone, you might as well wear a sign reading, Hey, I'm Up to Something Here."

"Yes, you're right. I guess it'll just have to wait till you're finished with your drug lords."

"I won't be gone long," he assured her again. "I'll be there in the morning, and I bet I'll be back by Monday night. Sometime Tuesday at the latest. And as soon as I'm home, I'll call you."

And I, she silently said, *will figure out something useful to do in the meantime.*

APRIL CAME AWAKE IN the darkness of her bedroom, her heart pounding. She'd heard a strange noise in the apartment. The sound of something sliding, like a window being opened or closed.

Lying there, not moving, listening intently, she told herself it couldn't have been a window.

Not that she always kept them locked up tight. She wasn't fond of air-conditioning, so she often left them open to the night air. But unless Spider-Man had climbed up the brownstone's exterior, the only third-floor window anyone could get even remotely close to was the one that opened onto the fire escape. And that one she did keep securely locked. Plus, it had chicken-wire glass.

After a few moments, she glanced at the clock, saw it was almost four-thirty, then quietly sat up in bed and reached for her cell phone—all the while listening for another sound.

There was nothing. Nothing except the noise of traffic in the city that never sleeps, noise drifting through the night from Amsterdam and Columbus.

She listened for another minute, telling herself she'd probably imagined the sound. After all, Spider-Man didn't really exist. And her place was as safe as Fort Knox.

That was what the landlord had assured her before she'd signed the lease, and she'd never had any reason to think otherwise. Still, she doubted she'd get back to sleep unless she checked things out, so she switched on the light and dug the can of pepper spray out of her purse. Then, the can in one hand and her cellular in the other, she inspected the entire apartment, assuring herself she really was alone.

Despite that reassurance, when she went back to

bed she couldn't fall asleep again. At six-thirty she gave up trying and had a shower. After that, she tidied up some loose ends in a client's file, killing time until it was a reasonable hour to make phone calls. Then she retrieved Paul's business card from her purse. If he hadn't caught a plane to Bogotá, he'd probably be smart enough not to answer any phone calls, but it was worth a try.

When she dialed his apartment, she got an answering machine and hung up. His cellular number connected her to voice mail, which she hung up on, as well. That only left her NBS to try. Once she reached its automated phone system, she buttonpunched her way to his voice mail there.

"I'm not available at the moment," it said. "So either leave me a message or press zero to talk to a real person."

She pressed zero, which led her to somebody else's voice mail.

Hanging up, she told herself she was only wasting time when she should be doing something productive. But what?

Talking to Resdoe or the senator was out. In the first place, she'd never be able to track either of them down on a Sunday. In the second place, whether she liked it or not, Paul had been right. Talking to them on her own would be a mistake. But there were a couple of people it might be a good idea to talk to.

The other day, when she'd been checking up on what Paul had told her, she'd popped Ken Gutteridge and Tom Walker's names into one of the search engines on the Internet. For Walker, she'd gotten an address and phone number in Bridgeport.

Gutteridge's name had taken her to a Web site for the Port's View Motel in Port Credit, Ontario, which he both owned and managed. And since she couldn't find any other address for him, she assumed he lived there, as well.

There was no guarantee, though, that they were the AWV Walker and Gutteridge. Possibly, Paul had simply searched on the Internet himself and found two names that were the same as the "informers'." If that was the case, his entire story about visiting them was a crock. As were the tape and signed confession.

"One mistake," she murmured to herself. If he'd made just one mistake and she caught it, she'd know that he was either FBI or a dead man's son out for revenge.

She picked up the phone once more and reserved a rental car, thankful that at least one of the two men was within easy driving range. Barely two hours later she was in a gas station on the outskirts of Bridgeport, buying a city map. Locating Lincoln Avenue on it, she started off again.

Bridgeport, she noticed as she drove along Main Street, was a town down on its luck. A lot of vacant buildings displayed For Lease signs and others had simply been boarded up. The sense of a town in decay was still prevalent when she finally spotted Lincoln ahead on the left.

She turned and began watching for Walker's house, which proved to be a run-down bungalow with an overgrown yard and a horde of kids playing road hockey on the street in front of it.

Hoping her car would be safe from their game, she

parked farther down the block and began walking back, assuring herself things would go just fine. If Tom Walker didn't have a clue who Paul Gardiner was, that would tell her all she needed to know. On the other hand, if this was the AWV Tom Walker, she might learn something.

Of course, she'd have to watch what she said. If that statement and tape were for real, he'd given them to Paul in confidence. He wouldn't like the idea that she knew about them. And since he'd flatly refused to tell Paul who the real bomber was, he'd hardly tell her. So she probably shouldn't even mention the bombing, just hope to get lucky with the questions she'd dreamed up.

Reaching the house, she rang the bell. If it was working she couldn't hear it, so when nobody responded, she knocked loudly on the screen door, feeling more ill at ease by the second. She might be good at lying, but unless it was essential, she usually felt guilty doing it.

She reminded herself that Walker was one of the men who'd accused her father, and that the truth wouldn't get her anywhere with him. So in a way, lying to him was unavoidable.

While she was complimenting herself on that bit of logic, she heard a lock turn and held her breath as the inner door slowly opened, revealing a man in pyjamas and a striped bathrobe.

"Yes?" he said through the screen.

"Mr. Thomas Walker?"

"Yes?"

She exhaled slowly. His voice had the slightly

raspy sound of the voice on the tape. And he had the shrunken, pasty appearance of a man dying of cancer.

"Mr. Walker, my name's April Kelly and I'm Paul Gardiner's research assistant."

He instantly looked wary.

"Paul asked me to tell you something before I say anything more," she quickly added. "I'm aware that he taped an interview with you, but I have no idea what it was about. All he told me was that it didn't relate to the segment we're doing."

He eyed her for a long moment, then slowly nodded.

She began to breathe more easily. He wasn't going to slam the door in her face, and she'd established that at least part of what Paul had told her was true. So far so good.

"I hope this isn't a bad time," she said. "But when we started putting the segment together we realized we should touch on a couple of other angles. Paul said he didn't think you'd mind talking to me, so if it wouldn't be too much of an imposition…"

"No, I'm not doing anything."

He unlatched the screen, then turned and began shuffling down the hall, moving like a ninety-year-old rather than someone in his fifties.

Closing the door behind herself, she followed him into the living room. It was as tired looking as he was, with magazines and newspapers strewn all over the couch.

He shoved a few of them aside, gestured for her to sit down, then eased himself into a recliner that faced the TV set. He switched it off as she dug a pen and notebook out of her bag. "You know," he said, "you remind me of someone, but I can't think who."

Her heart froze. She didn't think she looked *that* much like her mother.

"If we were in a singles bar, I'd think that was a pickup line," she told him, managing a smile.

When he wanly returned her smile, she said, "So, what we decided the segment still needs is something about the sorts of people that the protest groups attracted. In retrospect, we came up with three basic types, but we wanted to run our thoughts past someone who was there."

"Sure. Go ahead."

She gave him another smile. "Okay, it seems as if there were some people who saw the protest movement as a political process—men like Tom Hayden and Nelson Harmidarrow, who ended up going from protest politics to state politics."

When Walker didn't so much as blink at Harmidarrow's name, she added, "I guess you must have known Senator Harmidarrow? With both of you being in AWV?"

"A lot of people belonged to AWV. But yes, I knew Nelson. Not well, but I knew him."

She resisted the urge to ask whether, as her father had said, both Walker and Gutteridge would have lied to the feds to protect the man.

"So," she said instead, "could we say that people like Hayden and Harmidarrow were at one end of the spectrum and the lunatic fringe was at the other?"

"Yes, that would be a fair way of putting it. All the protest groups had their crazies."

"Were there any who you particularly remember

from AWV?'' she asked, willing him to mention John Bellavia's name.

''Not really,'' he said. ''It was a long time ago, and most of the kids I associated with were like me— college students who didn't think America should be in that war. But I guess that's the third type you and Paul came up with. Just average people who didn't like the war.''

''Exactly.'' She made a few notes so she'd look authentic, her disappointment growing. She was zero for two, and if he had nothing to say about Wayne Resdoe, it would be strike three.

''There's one other thing we want to include a bit about,'' she said, glancing up from her notebook. ''We know the FBI infiltrated the major protest groups, but were people aware of it at the time? I mean, were you careful about what you said and who you said it to?''

''Careful? I think *paranoid* would be more accurate. We weren't sure whether the feds had actually infiltrated or were only relying on civilian spies, but we knew we were walking a thin line between what was legal and what they'd jump on.''

''And were there specific people you suspected of being civilian spies? Or agents?''

While Walker thought about that, she tried not to look expectant. When he shook his head, she tried not to look disappointed.

''No, I think there was just a general sense that you should watch what you said to practically everyone.''

She made another note, and when she looked at him again he had his hand to his mouth and was pushing himself out of the chair. "Excuse me," he mumbled. "I need to take a pill."

Watching him hobble from the room, she wasn't quite certain how meeting him had made her feel. For as long as she could remember, she'd hated the two nameless men who'd claimed her father was the bomber. But now that she'd seen what was happening to Walker... Well, it was sad to see anyone in his condition.

She glanced slowly around the room, her gaze coming to rest on the end table beside the recliner. She hadn't noticed what was on it while he'd been sitting down, but now she saw that his phone was there. And beside it was a little directory—lying open.

For half a second, she hesitated. But she could hear tap water running, so she had time for a peek.

Quickly, she headed over to the table and looked down at the book. It was open to the *G* page, and there were only three entries on it. Garage, followed by a phone number. George's Pizza, with its number. And Ken Gutteridge, with the address and number she already had for the Port's View Motel in Port Credit.

Her heart skipped a beat. Walker didn't look in any shape to be fancying pizza or driving a car. So had he called Gutteridge recently? And if so, why?

ONCE SHE GOT BACK to the car, April took her cellular from her purse, called the Port's View Motel and asked for Ken Gutteridge. If she got him, she'd hang up, but she had to establish whether he was there.

The idea of going all the way to see him was crazy enough. She certainly didn't want to get there and find he was on vacation. Or that he was never anywhere near the motel on Sundays.

When a woman answered the call, April asked to speak to Gutteridge.

"I could put you through to his apartment," the woman said, "but I know for certain that he's out. He should be back by about four, though. He works evenings. Would you like to leave a message?"

"Thanks, but I'll call back." She pushed End, put down the phone and began looking for the airport on her map. Driving to Bridgeport hadn't been a major deal, but Paul had said Port Credit was a suburb of Toronto, which would mean a heck of a long car trip.

Pulling away from the curb, she assured herself this wasn't a completely crazy idea. That book being open at Gutteridge's name had struck her as an obvious omen. And just because she didn't normally act on impulse, there was no reason she shouldn't today.

Still, by the time she'd parked at the airport she was having serious second thoughts. But they were driven away when she discovered she was just in time to catch a plane that would connect with one to Toronto.

She took that as another omen. The fact that there were no flights back to Bridgeport tonight, which meant she wouldn't get back to pick up her car until tomorrow, was only a minor inconvenience.

"Okay, all set," the USAir clerk told her, handing over the ticket. "You'll fly to Baltimore with us, then on to Toronto with Air Ontario. That'll get you in just after four-thirty.''

She nodded, trying not to think about how much she'd had to pay for this last-minute booking.

''You'd better hurry,'' the clerk added. ''They've already called your flight.''

She thanked him, then headed for the gate and boarded. When the engines rumbled to life, she was still hoping she was doing the right thing. But she did have a feeling she was going to learn something useful from Gutteridge. And since she hadn't learned a darned thing from Walker…

No, that wasn't true, she reminded herself as the plane began rolling across the tarmac. Maybe he hadn't said anything useful about their suspects, but now she knew that Paul hadn't fabricated his story.

He hadn't fabricated the part of his story about having talked to Walker and Gutteridge, she silently corrected herself. That didn't mean she could start trusting him. Especially when she was still wondering whether he was actually in Bogotá or was playing games.

As desperately as she hoped he wasn't, she just couldn't be sure. But if he did ultimately prove to be one of the good guys…

Against her better judgment, she let her thoughts start wandering down that road. She was certain he was attracted to her. She could see it in his eyes and feel the chemistry between them. And saying she was attracted to him would be a distinct understatement.

When he was around, she was so intensely aware of him that she had trouble keeping her eyes off him. Even when he wasn't around… Well, she'd never before met a man who seemed to be almost constantly on her mind. So if he *didn't* turn out to be one of the good guys...

She prayed that wouldn't happen. And she refused to admit, even to herself, how upsetting she found the possibility that it might.

"WE'RE BEGINNING OUR descent into Toronto," the captain announced. "And the weather there is hot, hazy and humid."

Hazy, April thought, didn't even come close. She wasn't exactly a white-knuckle flier, but the plane was enshrouded in the sort of heavy gray clouds that always made her pray the radar system had been inspected recently.

"It's thirty-eight degrees, with ninety-percent humidity," the captain added.

"Thirty-eight degrees?" She glanced at the woman seated beside her, a Torontonian she'd been chatting with during the flight.

"We use Celsius in Canada. In Fahrenheit that would be...right around a hundred, I think. With these clouds, there'll probably be a terrific thunderstorm once it starts cooling down."

April nodded, then spent the rest of the descent hoping the storm would hold off until after she'd seen Gutteridge.

Her seatmate had told her that Port Credit wasn't too far from the airport, and once they'd landed, she looked for a taxi stand rather than a car rental counter. It proved to be a wise choice. Toronto in rush hour was the same sort of bumper-to-bumper nightmare as New York.

While they crawled south down one highway, then west along another, the meter endlessly clicking, she told herself that at least she was getting time to review what she planned to say to Gutteridge.

She'd stick with the story that she was Paul's research assistant, of course. Walker hadn't doubted it, so there was no reason Gutteridge should. And maybe if she said that Paul had asked her to follow up with both of them, and that she'd already visited Walker…

Yes, that was a good idea. Since Gutteridge knew Walker had admitted lying about the bomber's identity, he'd be worried that his old friend might have provided her with even more revelations. And his worrying might put him off balance.

Eventually, they took an exit that led to Lakeshore Boulevard and Ken Gutteridge's motel. The Port's View was modern and attractive and looked out on what the cabbie told her was the Port Credit Yacht Club.

"You gotta reservation?" he asked, pointing at the No Vacancy sign.

If she weren't so nervous, the question would have made her laugh. She might need a room for the night, but she'd rather stay at the motel in *Psycho* than here.

"Or you want maybe I should wait?" the cabbie offered.

"No, thanks, I'll be fine." After paying him, she climbed out of the air-conditioned cab into the muggy heat, then straightened her dress and took a deep breath.

Through the front window of the office, she could

see a middle-aged man behind the counter. Since it was well after five, he was probably Gutteridge.

She spent a minute sizing him up, this second man she'd hated, in the abstract, for as long as she could remember. He was average height, with a receding hairline, glasses and a potbelly. Thinking he looked far too ordinary for a man who'd helped destroy her parents' lives, she opened the door and stepped inside.

He glanced over at her—and suddenly looked as if he'd seen a ghost.

"My God," he whispered. "It's you."

She simply stared at him. She had no idea who he thought she was, but he looked so frightened that she felt scared herself. Then he regained his composure and asked, "What do you want?"

For a few horrible seconds, she couldn't come up with her opening line. "Well, I'm Paul Gardiner's research assistant," she said at last, "and—"

"Cut the crap. You're Jillian Birmingham. What do you want?"

Her mouth went dry. He clearly wasn't guessing. He knew who she was, so there was no point denying it.

But how did he know? And what had possessed her to come here?

Omens, she remembered, deciding on the spot that she was never going to take anything as an omen again.

"Did Gardiner send you?" he demanded. "And what the hell are the two of you up to, anyway?"

"I...Mr. Gutteridge, could we back up for a minute? How do you know who I am?"

"Never mind that. Why are you here?"

"No, first tell me... No, wait, we're not going to get anywhere like this. Why don't we take turns answering each other's questions."

"Fine. Ladies first."

"This is the nineties. Let's toss for it."

He eyed her for a moment, then pulled a quarter out of his pocket and flipped it to her.

"Heads or tails?" she said as she caught it.

"Heads."

She tossed the quarter, caught it against the back of her hand and looked at it.

"Tails." She held it out for him to see. "So how do you know who I am?"

"Joey?" he called into the office behind the counter.

A young man emerged.

"Take care of things until I get back," Gutteridge said. "Come on," he added to April. "As they say, a picture's worth a thousand words."

CHAPTER SIX

STILL SHAKEN THAT Gutteridge had instantly recognized her, April followed him to the far end of the motel, where the last two units had been converted into a fair-sized apartment.

"Have a seat," he told her. "I've got a tape you might be interested in."

Wondering what on earth he was going to show her, she perched nervously on the couch while he clicked on the television and stuck a tape in the VCR.

He pressed Play, then moved away from the set as an image of Paul appeared.

She was so taken aback that she didn't immediately notice he was standing beside a Budget car rental counter. Just as she did, she walked into the picture.

"My God," she whispered, nervously fingering her grandmother's locket. The tape was of her and Paul at La Guardia.

"So it *is* interesting," Gutteridge said. "I only wish there was sound."

Watching herself stop in front of Paul, she could almost hear his deep voice saying, "Jillian?"

On the screen, she nodded.

They both mouthed a few more words and then he smiled. Rather than a rush of warmth, his smile sent a chill through her. Why had he wanted a taped record of their meeting? Because he was FBI?

That seemed the only logical answer. For some reason the bureau had wanted her on video.

She blinked back hot tears, feeling angry, hurt and foolishly gullible. But there wasn't time to worry about how she felt. Or about the fact that Paul was dirty, lying pond scum. She had to come up with a plan for damage control, because this trip had been an enormous mistake.

If Gutteridge hadn't already contacted the real bomber, he'd be certain to now that Colin Birmingham's daughter had shown up at his door—unless she could figure out some nonthreatening explanation for why she was here.

Focusing on the TV set once more, she tried to come up with something Gutteridge would believe and watch the screen at the same time. The tape had progressed to where she and Paul were sitting in the coffee shop, where he'd been telling her about tracking down the men who'd claimed her father was the bomber.

"Don't miss the next bit," Gutteridge said. "There's some special editing."

Her gaze flickered to him, then she looked back at the television just as Paul smiled again. This time, she felt as if someone had stuck a knife in her stomach and was twisting it. He said something more, the tape faded to black for a second, then the last bit was repeated in slow motion.

"Can you read his lips?" Gutteridge asked. "It took me a few tries, but I finally made out that he's saying, 'Their names are Tom Walker and Ken Gutteridge.'" He clicked the remote, pausing the tape. "What was he talking about when he told you that?"

Thinking rapidly, she decided that he'd undoubtedly figured out the answer, so she'd better go with the truth. "He was talking about the Unique factory bombing. I said I'd never known the names of the men who claimed my father was responsible, and he told me. But where did you get this tape?" she added, not wanting to dwell on the bombing.

"It arrived by FedEx a few days ago."

"Sent by...? There must have been a name and return address."

"Yeah, but when I checked them out they were phony. You're getting ahead of me on questions, though, so why don't we try my original one again. What are you doing here?"

"I..." She paused, at a complete loss for words. She had nothing except the research assistant story, and he already knew that was a lie.

"If you tell me everything," he said, "I'll show you the note that came with the tape."

Oh, Lord, there was a note. And she'd have to tell him something if she wanted to see it. When not even a remotely plausible lie came to mind, she had to go with more of the truth.

"Okay," she said. "I wanted to talk to you because Paul told me that Tom Walker had changed his story. That he was saying my father wasn't really responsible for the bombing."

"And why would that make you want to talk to me? Why didn't you go see Walker?"

"I did. This morning. But... You know he's very ill?"

Gutteridge nodded.

"Well, he was so pathetic that I just couldn't ask him about it. I knew that if I did he'd be upset, because he'd discussed it with Paul in confidence. And when I couldn't make myself get into it with him, I decided to come and see what you had to say."

"Didn't Gardiner fill you in? I told him Walker was lying, which is the truth."

"I just…I guess I had to hear you say it for myself, because I can't figure out why in the world he'd make up something like that."

"Hell, I've been trying to figure it out ever since Gardiner asked me about it. And the only thing I've been able to think of is that the cancer's eating the guy's brain. He's called me a few times lately, and he hasn't always been too coherent."

Which meant, April thought, that Walker's book being open at the *G* page probably hadn't been significant after all. He'd just been phoning Gutteridge to talk about whatever.

Looking as sincere as she could, she said, "Deep down, I guess I knew that changing his story didn't make much sense, but I was hoping against hope that maybe…"

"Hey," Gutteridge said quietly, "I understand why you wouldn't want to believe your father was responsible, but I'm afraid he was. I mean, ask yourself this question. If it was somebody else, why didn't Walker go all the way and give Gardiner the real bomber's name?"

"I don't know."

She knew her father hadn't been the bomber, though. Never, in her entire life, had she doubted the truth of that. But why *had* Walker stopped short of telling Paul who the real bomber was?

"I want to ask you about something else," Gutteridge said. "How did you get involved with Gardiner?"

Involved. For a second, she couldn't keep from wondering just how involved they might have gotten if she hadn't found him out.

Forcing the thought away, she said, "He ran a classified ad trying to get in touch with me, and I answered it. Then he asked me to meet with him. And as you saw, I did."

"What did he want?"

"To talk to my father—to follow up on Walker changing his story. He thought I might make it happen."

"Did you?"

"No. I don't know where my parents are."

Gutteridge didn't look as if he believed that, but he merely popped the video out and said, "I assume you weren't aware you were being taped?"

"Of course I wasn't."

"Do you have any idea who'd have done it?"

She merely shook her head.

"Have you seen Gardiner since that day?"

"No," she lied, not wanting to give away any more than she already had. "When I said I couldn't help him out, that was it. I got the impression he was just going to let things drop," she added.

Gutteridge probably wouldn't buy that, but it was worth a shot.

"Well," she said, then paused. She'd been about to say she should be going, but she'd almost forgotten something important. "You said a note came with the tape."

"Uh-huh." He opened a drawer and produced a sheet of paper with a single paragraph typed on it.

By the time she'd finished skimming it, her hands were trembling. The message read, "The man in the tape is Paul Gardiner, an investigative journalist with NBS. The woman goes by the name of April Kelly and has a Manhattan business called Smooth Moves. But she's really Jillian Birmingham, Colin's daughter. And the two of them are going to get you."

She sat gazing at the words, trying to think logically. Aside from her parents, the only person who knew her real identity was Paul. But whoever he actually was, whatever he was actually up to, the last thing he'd want was Gutteridge knowing for certain that he represented a threat.

Of course, if he was FBI, by now the entire bureau could know who she was. But why would another agent send Gutteridge the tape?

While she was trying to come up with a plausible reason for that, another possibility occurred to her. Maybe someone else had learned who she really was. Someone not connected with the feds at all.

She had no idea who it might be or where he'd fit into the picture, but if there was someone else, then she might have jumped to the wrong conclusion. Maybe it hadn't been Paul who'd arranged to tape their meeting. Maybe he'd be just as surprised by all this as she was.

There were a hundred different thoughts tumbling around in her mind, but she latched tightly onto that one, and it started a fluttering sensation near her heart. If he wasn't one of the bad guys after all...

Almost afraid to let herself continue that line of thinking, she reread the note—this time catching something that hadn't registered the first time through.

"The man in the tape is Paul Gardiner," she read aloud, glancing at Gutteridge. "But you didn't need to be told that."

"Right. Whoever sent it must not have known he'd been to see me. But what about the rest of it? Are the two of you trying to get me?"

"No. I told you. Paul wanted to talk to my father and I said I couldn't help him out. That was it."

"And who knew you'd arranged to meet him?"

"Nobody. At least I didn't tell anyone."

"Then he must have, because somebody obviously knew."

"But..." She paused, reminding herself that the less information she gave Gutteridge the better.

"But what?" he asked.

"I don't know. I can't make any sense of this. That tape, on its own, is meaningless—although I find it awfully spooky that someone was spying on me. But the note saying that we're going to get you... Who would want to make you think we're a threat to you when we're not?"

Gutteridge pinned her with his gaze, and she had a horrible feeling that he could see she was lying. Could see that she'd love to get him, because by proving he'd lied, she would be proving her father was innocent.

"If you're not a threat," he said at last, "I have no idea who'd want me to think you are."

BY THE TIME APRIL had checked into a hotel near the airport she was exhausted. The promised thunderstorm was raging outside her window, and she'd have liked nothing better than to lie down and watch the lightning flash. But her father had asked her to keep him up-to-date on what was happening. And even if he hadn't, she needed help with thinking her way through everything she'd learned.

She glanced longingly at the phone beside the bed, knowing she couldn't use it. Creating a record of her parents' number, dialed from her hotel room, would be almost as risky as calling them on her cellular or from her apartment phone.

She didn't want their number showing up on any records linked to her, and with that in mind, she wearily headed back down to the lobby and found a pay phone.

"Hi, Dad," she said when he answered.

"Mouse." His voice told her he assumed she'd found out something.

And she had, of course, but it was hardly anything either of them had been expecting. Quickly, she filled him in, starting with Paul's alleged departure for Bogotá and ending with her visit to Gutteridge.

"So even though I started off thinking the tape meant Paul had to be FBI," she concluded, "by the time Gutteridge and I were done, I wasn't sure. I mean, if Paul is a fed, what reason could he have had for filming our meeting? And the idea of his sending the tape to Gutteridge seems even less probable. Especially with that note. But what do you think?''

There was a moment's silence, then her father said, ''Darling, I think that you shouldn't have gone to see Gutteridge on your own. Being alone with him in that motel room could have been dangerous.''

''Dad, it wasn't a motel room. I told you, he owns the Port's View and we were in his apartment there. And he'd hardly have done anything to me when people knew I was there with him.''

''You can never be sure what people will do.''

''Well…okay, you're right. I probably shouldn't have gone on my own,'' she said to avoid further discussion. ''But what do you think about Paul and the tape? Did he have anything to do with it or not?''

''He must have. Whoever shot it had to know where and when you were meeting him. And if you didn't tell a soul, he must have.''

''Not necessarily. If someone checked out who'd placed that classified, they could have had him under constant surveillance. And if they followed him to the airport with a camera ready to roll…''

''I guess that could be what happened. But we can't assume it was. Not as long as we aren't certain which side he's on. What about Gutteridge, though? He must have some idea who'd want to warn him.''

''Well, if he does, he wasn't telling me. So what should I do now? Just sit tight and wait for Paul to get back from Bogotá?''

''You mean, assuming that's where he actually is.''

''Yes. Assuming,'' she agreed unhappily.

Her father was silent again, then he said, "I think what you should do now is back off."

"What? You mean not even go to see Harmidarrow and Resdoe with Paul? But then we'd only have his version of what they say."

"No, Mouse, what I mean is that both you and I should simply forget this whole thing. Tell Gardiner you're out. That I've decided your mother and I are just fine the way we are. That I don't really care about proving my innocence."

"But you do! I know you do."

"Not as much as I care about your safety. Look, I don't know why anybody would want to make a tape of you or would warn Gutteridge that you're trying to get him, but I do know it's not good. So let's just quit while we're ahead, okay?"

"But—"

"Mouse, listen to me. I think you're right that it wouldn't have made sense for Gardiner to send that tape. Or for another fed to have. Which leaves us with your 'someone else' idea."

"You think that's it?"

"Yeah, I think it is."

"Someone like whom?" she asked, even though she was afraid she knew the answer.

"Like the bomber," her father said quietly.

Those words kept her awake for hours, until long after the thunderstorm was over. And when she finally fell asleep, they haunted her dreams. She woke up feeling as if she hadn't slept at all.

Hoping that some sunlight would make her feel better, she opened the drapes—and was greeted by heavy fog. Very heavy fog, she thought uneasily. The pea-soup kind that socked in airports.

Switching on the TV, she channel-surfed until she found a weather station. And sure enough, there were no flights getting in or out of Toronto.

Gloomily, she hit the shower. There wasn't a chance she'd make her connecting flight in Baltimore. And the next one didn't leave for Bridgeport until five o'clock, which meant by the time she'd driven back to New York, she'd have wasted the entire day and the evening to boot.

ALL GOOD INVESTIGATIVE journalists had a finely tuned sixth sense, and Paul's was making him more anxious by the second.

Glancing up through the deepening twilight, he saw that the third story of the brownstone where April lived was still in darkness.

That was hardly surprising, though. She couldn't have sneaked in past him. Still, he hadn't been able to stop himself from checking her windows every couple of minutes.

Forcing his gaze from them, he paced the width of the building once more, wondering for the millionth time where she was. And why he hadn't been able to get in touch with her since he'd left.

He'd phoned her yesterday, after he arrived in Bogotá, to make sure he'd convinced her to stay away from Resdoe and Harmidarrow while he was gone. But he'd gotten her answering machine at the apartment and her voice mail on her cellular number. And the messages he'd left, asking her to call him back, had gone unanswered. Then, when he'd phoned her from the plane on the way home and had still gotten machines, he'd begun feeling so uneasy that he'd come here straight from the airport.

He looked up at her windows yet again, thinking he should have worked harder to convince her there was a lot of potential danger in a situation like this one. And that if she made a bad move on her own…

Telling himself he was getting nowhere standing around worrying, he picked up his bag and the laptop's carrying case, slung their straps over his shoulder and started down the block in the direction of Amsterdam Avenue.

He didn't have any idea where her parents were living, but he suspected it would be within driving distance of their only child. And maybe, after his conversation with her father, April had decided she'd like to talk to him about their suspects. In person.

If that was it, he had nothing to be concerned about. And he could probably learn whether she'd rented a car in the past day or two by simply talking a good story to the clerk.

Reaching the corner, he turned onto Amsterdam, then breathed a huge sigh of relief when he got far enough up the block to see the rental place. April was just coming out of it.

He continued walking as she started down the other side of the street, wondering if she'd look over and spot him. She was wearing a white dress with a skirt that swirled around her knees as she moved. And high heels that emphasized how long and shapely her legs were. Just looking at them was enough to make him—

He suddenly stopped in his tracks, frozen by an explosion of noise.

Gunfire! As his brain identified it, people across the street were diving for the pavement—April among them. Ice-cold fear pierced his chest, then a surge of adrenaline jolted him to action and he dashed into the traffic at a dead run.

Brakes squealed. Horns blared. "Call 911," someone was screaming.

Then he reached April and his heart slammed against his ribs. She was starting to sit up. She wasn't dead.

"Are you all right?" he said, tossing down his bags and dropping to his knees beside her.

Her face was pale in the glow of the streetlights, and her eyes were dark with fear, but she nodded. "I...yes. I hit the sidewalk pretty hard, but I'm okay."

Wrapping his arms around her and pulling her close, he sat cradling her.

She was alive—soft and warm against him. But for a few seconds he'd known she could be dead. And they'd been the most terrible seconds he'd ever experienced.

He exhaled slowly, trying to get his heartbeat back to normal. When he breathed in again, her sultry scent made him want to hold her forever.

"What were you doing here?" she murmured.

Her breath, fanning his neck, sent a hot rush of desire through him.

"I was looking for you."

"Looks like you found me," she whispered.

The words started his heart racing erratically once more.

He hadn't forgotten that he couldn't let himself fall for her. Not this woman whose father might have murdered his. Yet she'd been almost constantly on his mind for the past couple of days, and now, the way she felt in his arms...

He realized he shouldn't keep sitting here holding her, but when she made no move to stand up, he continued to do precisely that. He was only vaguely aware of other people on the sidewalk, of sirens growing closer, car doors slamming and the rise and fall of voices.

Finally, a cop knelt beside them. "You two okay?"

Paul nodded.

"Is everyone else?" April asked.

"As far as I know."

"Did you get the shooter?" Paul said, pushing himself to his feet, then helping April up.

"Not yet. Did either of you see the car?"

"It was a drive-by?"

"Uh-huh. You didn't see what happened, huh?"

"I just heard the shots and hit the sidewalk," April said.

The cop took a notebook from his pocket. "Okay. I'll need to get your names and addresses and ask you a few more questions."

"Did anybody see the car?" Paul said.

"Not that I've talked to. Somebody might have, though."

But even if they had, he knew that wouldn't likely

be any help. Odds were, the car was stolen. And if it hadn't already been dumped, it soon would be.

What he didn't know was whether it had been a random shooting.

Logic said it had. Random drive-bys weren't exactly unheard-of in New York City.

His sixth sense, though, was warning him that there could have been an intended victim. And that it might have been April.

CHAPTER SEVEN

"THAT'S IT FOR NOW." The police officer closed his notebook.

"I'm sorry I couldn't be more help," April said. Then she and Paul turned and started down Amsterdam.

"Have you stopped shaking inside yet?" he asked.

She nodded, surprised to realize that she had. The drive-by had scared her half to death, but it had been over so fast that already it seemed more like a bad dream than anything else.

"It's funny," she said. "When you told me you had to go to Bogotá, I thought that sounded dangerous. But here you are, back and perfectly safe, while I almost got shot just a couple of blocks from home."

"It's the 'almost' that counts." He smiled, sending another of those rushes through her—this one hotter than ever.

The way he'd magically materialized had made her feel as if there were a guardian angel in her corner. And as frightened as she'd been, once he'd wrapped his arms around her and held her...

She was afraid to even think about how that had made her feel, but she couldn't stop herself. She'd felt safe and protected and...loved.

When the word whispered in the corner of her mind, she tried to suppress it. Bad enough she was physically attracted to the man. If she let down her emotional guard and he turned out to be the enemy, she'd never be able to handle it.

She glanced at the bags slung over his shoulders; he certainly looked as if he'd been away. But if he was the enemy, that's exactly how he'd make sure it looked.

"So, where've you been the past couple of days?" he asked as they turned onto West Seventy-fifth. "I called yesterday and left messages. Today, too."

Where had she been? The question made her stomach tighten. Almost getting killed had driven every last thought of the visit to Gutteridge from her mind. But she was going to have to tell Paul about it, even if she gave him a bastardized version of the truth, because she had to know what he made of the tape and note.

When she told him, though, he'd probably want to murder her, so instead of getting into it at the moment, she said, "You left messages about what?"

"Oh…just letting you know that I've got a couple of appointments lined up for us."

He looked very pleased with himself.

"Appointments with…?"

"Well, after I knew for sure I'd be getting back tonight, I not only got hold of Resdoe but connected with Harmidarrow's assistant, as well. We're set up to see two of our three suspects tomorrow."

"Really? You got something that fast with the senator?"

"Uh-huh. Never underestimate the power of network television. Everybody likes to see their face on the screen, especially politicians.''

"Well, that's great," she said. Then, before he could get back to his where've-you-been? question, she asked, "What about your trip? What happened in Bogotá.''

"We shot a terrific ending for our segment. The *tombos*—the cops—seized a cargo plane loaded with cocaine. And one of the drug lords was right there on the scene, so they had him cold. After a shoot-out and a car chase, that is.''

"Then it *was* dangerous," she said, unsettled by how much that concerned her.

"More for the photographer than for me. He was the one hanging out the window with his video camera. All I had to do was drive the car.''

"Ah. And I know how un-dangerous you are behind the wheel.''

When he laughed at that, she couldn't help smiling. He had such a deep, hearty laugh, it was infectious.

"You've only ridden with me once. And I was trying to lose a tail.''

Her smile faded. At this point, she was pretty sure that if someone had been tailing them, he *hadn't* lost them. Whoever had written that note had known she was living as April Kelly. And an obvious way to have learned that would have been by following them all the way to her apartment that day.

They'd reached her building, so she said, "You'll come in for coffee? To hear what I've been doing,'' she made herself add.

He trailed her up to the third floor, putting his

things down inside her door and looking around. She followed his gaze, trying to see the apartment through his eyes.

When the brownstone had been a single-family dwelling, the third floor had consisted of four bedrooms and a bathroom. Now, two of the former bedrooms were a combined living-dining room. One of the others was still a bedroom, the last her office.

"Spacious," he said.

"Except for the kitchen. I suspect it started life as a linen closet."

"All right, what I can see is spacious. And it looks comfortable. Although I wouldn't want to be your moving man," he added, gesturing toward her overstuffed sofa, then beyond it to the almost-antique dining room table.

"I know. They had a hard time getting some of my things up the stairs. But I like the way that big, heavy pieces of furniture make a place seem more permanent." When he glanced at her quizzically, she shrugged. "We moved a lot while I was growing up."

"That must have been tough."

"I got used to it. There was only once it was really hard."

"Oh?"

She hesitated, feeling strange about volunteering something personal when she rarely did so. "I was about nine years old," she finally said. "And we lived in an old house in the country. I don't know the details of why, but we had to leave very suddenly. In the middle of the night. Anyway, we had a big fluffy cat I'd named Marmalade."

"Who was orange," Paul said, making her smile.

"Yes, I wasn't a terribly original child. At any rate, he was a great cat. He had gorgeous green eyes and was really affectionate—followed me around and almost always slept on the end of my bed. But he'd stayed outside that night, and there was no time to look for him, so we had to leave him behind. I cried myself to sleep every night for weeks afterward."

The story made Paul's chest feel tight. He remembered how miserable he'd been the first year or so after his father had died, but her entire childhood must have been rough.

"It's strange that I still think about that cat, isn't it," she added softly.

"Maybe you should get another one."

"Maybe. I've considered it, but... Oh, I don't know."

He nodded, wondering if her childhood experiences had left her afraid of growing too attached even to a cat.

"Well," she said, looking at her hands. "I guess I'd better wash the dirt off before I make coffee."

Until then, he hadn't noticed that her palms were badly scraped. He glanced at her knees and saw they were, too.

"I think you'd better do more than wash the dirt off. Do you have any antiseptic?"

"I'll check, but I'm pretty sure I'm out." She turned and started down the hall.

He followed along, glancing into her bedroom as they passed it and immediately wishing he hadn't. Seeing her bed started him entertaining thoughts he shouldn't.

The bathroom was at the end of the hall and seemed to be the only room that had gotten short shrift during the conversion. Its floor was covered with those tiny black-and-white tiles that had been so popular way back when, and the bathtub was one of the old claw-footed jobs deep enough for a serious soak.

"You leave your windows open?" he asked, noticing the curtain was stirring.

She glanced over at it. "Sometimes."

"It's safe enough?"

"On the third floor it is. It's funny you should ask, though, because just the other night I heard a noise that made me think someone was at one of them. It scared me spitless," she added, rummaging through the cabinet. "But there's no conceivable way of reaching them short of a fireman's ladder, and I think somebody walking down the street with one of those would be a tad conspicuous."

"Yeah, I guess."

"I was right. No antiseptic." She closed the cabinet. "I sliced my finger along with a tomato last week, and I must have used the last of it."

"I've got some in my bag. I always travel with a first aid kit."

"I guess," she said, giving him a wry glance, "that when you play at car chases and shoot-outs, you just never know when a dab of antiseptic might come in handy."

Grinning, he went to get it, then headed back to the bathroom. April was sitting on the edge of the tub, gingerly dabbing at her knees with a wet washcloth.

Crouching beside her, he tried not to start thinking about what great legs she had. But that was pretty well impossible when they were only inches from his eyes.

As Paul began unscrewing the bottle's cap, April studiously avoided looking at him. Suddenly, her big old bathroom felt like a very intimate space. And he was close enough that she could smell his woodsy, masculine scent—a scent that was becoming more intoxicating with each passing second.

"Here, I'm at a better angle for this," he said, taking the facecloth from her.

She had to look at him then. And despite her best efforts, once she had, she couldn't force her eyes away.

He gently wiped her knee, then poured a little antiseptic on the scrapes.

It stung, but she knew that wasn't what was making her throat dry and her body hot. It was the way his head was bent over her knees, the way looking down at his dark hair made her want to run her fingers through it.

"Okay, let's have your hands," he said, finishing with her other knee and looking up.

When he did, she had an almost overwhelming urge to lean forward and kiss him. But that would make things even more complicated than they already were.

"I can manage my hands," she said softly. "But thanks. It only hurt a bit."

"No problem." He shrugged, just a little too casually. Then he stood up, handed her the bottle and walked out of the room.

She sat gazing through the empty doorway, wishing she knew whether being honest about what she'd been up to would simplify things between them or only make them more complicated.

"DECAF?" APRIL ASKED, looking over to where Paul was leaning against the kitchen doorway.

"That's probably a good idea," he told her. He hadn't gotten much sleep in the past couple of days, so the last thing he needed was caffeine.

Glancing around the room, he decided she might not have been joking about the kitchen having begun life as a linen closet. There wasn't room for even a small table.

While he was imagining her eating alone at that enormous dining room table, she looked over again. "Why don't you go on into the living room and sit down. I'll just be a minute."

"Oh, I sat for too many hours on the plane." Besides which, he couldn't quite make himself stop watching her. She'd taken a couple of minutes to change into jeans and a shirt, and the way those jeans fit would have made it impossible for him to keep his gaze off them—if it weren't for her neck.

Her hair was very short at the back and he found the slender curve of her neck incredibly arousing.

Hell, the truth of the matter was that he found practically everything about her arousing. Which explained why, back there in the bathroom, he'd almost forgotten she was off limits.

It was a damn good thing he hadn't, he told himself firmly. Maybe the chemistry between them was more potent every time they were together, but he sure as hell wasn't going to do anything about it. Not unless he was one hundred percent convinced her father hadn't planted that bomb.

As the last of the coffee trickled into the pot, she turned and caught him watching her. When she held his gaze, he half expected the air to start crackling.

Finally, she cleared her throat and said, "Black, right? That's how you were drinking it at the airport."

"Uh-huh. Black."

Turning away again, she picked up the pot. As she did, he forced himself to head for the living room.

She followed along, handed him his coffee, then sat down—not beside him on the couch, but in one of the two big chairs facing it.

After taking a sip from her mug, she murmured, "So. I was going to tell you where I've been."

"Right," he said, even though he'd forgotten that he'd asked her. Hell, if he wasn't careful, the next thing he knew she'd be making him forget his name.

"I went to Bridgeport. To visit Tom Walker."

He tried not to show any reaction, but she wouldn't have surprised him more if she'd said she'd gone to the North Pole to visit Santa.

"Oh?" he said as casually as he could. "Why?"

She stared at her sandals for so long that he was about to repeat his question. But just before he did, she looked at him again, her expression anxious.

"I'm going to tell you the truth, Paul. Until right this minute I wasn't sure I would, and I'm still not sure it's the smart thing to do. But…"

"But what?" he prompted.

Slowly she shook her head. "I don't really know

what it is. Maybe I've had to lie so many times in my life that I'm sick of doing it. Or maybe it's something else entirely. But whatever the reason, I don't want to lie to you right now. So I'm not going to say I was just hoping Walker would tell me who the bomber was.

"I went to see him because I wanted to be sure he was for real. That his confession was for real. That what you told me about him was true."

"I see," he said as evenly as he could. "What were you figuring? That I got someone else to record the tape with me? That I signed his statement myself?"

He'd tried not to sound angry, but the look on her face told him he'd failed.

"I wish you wouldn't take it personally," she said in a quiet voice.

"Oh? And how am I supposed to take it?" He stopped right there and ordered himself to count to ten. After all, he'd been aware from the start that she'd be afraid to trust him. And he knew she'd be wise not to. But even so, it had bothered him almost from day one that she hadn't. And right this minute, the idea of her checking up like that was bothering the hell out of him.

"Paul, just listen to me for a minute. My parents went underground when I was two years old. And from then on they taught me to be wary of strangers, not to trust anyone until I was absolutely sure of them. So when you walked into my life, out of nowhere, and asked me to help you... Look, for all I knew, you were a fed and—"

"A fed," he repeated. Even though he'd realized

that possibility would occur to her, he'd assumed that by this stage of the game she'd have decided he wasn't one.

"How can I know that anything you tell me is the truth?" she asked. "How could I even be sure you were really going to Bogotá? That you didn't just want to go see Resdoe and Harmidarrow on your own?"

"What? You didn't even believe that? Dammit, April, I haven't lied to you once. Not once."

"Maybe not," she murmured. "But how can I be certain? Paul, I want to believe you. I really do. What I'm trying to explain is that under the circumstances I'd be suspicious of the pope. I have to be cautious, because if I decided to fully trust you and it was a mistake…"

He took a slow, deep breath, telling himself he *should* try not to take this personally, that she was caught between the proverbial rock and hard place.

"Can you understand what I'm saying?" she asked. "Can you see what an impossible position I'm in?"

"Yes." Like it or not, he *did* see.

"Good," she said, suddenly looking even more anxious. "I'm really glad, because it'll help you understand what I did after I saw Tom Walker."

THE MORE OF HER STORY April told, the worse it got.

Paul had decided not to interrupt with questions, that it would be better to save them until later and he just try to absorb the facts. But he'd have had to be a sponge to absorb everything she was saying, and by the time she was winding down—telling him that she'd discussed the whole mess with her father last night—he'd pretty much stopped listening and was trying to figure out what the hell to do.

The most troubling aspect, of course, was that if things hadn't already been dangerous, her visit to Gutteridge had ensured they were now. The videotape and note would have had Gutteridge antsy as hell before April showed up. And when she did, odds were it was enough to spur him into action. That probably meant she *had* been the intended victim of that drive-by, and Gutteridge had set it up.

But how? How could he have learned she had a car to return in Manhattan, let alone which rental outlet she'd used?

An answer came, and it wasn't a happy one. Someone Gutteridge was in contact with must have been keeping an eye on her. After she'd left his motel, Gutteridge had called that someone and they'd arranged for the drive-by, arranged for whoever was going to do the shooting to wait at the rental place for her to return the car. And after she had...

Realizing she'd stopped speaking, he focused on her. "I'm sorry. I missed the last bit."

"It was nothing. Just that the plane didn't land in Bridgeport until dinnertime. And I still had to drive back here after that."

She curled her legs up beside her in the chair. "Paul, I'm more sorry than I can tell you. I know I really screwed up. But when I saw Walker's book lying open, I was certain that if I went to see Gutteridge, I'd learn something."

"And you did. If you hadn't gone, we wouldn't

know about the tape and all." He hesitated, knowing he'd upset her if he said he figured she'd been the target of that shooting. But there was no way around telling her.

Her eyes grew darker as he spoke, and when he'd finished, she murmured, "I guess that adds up. But we can't be certain the shooter was after *me*."

"No, we can't."

"If he was, though, if there is someone working with Gutteridge... Paul, something doesn't make sense here. Surely someone working with him wouldn't have sent him the tape. I mean, as I said, the note with it was downright threatening."

Paul studied her across the coffee table. He hadn't considered that, but it was a good point. There had to be more than one person involved in all this. And at least one of them *wasn't* on Gutteridge's side.

Just as he was thinking that, she said, "I feel as if we're in the middle of a conspiracy."

Her voice caught a little, and if she'd been sitting beside him, he'd have taken her in his arms to comfort her.

Since she wasn't, he merely shook his head and said, "Let's try to figure out who *did* send the tape, who caught us on camera that day."

"I've been trying to. And it makes sense that it was someone who knew Gutteridge was one of the informants, who knew that if he found out we were trying to get at the truth, it would worry him. And it had to be someone who knew where he's living, where to send the tape."

"There can't be many people who'd fit that bill."

"No, there can't. But without knowing who any

of them are..." She shook her head, her frustration obvious.

"Okay, let's back up a step and try to figure out who they could be. After you told your father you'd been to see Gutteridge, did he say anything that might give us a clue?"

When she didn't reply, he said, "April? What did he say?"

She gave a little shrug. "He said I should quit while I was ahead. He wanted me to tell you I was backing off, because he's decided he doesn't really care about proving he's innocent. He does, though. He's just worried about my safety."

He wasn't the only one, Paul thought.

"By the time I'd finished filling him in," she continued, "he was certain that Gutteridge must have contacted the real bomber after you told him Walker admitted lying. And that it was the bomber who taped our meeting."

"It wouldn't have been him personally."

"Why not?"

"Because our suspects are a senator, a senior special agent and a nutcase who lives in California. None of them would have been standing around La Guardia videotaping us."

"How do you know John Bellavia lives in California?"

"I located him while I was waiting for the drug bust to go down. You can search databases as easily from Bogotá as from anywhere else."

"And what did you learn about him?"

"Nothing much so far. But I've got somebody digging around for me out there—a journalist buddy who's with the NBS affiliate in L.A. I also checked out your father's story about Resdoe infiltrating AWV for the feds, and my contact says the records show he didn't join the bureau until 1973. So the Network must have gotten the wrong information."

"The Network got the wrong information? How about your contact didn't get the right information? I'll bet a lot of agents' personnel records aren't accurate. They don't call the feds Fibbers for no good reason."

Paul nodded slowly. It was damn hard to get an accurate picture of things when you couldn't be sure what was fact and what was fiction.

"I guess you're right," he said at last. "We'd better not rule Resdoe out just yet. But let's get back to your father's theory and assume it was the bomber who had us taped. Then he turned around and sent the tape to Gutteridge because...?"

"We couldn't figure that out. I mean, he'd obviously be worried that Gutteridge might decide to back up Walker's statement. But we couldn't see how warning him that you and I are out to get him would encourage him to keep quiet."

"No. Logically, it would do just the opposite, wouldn't it—make him wonder if he should come clean as a preemptive move."

For an instant, April looked hopeful. Then the look faded and she said, "But there isn't much chance he'd actually do that, is there. If he admitted the truth, wouldn't he end up in jail? For sending the feds after the wrong man in the first place?"

"Unless they gave him immunity in exchange for the real bomber's name."

"Do you think they would?"

"I don't know." *Because I'm not a fed,* he wanted to add. He didn't, though. By this point he'd realized that his denying it wasn't going to convince her. It was a conclusion she'd have to reach on her own.

But, for all he knew, she might have decided to take her father's advice and back off. And if that was the case, they'd be having nothing more to do with each other, so it really wouldn't matter what she believed about him.

"You haven't told me how you left things with your father," he said. "Did you say you *would* call it quits?"

"I said I'd have to think about it."

Her gaze briefly met his, and even though she didn't say another word, he knew she wanted to hear what he thought she should do. But he wasn't sure what he thought.

In the beginning, he'd only agreed to let her tag along because they'd forced him into it. And right now, she seemed so nervous that if he told her he should handle things alone from here on in, she'd probably say "Okay."

He had a problem with that, though. The way things stood, he'd just as soon keep an eye on her. After all, he'd started this, and if anything awful happened to her because of it, he'd feel responsible.

He glanced over at her again, curled up in the chair and looking so desirable that his heart began to thud against his ribs. As much as he hated to admit it, and despite how hard he'd been warning himself off, there was another, stronger reason he didn't want anything awful to happen to her.

"What about you?" she asked, breaking the silence. "Whether I hang in or not, if you keep digging, you'll be at risk."

"Well…" He hesitated, trying to figure out the best way to play things from here. "You know what?" he said at last. "I think we'd better talk to the cops again. About that shooting."

"Really?" she said uneasily. "Even though we can't be certain I was the target?"

"I think it would be a good idea, because if you were… Look, I don't want to scare the hell out of you, but if they tried to kill you once, they might try again."

Her face grew pale, but all she said was "And telling the police what we suspect would get us where?"

"Well, if they paid Gutteridge a visit, or if the feds did, he and whoever else is involved would think long and hard before they actually did try anything more."

For a few seconds, she simply continued to look at him. Then she said, "You're serious, aren't you. You want me to tell the cops, or the feds, that I'm Colin Birmingham's daughter. That I know where he is."

"Well, no, I didn't mean where he is, but—"

"Paul, there's no way in the world I can tell them anything. Aside from the risk to my parents, I'd probably get charged with, oh, obstructing justice or something. At the very least."

"But if—"

"No. I don't even want to discuss it. And you can't involve the law, either. You gave me your word. You promised that if I put you in touch with my father you'd keep everything in the strictest confidence.''

"Dammit, that was before somebody tried to kill you!''

"Maybe somebody did. You don't know that for sure. Maybe it was exactly what that cop figured. A random drive-by.''

"That's not what he'd have figured if he'd known who you are,'' he muttered. ''And what you've been doing.'' He pushed himself up from the couch and paced across to the window.

As he stood staring out into the night, April said, "You figure we should both just let this go, don't you.''

"I told you what I figure,'' he said, turning away from the window. ''We should talk to the cops.''

"I can't,'' she said quietly.

Shaking his head, he tried to decide what the second-best option was. If the bomber was running scared, if the man who'd killed his father was worried that they might catch up with him, there must be a chance they could. And if they were in danger whether they kept on trying to find him or not...

"What are you thinking?'' April asked.

He eyed her for a moment, wishing he knew which way things would be safer for her. ''I guess I'm thinking it might be too late to back off. That even if we did, Gutteridge and the bomber might not believe we really had.''

"And they'd still try...something more?''

"I'd say it's a strong possibility.''

"And they know where to find us.''

"Uh-huh. So we're probably in a 'damned if we do, damned if we don't' situation. Which means that maybe our best bet is to just keep going and hope to hell we find something that'll let us nail them. What do you think?"

She looked uncertain, but said, "If you figure that pressing on is our best bet, then I think we should keep our appointments with Resdoe and Harmidarrow tomorrow."

CHAPTER EIGHT

APRIL WALKED PAUL to the door of her apartment, aware that while they'd been talking about how to play things from here, the fact he could be a fed had completely slipped her mind.

That worried her, because it meant she was subconsciously starting to trust him, something she couldn't let herself do.

"You're sure you don't want me to call a cab?" she asked him.

He shook his head and picked up his bags. "It'll be quicker to get one in the street."

"But it might be safer to—"

"Hey, I thought we agreed we were going to be careful but not paranoid."

"Right. We did."

"But do me a favor?"

"What?"

"Lock all your windows?"

"And that's not being paranoid?"

He smiled. "Just do it, okay?"

"Okay." She opened the door, resisting the urge to offer him another cup of coffee. It might make him realize how uneasy she felt about being left on her own, and she'd just as soon he didn't think she was a scaredy-cat.

"So, I'll see you in the morning," he said, pausing in the doorway. "And don't wait out in the street, okay? I'll buzz when I get here."

She suspected his concern wasn't just good manners showing, and that made her even more uneasy.

"I really wouldn't mind meeting you there," she told him. "It's completely out of your way to pick me up."

He shrugged. "We'll both have had more time to think by then, so comparing notes before we see Resdoe makes sense."

"Yes, I guess you're right." And walking into the bureau's building with Paul wouldn't be a bad idea. She'd see whether anyone recognized him or not. Of course, she knew he had at least one contact there, but if a lot of people seemed to know him...

She considered that for a few seconds, then realized she didn't have a clue whether it would mean anything or not. After all, he'd mentioned that not a month went by without his consulting the feds about one case or another.

"Well...'night," he said, stepping into the hall.

The warmth in his dark eyes made her heart flutter, but she simply said, "'Night."

He walked away a few steps, then looked back. "Don't forget to lock up."

"I won't."

When he started down the stairs, her gaze lingered on him until he vanished around the landing. Once he had, she closed the door, turned the deadbolts and dropped the security bar into place, then went to lock the windows. After that, deciding she was too wound up to sleep, she poured herself another mug of decaf and headed for her office to check the messages on her machine.

There were the ones Paul had left, one from a friend, plus a couple from clients. Making a mental note to return the calls in the morning, she wandered back to the living room and turned on the late-night news. With any luck, seeing what was going on in the rest of the world would take her mind off what had been happening in her own little corner of it.

As she sank into a chair, one of the station's roving reporters was saying, "And here in New York, there was a bizarre incident on the Upper West Side."

She sat up straighter and focused on the picture. The reporter was standing close to where the drive-by had occurred.

"Earlier this evening," he continued, "a drive-by shooting on Amsterdam Avenue had passersby diving for cover. No one was injured, and crime scene investigators have discovered why. The perpetrator was shooting blanks, not real bullets. Live from the corner of Amsterdam and West Seventy-sixth, I'm Benjamin Wright."

The picture cut back to the studio. "In other local news," the anchor began, but April barely heard him. If the bullets hadn't been real, then nobody had been trying to kill her after all. Did that mean she and Paul had added things up wrong? Maybe the shooting hadn't had a thing to do with her. Maybe it had just been some kid looking for laughs and—

Her buzzer sounded, making her jump, but she didn't get up from the chair. Nobody she knew would arrive unexpectedly at this time of night. Unless Paul had come back.

That possibility in mind, she headed to the intercom and asked who was there.

"Clancy's Couriers," a man said. "Delivery for apartment three. Ms. April Kelly."

"At this time of night?"

"It's got one of our special delivery stickers on it, ma'am. We deliver those as soon as we get them. Twenty-four hours a day."

"Well, just leave it on the top step," she told him. "I'll come right down and get it." No way was she opening the door to a stranger.

"Sorry, ma'am," he said. "I gotta have a signature."

"Who's it from? Is there a return address?"

There was a moment's silence, then he said, "Yes, ma'am. It's from a company called Personalized Videos."

Uneasiness crept through her. First Gutteridge had gotten a video, and now there was one for her? She had to know what was on it.

"All right," she said, pressing the lock release. She grabbed her purse from the hall table and dug out the can of pepper spray. Then, heart pounding, she unlocked her door, cracked it open on the security chain and stood listening to the footsteps thudding up the stairs.

The young man who appeared was dressed like a typical bicycle courier and was carrying a brown padded envelope just the right size to contain a video.

"ID?" she said through the crack.

He gave her a pained look but produced a card.

She checked it, then opened the door to the full length of the chain, giving him enough space to hand her the package and his clipboard. After putting the package on the table, she signed his delivery sheet.

"Have a good night," he said when she handed back the clipboard.

"You, too." Closing the door, she relocked it and stood staring at the padded envelope. On the lower right corner, someone had printed Open Me Now.

Nervously, she ripped the package open, aware that the hairs on the back of her neck were standing on end.

"Relax," she whispered to herself. "It's only a videotape." She turned it over and read the message printed on the label.

Watch Me Now, it ordered.

Desperately wishing it had arrived ten minutes earlier, while Paul was still here, she headed into the living room, stuck it in the VCR and switched the television to the video channel.

Then she retreated to her chair and grabbed the VCR's remote from the coffee table. Taking a deep breath, she pressed Play.

"Oh, Lord, déjà vu," she murmured as Paul's face appeared on the screen. On this tape, though, he wasn't at the airport. He was on a street, getting into his Cherokee. As he pulled away from the curb, the picture froze for a few seconds, giving her a still shot of the license plate before the Jeep began moving again. Then it disappeared from the screen, leaving her wondering what kind of message she was supposed to be getting.

Suddenly the tape cut from the street scene and

another man appeared on the screen. A man with a balaclava hiding his face. Seeing him sent a shiver through her.

She pushed Pause and listened to the silence in the apartment, telling herself that it was as safe from intruders as it could possibly be. Then, knowing that if she actually heard an unexpected sound she'd jump out of her skin, she made herself press Play once more.

The man wearing the balaclava began walking, and she could see that he was in an underground garage. She watched as he approached a black Jeep Cherokee and the picture focused on its license plate.

"Oh, Lord," she whispered again. It was Paul's car.

The camera panned back to the man. He looked around, then carefully put down the sports bag he'd been carrying and began fiddling with the lock on the driver's door. Even though he was wearing gloves, he had it open within seconds. Reaching inside, he popped the hood.

Her heart began hammering when he stepped to the front of the Jeep and lifted the hood. Picking up the sports bag, he gingerly removed something from it, then turned toward the camera and gave a thumbs-up. A moment later, his image was replaced by a single printed word.

BOOM! filled the screen in big letters.

She stared at them, her hands trembling so hard she almost dropped the remote.

The bomber was striking again. He'd killed Paul's father, and now he was going to kill Paul.

"No!" she said out loud. She couldn't let that happen. She had to do something.

Racing to the hall, she grabbed her purse and searched through it for Paul's business card.

Her entire body was trembling as she hurried back to the living room and called his cellular number, praying he had the phone turned on.

It started ringing, and when he didn't answer right away, tears began stinging her eyes. She was going to get his voice mail.

Then he answered.

She tried to speak and couldn't.

"Paul Gardiner," he said a second time.

"Paul!" she managed to say.

"April?"

His voice sounded concerned, but he was the one in danger.

"Paul," she said once more. "Where are you?"

"In a cab. On my way to NBS."

She sank onto the couch, her knees suddenly so weak she couldn't stand. He was safe.

"I've got to pick up my car."

"What?" she whispered.

"I left it in the NBS garage while I was away. I'm just going to get it."

STICKING HIS CELL PHONE back into his pocket, Paul leaned anxiously forward in the taxi.

"Change of plans," he told the driver. "Head back up to West Seventy-fifth. And the faster you get me there, the bigger your tip."

"You got it."

As the cabbie cut sharply through the traffic to

make his turn, Paul stared out into the darkness and worried.

"I need you here," April had said. "Right away. And whatever you do, don't go anywhere near your car."

She'd sounded in a total panic, yet when he'd asked if she was all right she'd said she was fine. Obviously, though, she wasn't. And apparently, neither was his car. But how did she know that?

The one possibility he could think of was that someone had phoned her about it. But who would call her about his car?

Almost nobody was even aware they knew each other. Only her parents, Walker and Gutteridge, and whoever had been spying on them. And since that was probably someone working for the bomber...

He swore under his breath. He and April had gotten themselves involved in one hell of a game of cat and mouse, and unfortunately, they weren't the cat.

"What number?" the cabbie asked, turning onto West Seventy-fifth.

Paul told him, then scanned the street outside her building as they neared it. He saw nothing unusual, but he doubted that meant a thing. In the dark of night, there were a hundred potential hiding places.

Paying the fare and adding a healthy tip, he grabbed his bags from the trunk and headed for the brownstone. He'd been too busy checking the street to look up and see if April was watching for him, but she must have been, because the lock buzzed as he reached the door.

He jerked it open and took the stairs two at a time. When he got to the third floor, she was standing in her doorway, looking as if she were about to burst into tears.

"What's wrong?" he demanded as she stepped back to let him in.

"I thought you were going to die."

Her words chilled his bones, but the look on her face made his blood run hot. If the thought of his dying had her this upset...

Pushing the door closed with his heel, he dropped his bags, wrapped his arms around her and pulled her close. The soft warmth of her body started his blood running even hotter, and the sultry scent of her perfume made him crazy with wanting her.

"Oh, Paul," she murmured against his chest. "If I hadn't been able to reach you, you'd have been killed."

"Tell me what happened," he said, stroking her hair.

She looked up at him, her eyes luminous with tears.

He tried his damnedest to remember why he didn't want to get involved with her, but when he couldn't, he simply lowered his mouth to hers.

Her lips felt as lush and soft as they looked— softer than soft, warmer than warm—and she tasted of sweet coffee and hot desire. Smoothing his hands down her back, he drew her even more closely to him. He wanted to feel every inch of her body pressed against his—the fullness of her breasts against his chest and the tantalizing curve of her backside beneath his hands.

He was so hard with longing that she couldn't help but know, and as he pulled her lower body even more tightly to his, she moved against him and whispered, "Oh, Paul."

Her breath was deliciously warm against his mouth and her need was unmistakable. At that instant, he could easily imagine what paradise was like.

Then she murmured, "Paul, we have to stop. You have to look at something."

As she eased out of his arms, he wanted to tell her he was already looking at the only thing in the world that mattered right now.

Before he could say a word, though, reality came crashing back and he remembered why he was here. She'd thought he was going to die.

"JEEZ," PAUL MUTTERED as BOOM! filled the screen. "Really creative, huh?" he added, giving April a wry look. "Maybe we're dealing with a wannabe filmmaker."

His words made her shiver inside. They both knew it was a killer they were dealing with.

"What do we do?" she asked once the set went gray.

"Get the bomb squad to NBS."

Her expression must have told him how she felt about calling the police, because he reached for her hand and gave it a squeeze.

"Hey, we've got no choice. If there's a bomb in my car, it has to be defused before it goes off and kills somebody."

She nodded. She'd already known there was no choice. But the police would have a million questions, and since the tape had been delivered to her,

Paul wouldn't be the only one they'd expect answers from.

"I don't have a good contact on the bomb squad," he said, looking through the notebook he'd taken from his pocket. "But I'll call somebody high up in the police force."

When he began punching a number into his cellular, she closed her eyes and told herself to think about anything except the fact that he'd almost been killed.

A few moments later she was recalling the way he'd kissed her, and how incredible he'd made her feel. It had been so wonderful... So wonderful she didn't think she could bear going back to where they'd been before the kiss. Kissing him seemed to have opened an emotional floodgate within her, and shutting it again would be impossible.

That realization was exhilarating and terrifying at the same time.

She'd been absolutely determined to keep their relationship platonic. But despite the warnings still whispering in her mind, her determination seemed to have vanished.

Opening her eyes, she sat gazing at his rugged profile and wondering how she could possibly be thinking about kissing him at a time like this. But everything about him exuded sex appeal. She adored the way his hair curled onto his neck. And his strong jawline made her fingers want to trace it—even at a time like this.

He finished his call, then said, "There'll be a couple of detectives here shortly."

"And exactly what do we tell them?" she asked, forcing her thoughts back to the tape.

"I guess everything. As I said before, once whoever's playing games learns the cops are involved, they'll know it'll be a lot more risky to do anything to us. And hell, first you almost got killed, then me. And since we can't count on our luck holding, we—"

"No, wait. I didn't almost get killed. That drive-by wasn't for real. The bullets were blanks."

"What?"

"There was an item on the news—right before the tape arrived. After that, I forgot all about it. But it means nobody could possibly have been trying to kill me."

"That's right," he said slowly. He looked over at the television, then back at her. "And whoever's responsible for that tape had it delivered in plenty of time for you to warn me. Put those two things together and what do you have?"

"Somebody not really trying to kill us? Just trying to scare us off?"

"Exactly."

"But why go to so much effort? Why not just send us a note saying that if we don't stop poking around, we're dead?"

Paul shook his head. "I don't know."

"But…if they're only trying to scare us, then can't we simply tell these detectives we don't have a clue what's going on?"

"No, that would be too—"

"Wait. Listen for a second. If the police learn who I really am, I'll have to reinvent my identity again.

Otherwise, I'd never be certain it was safe to see my parents, and... Paul, it would mean giving up my business, probably having to start over in some other city. So couldn't we at least avoid telling them that I'm Colin Birmingham's daughter?"

"I'm not sure," he said slowly.

"Let's think about it for a minute. What do we absolutely have to tell them?"

"Well, they'll definitely ask if I have any idea why someone would put a bomb in my car. And I'll have to say it might have been symbolic, because I've been investigating the Unique bombing."

"Why even mention that?"

"Other people know I've been looking into it, so I have to say something about it in case someone else does. But I guess I could give the impression that I haven't done much work on it—nothing beyond checking the NBS archives and talking to someone at the bureau."

"What if they learned you'd done more?"

He shrugged. "Journalists can always fall back on their right to keep sources confidential, so if they found out I've talked to Walker and Gutteridge, it wouldn't be too big a deal. And it would buy us some time.

"Unless..." He caught her gaze and held it. "Maybe we should reconsider calling it quits. I'm afraid of something happening to you," he added softly.

The words sent a slow, sweet warmth through her. And when he draped his arm across her shoulders and pulled her close, it made her wish the rest of the world didn't exist.

"Well?" he murmured. "What do you think?"

"I'm afraid of something happening to both of us," she admitted. "But if they *are* only trying to scare us…" She hesitated, but only long enough to firm her conviction. "Let's give ourselves a little more time before filling in the police," she said, praying that wouldn't be a mistake. "Let's tell them you've been looking into the bombing, but hold back on the details."

"I just wish we were certain that was the best way to play it."

"I know." But they were short on facts and long on speculation, which made it awfully hard to be certain about anything.

"Okay," he said at last. "We'll give ourselves until after we've talked to Resdoe and the senator and see where we're at then."

Her heart beating rapidly, she tried to think of what other parts of their story they needed to think about before the police arrived.

"What about the drive-by?" she asked after a minute. "Even though the bullets weren't real, do we mention I was one of the people diving for cover?"

"No, let's try to keep them focused on me, keep you out of it as much as possible. But they'll want to know what our relationship is—why the tape would get delivered to you."

"Can't we use the research assistant story?"

"Uh-uh. Resdoe and Harmidarrow aren't likely to check that out. They'll take it at face value. But when it comes to a car bomb, the cops are going to be pretty thorough. And it would take them about three seconds to establish you're not with NBS."

"Well...why not say I'm your girlfriend? And that I've been working on the story with you because I thought it was interesting."

He looked pointedly at his arm, still around her shoulders, then smiled. "My girlfriend, huh?"

She couldn't keep from smiling back.

"Well..." he said. "I can't think of any reason they'd doubt that. I mean, just look at us."

That almost made her laugh out loud. Just look at them indeed—sitting here gazing at each other with foolish grins on their faces.

Then, slowly, Paul leaned nearer and kissed her. His mouth, hot and hungry against hers, started a throbbing ache down low inside her.

As he deepened the kiss, the ache grew more intense. She pressed herself against him, her body heavy with longing, yearning for his touch. He trailed his fingers down her throat, sending fresh ripples of arousal through her, then slid his hand across the curve of her breast and began caressing her nipple with his thumb.

Raw desire shot through her, almost making her moan. She'd never felt the way he was making her feel, as if she wouldn't be a complete woman until they'd made love.

But that couldn't happen right now. Not with a couple of police detectives on their way.

"Paul?" she murmured.

"Mmm?"

Before she even had time to remind him about them, the front door buzzer sounded.

CHAPTER NINE

BY THREE O'CLOCK in the morning, April was dead on her feet and Paul looked every bit as exhausted. But the police detectives were still camped in her living room—at the moment, waiting to learn whether Clancy's Couriers was for real.

"Okay, thanks for checking," Tino DiMarco said at last. He put down his phone and glanced at his partner. "No such business."

"But the courier had ID," April said. "The phony courier, I guess I should call him."

"The smart ones are thorough," DiMarco told her. "He must have been waiting outside until he saw you leave," he added to Paul, "then delivered the tape after you'd hailed your cab and were gone."

Waiting outside. Waiting and watching. It was an unsettling thought.

From now on she was going to have eyes in the back of her head. And if she caught somebody watching her, she'd... Well, what she did would depend on the situation, but she intended to stay on full alert.

"Does any of this make sense to you?" Paul was asking DiMarco. "I mean, what kind of nutcase plants a bomb in someone's car and then warns him about it?"

"Maybe somebody else warned you."

"Somebody else who just happened to be in the NBS garage, with a video camera, while the guy was doing his thing?"

The detective shrugged. "A lot of weird stuff goes down in this city, and sometimes it takes a while to make sense of it." He closed his notebook and looked over at his partner again. "Anything else you want to ask about?"

When the younger man shook his head, April tried not to let her relief show. But she desperately wanted them to leave, because as unlikely as it was, she kept expecting one of them to ask if she just might happen to be Colin Birmingham's daughter.

DiMarco picked up the tape and the padded envelope it had arrived in—now both encased within plastic evidence bags—and rose.

"You two be careful for the next little while," he told them.

"And if I were you," his partner added to Paul, "I'd forget all about following up on that old factory bombing."

The four of them had started toward the door when DiMarco's phone rang. He fished it out of his jacket and answered it.

"Really," he said after a few seconds. "Yeah, it sure as hell is. Well, we're still with them, so I'll tell him. And thanks for letting us know.

"Curiouser and curiouser," he said, tucking the phone back into his pocket. "You can pick up your car whenever you like," he added to Paul. "It was perfectly clean."

"You mean there wasn't any bomb?"

DiMarco shook his head. "Not the slightest sign of one. But they've moved the car to a police pound for safekeeping—just in case somebody's got any other funny ideas. The one down by Battery Park. You know where it is?"

"Yeah, I got towed from a no standing zone last year. Cost me a fortune."

"Well, you won't have to pay to get it out this time. But this whole thing..." He slowly shook his head, his expression saying that he considered "this whole thing" a damned waste of time.

"You don't have any friends who are into elaborate practical jokes, do you?" he finally asked.

April forced a smile, but she was certain neither the drive-by nor the bomb scare could be explained away as a practical joke. She only wished she knew exactly how they could be explained.

While he and April were seeing DiMarco and his partner out, Paul couldn't stop wondering what was going to happen once the detectives were gone.

Things might have gotten pretty passionate before they'd arrived, but he wasn't sure whether the ground rules had actually changed or it had merely been a heat of the moment thing.

The last he'd heard, April didn't trust him—she hadn't ruled out the possibility that he was a fed. And even if she'd decided he wasn't, he still had doubts about the wisdom of letting their relationship change. Maybe he'd had a memory lapse earlier, but now he remembered why getting involved with her would be a bad idea.

Surely Colin Birmingham couldn't be the bomber, though. That would mean he was terrorizing his own daughter. Besides which, how could anyone living underground possibly have orchestrated two customized videotapes and a drive-by shooting in such a short time frame?

He was telling himself it would be virtually impossible, when April called a final goodbye after the detectives and closed the door.

"Alone at last," he said, carefully keeping his tone light and nonsuggestive.

She gave him an anxious smile that told him she was as uncertain about where they went from here as he was.

"What do you think?" she said.

"I think the good news is that there wasn't really a bomb. Add that to the blank bullets and we can be sure nobody was trying to kill either of us."

"I guess. But now that the bomb's turned out to be a hoax, will the police even bother trying to learn who was behind it?"

"Well, it's sure not going to be high on their priority list. And neither's finding a drive-by shooter who was using blanks."

April stared at her shoes for a minute, then looked up again. "Do you think he's got any other nasty surprises in the works?"

"I don't know. But I think DiMarco gave us some good advice, that we should be damned careful."

She nodded slowly. "He also said we should forget about following up on the bombing."

"Yeah." He caught her gaze and waited to hear how she felt about that now. Maybe the latest episode had been the final straw and she'd decided she'd had enough.

As for him, he didn't know what to make of half the things that had been happening. But with each new event, he was becoming more convinced that there was something to find. And he wanted to find it.

"You haven't changed your mind, have you?" she said. "You still want to see this through."

"Yeah, I do. I'm a journalist after a story, remember?"

April nodded again, praying that was all he was. She still had no way of being certain. But despite her best intentions, she'd fallen hard for him. And surely, as good as she was at reading people, she couldn't be feeling this way about a man who was lying to her.

"I don't want to quit, either," she said. "For as long as I can remember, I've been afraid that one day the feds would catch up with my parents. And even though they try to hide it, I know they've always been afraid, too."

"Then I guess," he said quietly, "we're still keeping our appointments with Resdoe and Harmidarrow."

"Yes."

For a long minute, Paul merely looked at her, while her heartbeat accelerated and her desire intensified. The hallway was so quiet that she could hear her heart as well as feel it beating. She wondered if he could hear it, then realized she hoped he could. As dangerous as her feelings for him might be, they were too strong to deny.

He gazed at her for a few more seconds, then

glanced at his watch. "It's late. I guess I'd better get going."

He didn't move, though. He simply looked at her once more.

The naked desire in his eyes started her insides melting. She wanted him so badly that every sensation she was feeling was centered low in her belly, and every lingering doubt was fading like smoke in the wind.

"Well," he said at last. "As I said, I'd better get going."

She resisted for a final second, then whispered, "Stay?"

A slow, sexy smile spread across his face. "I thought you'd never ask," he murmured, reaching for her hands and drawing her to him.

His lips brushed hers, his breath warm against her mouth, then he cradled her face in his hands and kissed her—deeply and possessively, making her feel as if she were falling toward him even though their bodies were already pressed closely together.

Her fingers curled in his hair as she kissed him back. And then he was kissing her cheeks, her nose, her forehead and the pulse at the base of her throat.

His lips lingered there, the heat of his kiss sending a surge of need through her.

"Oh, Paul," she whispered. "Please tell me you have protection."

He said he did; she wordlessly led him to the bedroom.

They stopped in the moonlit darkness and, her fingers trembling, she removed her grandmother's locket. Once she'd put it on the bedside table, he took her in his arms again. Then, kissing the corners of her mouth, he dug a condom from his wallet and gently eased her down beside him on the bed.

After that, nothing was gentle. Raw primordial desire had them naked in seconds, and nothing in the world could have kept her from reaching for him.

He was all long, lean muscles and hard maleness, and she was so far beyond being able to resist him that she'd rather die than not have him.

When she smoothed her hands across the firm wall of his chest, he trapped one of them over his heart. It was beating as excitedly as her own. Cupping her breasts, he began to nuzzle them greedily, kissing and teasing, making her hotter than hot.

Ravenous with need, she reached down and wrapped her fingers around him, and impossible as it seemed, her hunger grew. Touching him that way made her want him even more desperately.

When he slipped one hand between her legs, she arched against it, so aroused that she could have come with nothing more than his touch. But she wanted more.

"Paul," she breathlessly whispered, "don't wait."

He put on the condom, the seconds passing with agonizing slowness, then he slid deeply inside her.

It made her moan with desire. She arched beneath him, her rhythm as fierce as his, while dark heat consumed her and her breathing became mere gasps for air. Hotter and hotter, higher and higher, her body one with his. And then mindless, frenzied sensations exploded inside her and she climaxed, shattering into a million fragments as the tremors seized her.

Each time Paul drove into her, fresh shock waves

tore through her. By the time he came, she couldn't breathe at all, could only cling tightly to him, her body hot and damp and spent.

The occasional tremor still seizing her, she lay beneath him, reality slowly stealing back. The reality of Paul's weight on her, of their sweat-slicked skin pressed warmly together, of her breasts crushed against his chest, his male scent in her nostrils and the musky scent of sex in the bed.

They were intoxicating, sleep-inducing smells that made her feel as if she'd never have the energy to move again. But it didn't matter. There was nowhere she wanted to be except here.

Eventually, when she was breathing almost normally once more, she trailed her fingers down Paul's back.

"Mmm?" he murmured against her throat. "Too heavy?" He eased his body off hers and curled her against him with one lazy motion, then tenderly kissed the back of her neck.

"That was...pretty amazing," she whispered.

"Only *pretty* amazing?"

She could feel him smiling and it made her smile.

"Maybe with a little practice," she teased, "we could make it absolutely amazing."

"Absolutely might kill me." He kissed her neck again, told her it was the sexiest neck in the entire world, then snuggled solidly against her, as if he wanted her exactly where she was when he woke.

While his breathing assumed the deep, regular rhythm of sleep, she lay awake in the darkness. He felt so right in her life, in her bed, that she was happier than she'd ever been. But in the corner of her mind, a tiny fear had begun worrying away at her.

She'd let him further into her life than she'd ever let another living soul. And if she'd made a mistake...

Closing her eyes, she told herself she hadn't. Nothing that felt this right could be wrong.

THE FBI's NEW YORK field office was located in Federal Plaza—on Broadway between Duane and Worth, south of Canal and north of City Hall. Fortunately that was within easy walking distance from Paul's apartment, because it was often faster to walk than drive in Manhattan.

Even so, by the time he and April had picked up his car from the police pound, then gone to his place so he could get cleaned up, they were barely going to make it to Wayne Resdoe's office on time.

Of course, he thought, smiling to himself as they waited for the elevator, they wouldn't be cutting things this close if they hadn't lingered in bed, making love, until the last possible moment. Simply thinking back to that made him wish they were still there.   He glanced over at the FBI crest on the wall—a screaming eagle holding the banner of justice in its talons. Given what he knew of Wayne Resdoe, though, ensuring justice prevailed wasn't his priority. With Resdoe, looking out for number one came first. When an empty elevator arrived and they stepped inside, he reminded April to be careful with the guy.

"He's sleazy but smart," he added as they started upward. "And if he decides to ask around about anything we say, he won't have a hard time getting answers. So be as honest as you can.''

"Paul, you're only making me more nervous. I know not to say anything that might trip us up. But if he was behind the bombing, if he's responsible for the tapes and the drive-by, he already knows all there is to know, including who I really am. And the same goes for Harmidarrow, if he's the one.''

Reflecting—not for the first time—that they were involved in a very complicated game, Paul wrapped his arm around April's shoulders and gave her a reassuring hug. "I guess the only thing we can do is watch him and see how much we think he knows.''

She nodded, looking anxious as hell.

As the elevator began to slow, he gave her a quick kiss. Then, tough as it was to make himself stop touching her, he stepped away. It would hardly be appropriate to walk into Resdoe's office holding her hand, even though they'd decided to forget about the research assistant story and stick with the girlfriend one they'd given DiMarco and his partner.

As he'd just told April, if Resdoe decided to ask around, he'd get answers. And a whole lot of people would know she wasn't his research assistant, whereas nobody could be sure she wasn't his girlfriend.

But...hell, at this point she *was* his girlfriend, wasn't she? Probably that wasn't the right term when it came to people their age, but whatever the right word was, April was it. He smiled to himself once more, then the elevator doors opened.

They had to pass the scrutiny of a receptionist-cum-guard, who directed them toward a hallway and told them Resdoe's office was the last one on the left. Paul's gut began to tighten as they neared the end of the hall. He found the prospect of facing Resdoe, knowing the agent might have been responsible for his father's death, deeply disturbing.

But it was only a possibility, he reminded himself. Maybe Colin Birmingham's suspicions about Resdoe's involvement were way off base.

As they reached the last office, Resdoe glanced up from behind his desk and waved them in through the open doorway, half rising in greeting.

Paul immediately tensed, then he told himself to take it easy.

"Paul. Nice to see you. It's been a while."

"Right. It has. This is April Kelly." He nodded in her direction. "April, Special Agent Wayne Resdoe."

"Wayne. Just call me Wayne."

While his gaze lingered on April, Paul gave him a quick once-over. It had been more than a year since they'd last run into each other, but the agent's appearance hadn't changed in the least. In his early fifties, he was about five-foot-ten, with brown hair that was turning gray—basically the fade-into-a-crowd type that the FBI liked its agents to be. He didn't look as if he had it in him to jaywalk, let alone mastermind a bombing. But, as everyone knew, looks could be deceiving.

Gesturing them into the visitors' chairs, he sat back down himself. "Should I take it you're working on this Vietnam piece, too?" he asked April.

"Only unofficially," she said as Paul opened his briefcase.

"Oh?"

"April's not with NBS," he volunteered. "She's a friend." He gave her such a warm glance that Resdoe couldn't possibly help realizing he meant "girl-friend." "But when I told her about the segment, she said she'd like to help research it."

Resdoe eyed her curiously.

"At heart, I'm a frustrated journalist. I've even taken a couple of writing courses," she elaborated, neatly sidestepping the issue of why she might be interested in this particular story.

Paul began to relax. He kept forgetting that she'd spent her entire life being careful about what she revealed, but it didn't look as if Resdoe was likely to give her any trouble.

Taking his tape recorder from his briefcase, he said, "You don't mind if I record the interview, do you?" When the agent shook his head, he set the recorder on the desk and turned it on.

Resdoe leaned back in his chair. "So, what got 'Today's World' thinking about the Vietnam era? It's practically ancient history."

"Yeah, but a lot of baby boomers were part of that particular history. And they're a huge marketing target, which means whatever interests them interests our sponsors."

Resdoe nodded. "And why did you want to inter-view me about it?"

"Because of your involvement with AWV. We're going to do a bit on each of the major protest groups."

"But why me? Why not someone with a high pro-file? Like Nelson Harmidarrow, for example?"

Hearing the name of one of their other suspects pop out of Resdoe's mouth took Paul completely by surprise and immediately made him wonder if Resdoe was their man, if he knew exactly what they were up to and was toying with them.

Of course, it could have been nothing more than an innocent question. Harmidarrow did have the highest profile of any ex-AWV member. Still, just happening to mention him...

"Isn't it strange that you should suggest interviewing the senator," April said, "because we're seeing him after lunch."

Paul glanced at her appreciatively. He hadn't responded quickly enough, so she'd jumped in and bailed him out.

"But we felt it was important to talk to you, as well," she added.

When Resdoe said "Oh?" again, Paul held his breath, but April didn't miss a beat.

"Yes. Paul finds it really interesting that you were part of an antigovernment group, and then a few years later you joined the bureau."

Resdoe shook his head. "Let's set the record straight about something. AWV wasn't an antigovernment group. We weren't anarchists. We simply didn't agree with the government's policy toward the war."

"Then what about..." Paul dug out his notebook and flipped through it, as if the subject he wanted to raise wasn't right on the tip of his tongue. But Resdoe had just given him a perfect opening.

"Oh, here it is," he finally said. "If you weren't anarchists, what about the bombing of that napalm factory?'' He glanced back at his book for a second. ''The Unique Technologies factory.''

There was a split second's hesitation before Resdoe said, ''That should never have happened. And it wasn't really an AWV protest. In fact, it almost destroyed the group.''

''Oh? How was that?''

''Well, the bombing was a one-man show—Colin Birmingham making his own personal statement. And part of the fallout from it was that Nelson Harmidarrow decided to leave AWV.''

''Why?'' Paul asked.

''Nelson was totally against violent protests,'' Resdoe explained. ''When he learned there were whisperings about his involvement in the bombing... Well, I think that was just too much for him to take, and it made him wash his hands of the group.''

''Whisperings about his involvement?'' April repeated.

''Be very careful you don't misquote me on this,'' Resdoe said, shooting Paul a warning look. ''If your segment gives even the slightest suggestion that I figured Nelson knew about that bombing beforehand, let alone condoned it, I'll sue your ass off. Is that clear?''

Paul nodded. ''But that's what some people believed?''

''I won't even go as far as to say I think anyone truly did. But Nelson was so prominent in AWV that he almost always knew about planned protests, so some people...wondered.''

''Wondered and whispered,'' April said.

''Yes.''

And did that ·explain why Harmidarrow was on Colin Birmingham's list of suspects? Paul asked himself. Was it only because Birmingham knew that Harmidarrow was normally aware of planned protests? And because there'd been whisperings?

Turning his attention back to Resdoe, Paul found himself wishing he knew exactly how smart the guy was. Had he simply been telling them about the way things were, or had he been neatly ensuring that they knew people had wondered if Harmidarrow'd had any part in the bombing? After all, if it was Resdoe himself who'd been behind it, he'd make a point of saying anything and everything that would throw suspicion off him and onto others.

"At any rate, as I said," Resdoe continued, "that bombing almost destroyed AWV, because once Nelson was gone there was a lot of infighting. There'd always been a pro-violence faction in the group, and he'd been the voice of reason, the one who managed to keep the protests peaceful. Actually, I was surprised that the group remained as nonviolent as it did after he left. That sure wouldn't have been the case if Colin Birmingham had still been around."

"No?" Paul said, refusing to let himself even glance at April.

"No," Resdoe told him firmly. "Birmingham had a lot of prominence in the group. I don't mean the son-of-a-bitch was in Nelson's league, but he had his supporters. And if he'd still been around without Nelson there to keep him in line, AWV would have probably become more militant than the Black Panthers."

At Resdoe's pronouncement, Paul just couldn't keep his gaze from flickering to April.

Amazingly enough, she looked as if Resdoe were talking about a total stranger—except for her hands. Resting in her lap, where the agent couldn't see them, they were clasped so tightly together that her knuckles were white.

CHAPTER TEN

AS TENSE AS PAUL had been on the way into Wayne Resdoe's office, he was wound ever tighter on the way out. Fortunately, he and April weren't alone in the elevator on their trip down to the lobby. That gave him time to think before they talked, which was good—even though he didn't like the thoughts that were snaking around in his mind.

Maybe April believed her father had been against violent protests, but that didn't wash with what Walker and Gutteridge had said. And Resdoe had made him sound like a downright menace to mankind.

Of course, he wasn't forgetting that Resdoe might have been behind the bombing. And if that was the case, he'd have tried to make Birmingham out to be evil incarnate for the same reason he'd have purposefully cast suspicion in Harmidarrow's direction.

But if he wasn't guilty, and if what he'd said about Birmingham was true...

Paul frowned, telling himself he'd hardly gotten a news flash. He'd known all along that Colin Birmingham might have been the one; the thought shouldn't be so upsetting at this stage of the game.

It was though, because now... Well, what the hell was going to happen if he'd gone and fallen in love with the daughter of the man who'd murdered his father? Because if this wasn't love, he didn't know what was. And right this minute that was scaring the bejabbers out of him.

Scaring the bejabbers. His father used to use that expression, and as a child it had always sent him into a fit of laughter. He hadn't thought of it in years, but right now, every single one of his thoughts was focused on either his father or April's.

He glanced at her, standing stiffly beside him, her mouth tightly set and her face flushed. As much as Resdoe's little tirade had rattled him, it had clearly bothered her a lot more. So even though he couldn't quite ignore his fear about her father's involvement in the bombing, he shifted his briefcase and reached for her hand. When he gave it a reassuring squeeze, she managed a smile, but it was obviously going to take a lot more than a squeeze to turn her into a happy camper.

April took a deep breath as the elevator slowed and stopped at the main floor. Then, her hand firmly in Paul's, they headed through the lobby and out of the building.

Once they reached the sidewalk, she stopped dead. She was so upset she wasn't sure she could carry on a coherent conversation, but she intended to try.

"Well?" she asked.

"Well what?" he said, not meeting her gaze.

The fact that he couldn't look her in the eye upset her even more. "You didn't believe him, did you?

"Did you?" she demanded when he said nothing. "Dammit, Paul, you be honest with me and tell me what you're thinking."

"All right," he said slowly. "To be honest, I'm thinking a whole lot of different things."

"I certainly hope one of them is that Resdoe was lying. Because at worst, he was behind the bombing and he's lying as part of his cover-up. And at best, he's merely toeing the party line—saying my father was into violence because it makes their so-called case against him seem stronger."

She waited for Paul to say that, yes, obviously Resdoe was lying. When he didn't, she continued to stand there while seconds passed like hours.

"There's something I have to tell you," he finally said.

She nodded, even though those weren't the words she'd wanted to hear and his serious expression said she wouldn't like whatever was coming.

"Okay, when Tom Walker told me that he and Gutteridge had lied, that your father wasn't the bomber, I asked why they'd claimed it was him."

"Yes, I remember that from the tape."

"No, this wasn't on the tape. I'm not talking about the reason they lied, not about whether someone paid them to or whatever. I asked Walker why the real bomber told them to lay the blame on your father, why him and not someone else. At any rate, Walker told me he'd assumed it was because people wouldn't have much trouble believing Colin Birmingham could have done it."

"What?" she whispered.

"And Gutteridge told me basically the same thing. Of course, he was still sticking to the story that your father was guilty, but both of them talked about how everyone knew where your father stood when it came to protests.

"They told me he used to say... I'm trying to re-member the precise words, because both of them put it the same way, as if they were repeating something they'd heard more than once. I think the phrase they used was that the end result justified any sort of pro-test."

"But..." A hot, angry pounding had started in her head, making it difficult to think.

"But of course they'd say something like that," she said at last. "They were the ones who accused him, so they'd have wanted to make it sound as if he'd have been likely to do it. I'll bet if we asked other ex-AWV members we'd hear the truth. They'd say..." She paused, the pounding in her head grow-ing worse as her mind flashed back to that last visit to her parents.

Could this be what she'd overheard them talking about? Had they been worried that if she got in-volved in Paul's investigation, she'd learn her father had actually taken part in violent protests?

She thought about all those old newspaper articles she'd read as a teenager. And she remembered that when she'd told her parents she was going to look through the library's microfilms for the coverage on the bombing, they hadn't wanted her to.

They'd warned her the papers had been full of lies. And she'd believed that when she'd read the articles, because she'd always been told a different story.

But had her parents' story been entirely accurate?

"So?" Paul prompted.

"I don't know," she murmured. "My father isn't

guilty. If he was, the last thing he'd be doing is trying to help you find the real bomber. He'd never have even agreed to talk to you. Right?''

"It wouldn't have made much sense," he said slowly.

"It wouldn't have made any sense."

Unless, Paul reflected once again, her father was hoping an investigative reporter would want a major story very badly. So badly that he'd go along with creating "evidence" that pointed to a different suspect.

He considered mentioning that possibility, then rejected the idea. It would only make April more upset than she already was.

"I guess," she said at last, "it's possible things weren't quite the way my parents explained them. Maybe they changed a few details. But, Paul, I've always believed they were totally honest with me, and if they weren't... Well, I've got to know exactly what the truth is. And the sooner the better."

APRIL AND PAUL WALKED up Broadway until they reached a pay phone. Then, while Paul waited, she deposited a handful of quarters and punched in her father's work number—automatically checking over her shoulder to make sure he couldn't see what it was.

When she realized what she'd done, it gave her a strange feeling. Had she simply checked out of habit? Or had she fallen in love with a man she still didn't entirely trust?

Before she had time to think about that, her father

picked up and she explained why she was calling. There was a long silence after she finished.

At last her father said, "Mouse, I've always told you I had absolutely nothing to do with that bombing. And it's the God's honest truth."

She exhaled slowly, telling herself she shouldn't have had even the tiniest doubt.

"That part of Resdoe's story was total garbage," he added. There was another silence before he cleared his throat and said, "As for my supporting violent protests, he was exaggerating—greatly. What your mother and I have always told you isn't exactly accurate, but it's a lot closer to the truth than his version of things."

Her hands had grown so damp she had to clutch the receiver more tightly to keep it from slipping.

"You mean you lied to me," she managed to say. "You mean you always said I should only lie when I had to, but all along you were lying to me when you didn't have to."

"Mouse...listen to me. When I was active in AWV, I was very young. A lot younger than you are now. And I already had friends who'd been killed in Vietnam. That made the war seem awfully personal. And, yes, at the time I did believe that the violence of the war justified violent protests. We thought anything that would end the killing was justified. And I wasn't particularly circumspect about keeping my opinions to myself.

"But after the Unique bombing... Even though I wasn't involved, it wasn't inconceivable that I might have been. And I realized that if I'd been responsible for those deaths, I'd never have been able to live with myself.

"That was enough to make me rethink my beliefs. So if we hadn't been forced to go under, if I'd remained active in the group, I'd have been talking a whole different philosophy. And as far as you're concerned, when you got older and we had to explain why we were always on the move, we couldn't see any point in... Well, we did what seemed best and changed that one detail."

"But why didn't you tell me the truth later?" she asked, feeling shaky inside.

"Because we couldn't see any upside to it. We could only see the risk that you'd..."

"That I'd what? Stop loving you?" Her throat had grown tight, and her eyes were full of tears. "Dad, I..." The tears spilled over and she couldn't go on.

Outside the phone booth Paul was watching her anxiously, so she wiped her eyes and gave him a little shrug to say she was okay.

"Oh, Mouse," her father said, his voice cracking. "Oh, Mouse, ever since you told us about Gardiner, ever since you insisted you were going to tag along with him, we've been worried about how you'd handle this if somebody said enough to convince you that..." Her father fell silent for a long moment. "I just hope you can understand we did what we thought was best," he said at last. "We've always done what we thought was best for you."

"Yes, I understand," she made herself say. "And I'm okay with it." With any luck she actually would be, once she'd had a chance to think. "But I've got to go."

"Darling, call us again soon. Your mother's going to be worried sick until she's talked to you."

"Tell her I said everything's fine."

April hung up and stepped out of the booth.

"Are you all right?" Paul asked, resting a hand on her arm.

"I will be. Do you want to know what he said?"

"Yes, but not now. Don't look away from me, but someone's following us."

It took her a second to absorb that information. Then her anxiety level started climbing—and the conversation with her father already had it sky high.

"He was in the lobby of the bureau's building," Paul was saying, "and he came out just after we did. I noticed him because of the surprised way he glanced at us, as if he'd expected us to already be on our way instead of standing right outside. And when we headed up Broadway, he did, too. He's been lurking in a doorway back there while you were on the phone."

"What do we do?"

"Find out who he cares more about following. Then we'll try to learn who he's working for. You start walking north again. I'll head back past him and we'll see which way he jumps."

"Paul, I don't like that idea," she said, fighting against the growing fear inside her. "If he follows me I—"

"It'll be okay. If he follows me, I'll stop and see what he's got to say for himself. If he follows you, I'll turn around and catch up to him. I won't let him get near you."

"But what if he has a gun?"

He didn't answer, merely gave her a quick kiss on the forehead, then said, "Get going and don't look back."

When he turned and began walking away, she started up the block, her heart racing a mile a minute.

Seconds later, Paul was walking purposefully past the doorway, not letting himself so much as glance into it. A few buildings further on, he stopped and checked out a window, then surreptitiously looked to his left.

April was half a block away from him now. The guy in the T-shirt and jeans was trailing her.

Adrenaline pumping, he started after them, walking so rapidly that his briefcase banged against his leg. He'd closed in about halfway when the guy looked back and spotted him—then took off at a dead run.

Paul began running, too, charging up the block while people scattered before him. Just as he raced past April, the guy darted into a coffee shop. Reaching it, Paul wheeled inside.

A quick glance around told him his man had vanished.

"Someone just ran in here," he said to the woman behind the counter. "Where'd he go?"

She shrugged. "He didn't ask for the key to the men's room."

"The back door's through there?" he asked, pointing in the direction where he figured it had to be.

"Yeah, but that's private. You can't..."

He was halfway to the back before her words trailed off. Bursting out into the alley, he spotted his quarry at the top of a fire escape. The guy clambered onto the roof and started running again.

Paul headed up after him, but when he reached the roof there was no one in sight. He stood there for a minute, carefully looking around.

When he couldn't see any potential hiding places, he swore to himself and started back down to the ground.

THEIR APPOINTMENT WITH state Senator Nelson Harmidarrow wasn't until three-thirty in the afternoon, which gave April and Paul forever to eat lunch.

By the time she'd filled him in on what her father had said, and the waitress had brought their food, April found she could only pick at hers. She was still too upset to eat. No matter how often she told herself that she could understand why her parents had never explained the complete truth, she felt betrayed that they hadn't. And learning that her father, whom she'd always idolized...

She stabbed at a french fry. Maybe she just needed time to let the dust settle. She probably wouldn't be half this upset if there hadn't been such a huge accumulation of other upsetting incidents: those damned tapes, the drive-by, and now being followed.

Followed again, she corrected herself. Or *still* might be a better word. Whichever, knowing that someone had been watching her every move gave her the creeps.

"Hey," Paul said, reaching across the table and resting his hand on hers. "You sure you're all right now?"

She forced a smile. "You mean for a woman

who's being stalked in the streets? And whose father just admitted that he would probably have been capable of a bombing in his younger years?''

Paul gave her a smile of his own. ''Yeah, that's exactly what I mean. But at least he only said he *might* have been capable of one, not that he was involved in one.''

''Thank heavens,'' she murmured, trying to ignore the nagging fear that her father might not have been telling her the entire truth. Only an hour or two ago, she'd been certain he'd never lied to her about anything. But now that she knew he had…

She stopped that line of thinking in its tracks, reminding herself again that he would never have talked to Paul if he'd had anything to do with the bombing.

''You know, we've got tons of time before we see Harmidarrow,'' Paul said. ''Do you want to head back to my place and check my E-mail? See if my buddy in California's come up with any info on John Bellavia?''

''Good idea.''

It seemed highly unlikely that a man who lived in California would have anything to do with what had been happening here. But since there was no apparent rhyme or reason about so much of what had been happening, who knew?

Paul paid the bill and they walked the few blocks to his place, which was in an old but tastefully updated building on Franklin Street.

The minute they stepped inside his apartment, he wrapped his arms around her and pulled her close.

"When this is over," he whispered, "I'm going to do nothing but hold you for an entire month."

"Only a month?" she murmured, resting her cheek against his chest and wishing with all her heart that they'd met under different circumstances. Normal circumstances. Wishing with all her heart that they had nothing more to worry about than where to eat dinner tonight.

"I guess we'd better check that mail," he said at last.

"I guess."

He didn't let go of her, though. Not until he'd given her a lingering kiss that left her longing for more. Then he took her hand and led her down the hall.

Like her, he used one of the two bedrooms as an office, and while his computer booted she glanced slowly around, her gaze coming to rest on the photographs sitting on a shelf of his bookcase.

For an instant, she thought the center one was of him, holding a little boy on his shoulders. Then she realized it was an old picture. But the man looked so much like him...

When she glanced at him, he was watching her. "My father and me," he said.

"I guessed." She turned back toward the photograph with a lump in her throat. He'd been five when his father died, and the picture must have been taken not long before that.

He looked so happy in it she couldn't help wondering how unhappy he'd been afterward, how much it would hurt to have a parent die when you were just a little kid.

"And that's your mom and dad," she said, looking at the wedding picture.

"Uh-huh." He eyed it for a second, then glanced at her locket.

"My turn for the family photos," he said. "You mentioned there are pictures of your grandparents in that."

She tried to open it, and when she couldn't manage to, she undid the clasp and took it off.

"That's strange," she said, trying again. "I opened it right after my mother gave it to me and it wasn't stiff at all. But now..."

"Here, let me try."

When she handed it to him, he had no more success than she'd had.

"It's probably just the humidity. I could use my Swiss Army knife and—"

"A knife?" she said, grabbing the locket back in horror.

"What? You have no faith in me?" he teased.

"Not when it comes to jewelry repairs. A knife might damage it. If it doesn't loosen up on its own, I'll take it to a jeweler."

"Up to you," he said, turning to his computer and bringing in his E-mail. "Okay, here's what we're looking for," he said after a minute. "Mail from my buddy, Ross, in L.A."

As the message popped onto the screen, she moved closer and began reading along with him.

Hey, East Coast,

I've turned up a fair bit of info on John Bellavia. If you need more, let me know and I'll

give it a shot, but what I've got thus far is that
he's fifty-four and has an IQ that's practically
off the upper end of the scale. He lives in Mal-
ibu and is positively loaded—thanks to a trust
fund and inheritance, not through any effort of
his own.

"Your father mentioned his family was filthy
rich," Paul reminded her.

He doesn't work, per se, but calls himself an
artist and is represented by a third-rate gallery
in L.A.—the Montique Gallery.

Since his paintings are garbage, he probably
rents the wall space to have them hung. The
gallery sure can't be earning much on commis-
sions from him.

Okay, now we start getting into the more interesting stuff. He's been under psychiatric care
for as far back as I could dig. Apparently he has
decided psychopathic tendencies, so it wouldn't
seem to me that he can be very treatable, but
every so often he gets checked into a private
clinic for a month or two at a stretch.

"Your father called that one, too," Paul said,
scrolling the next part of the message up onto the
screen.

April nodded, then continued reading.

Lately, he's also gotten involved with some self-
help program and seems to be pretty fanatical
about it. At any rate, he's a real Jekyll and

Hyde, sometimes smooth as silk and charming as all get out, other times coming on like Jack Nicholson portraying a psycho.

He's also a news junkie—subscribes to *Time*, *Newsweek*, *Nation's Business*, the *L.A. Times*, *New York Times*....

The list went on, but her gaze froze on the *New York Times* at the exact instant Paul said, "He subscribes to the *Times*."

"And suddenly," she said, "it doesn't seem quite so unlikely that someone in California might have something to do with what's been going on here."

"It sure as hell doesn't. Especially not when the someone's loaded. He could be paying a dozen guys to follow us around."

"But why?"

Paul shook his head. "He sees your name in a want ad and... You don't think he could still be obsessed with your mother, do you?"

"After all these years? No. Not unless he was..."

"The kind of guy who spends a fair bit of time in a private clinic?"

"We're probably adding two and two and getting a hundred and seven," she said. "But let's see what else your friend found."

She anxiously eyed the screen as Paul scrolled up the next bit of print.

I've saved the best—or maybe I should say the worst—for last. Bellavia has a history of stalking women.

"Oh, Lord," April whispered.

"Hell, I figured your father was exaggerating," Paul said. "But he told me that these days the guy would be labeled as a stalker."

His lawyer's always managed to keep him out of serious trouble with the law—plays on the excuse of Bellavia's mental problems and—no proof here, but I suspect—pays off the right people. At any rate, as far as I could learn, Bellavia's never physically harmed anyone. But several women have gotten restraining orders against him.

They seem to work. I guess his lawyer's convinced him that he'd end up doing time if he started ignoring court orders. But he's persistent as hell. As soon as an order runs out, he's back on the woman's doorstep. Some of them he's been hounding for twenty years or more.

"Oh, Lord," April whispered again. "If he's been hung up on other women for twenty years, he could easily still be obsessed with my mother."

"Yeah, this sure doesn't make it sound like such an off-the-wall possibility, does it."

Paul scrolled the print upward again, and they saw they'd reached the end.

Well, East Coast, hope this helps. And if you do want more, let me know specifically what.

Best,

Ross

"What do you think?" April asked, trying to ignore the uneasy feeling that reading about John Bellavia had given her.

Paul shook his head. "Let's try things from the top again. He sees the ad with your name in it."

"Ostensibly from my brother," she reminded him.

"Right. So he assumes your parents had another child after they went under. And if he's still obsessed with your mother, he figures that if he could find her kids, then he can get to her through them."

"You think we're really reaching here?"

"Maybe. But given what Ross had to say, I wouldn't be surprised if we're not. And if we aren't, once he sees the ad, he hires a detective, who learns it was me who placed the ad."

"And that you're not my brother at all."

"Uh-huh. He checks into who I really am."

"And if he looks further, he finds out that you've been talking to people about the bombing."

"Right. But regardless of what he's learned, he follows me, tapes our initial meeting..."

"And then sends the tape to Gutteridge. But why?"

"I don't know. This is the place we got stuck before, isn't it. When we decided that the bomber was responsible for the tape, we couldn't make any sense out of his sending it to Gutteridge—unless it was to convince him not to talk."

"But how does taping us at the airport fit in with the drive-by and the other tape?" April asked. "Whether Bellavia's the bomber or not, if he's actually trying to find my mother, where does he think scaring us half to death will get him?''

Paul raked his fingers through his hair. ''I haven't got a clue,'' he said at last. ''But look,'' he added, glancing at his watch, ''we'd better get going. With any luck, the senator will say something that helps us.''

''Let's hope so,'' she said. She wasn't going to hold her breath, though.

Talking to Gutteridge and Resdoe had only left her more confused than she'd been before she'd seen them. Why should she expect anything different from talking to Nelson Harmidarrow?

CHAPTER ELEVEN

WAYNE RESDOE MIGHT WELL have been the reincarnation of a snake-oil salesman, but Nelson Harmidarrow was cut from entirely different cloth.

An Alan Alda type, he exuded such charm and sincerity that April could see why the voters had elected him with a huge majority. She suspected she'd have trouble keeping in mind that he might be the one behind the bizarre things that had been happening.

After putting her and Paul at ease in two seconds flat, he quickly got to the subject of their meeting. "My assistant tells me your program is on the Vietnam era."

"It'll just be a segment, not the entire hour," Paul told him. "But we want to touch on a lot of different aspects. And what we'd specifically like to talk about with you is AWV. This okay?" he added, removing his tape recorder from his briefcase.

The senator nodded. "I assume you're aware that I was only involved with AWV until 1970? I can't really discuss the later years."

"That's all right. We'd primarily like to hear how it got started."

After Harmidarrow talked about that a little, Paul

asked him a couple of other general questions and then eased into the true purpose of their visit.

The second he uttered the words "Unique factory bombing," April thought Harmidarrow seemed marginally uneasy.

Nothing showed in his expression, but he ever-so-casually straightened his already straight tie and rolled his chair an inch or two farther back from his desk, putting a tiny bit more distance between himself and them.

"That was a terrible incident," he said. "And one that a lot of the group's members couldn't condone, myself included. It was the reason I severed my association with AWV."

Paul nodded. "As one of the leaders, you must have felt... What's the word I'm looking for? Disillusioned, maybe? That someone in a basically peaceful protest group would link its name with a crime like that."

"Yes. I was disillusioned, disheartened, angry. I felt we'd been making real progress, but that bombing turned public sentiment completely against us.

"I'm not saying it shouldn't have," he added quickly. "It was a horrible crime. I'm just saying that suddenly everyone perceived all of us to be radical militants when the bombing couldn't have involved more than a few people."

"A few people?" April said before she could stop herself.

When Harmidarrow looked at her curiously, she knew she had to explain. "From our research, we got the impression that nobody except Colin Birmingham was involved."

"The bureau issued statements to that effect at the time," Paul added.

"Oh, yes, of course." Harmidarrow gave them a shrug that suggested he had too much on his mind to remember all the details from so long ago.

"Would you mind my asking you something off the record?" Paul said. "Just to satisfy my curiosity?"

"I guess not," the senator told him. But April knew he was too savvy to believe anything was ever truly off the record.

"What did you think of Colin Birmingham? Your personal opinion."

"Well...we certainly weren't friends. There were things we didn't see eye to eye on. He was a rabble-rouser, and I didn't like to hear anyone in AWV suggesting violent protests would be more effective than peaceful demonstrations. But I always assumed his bark was worse than his bite."

"Then do you figure there's any chance he wasn't the bomber?" Paul asked.

April held her breath, slowly releasing it when the senator shook his head.

"I don't think it's likely," he said. "The bureau rarely makes mistakes."

She resisted the urge to take issue with that. There was no way he was going to say anything critical of the feds in front of a journalist, regardless of what his real opinion was. When she glanced at Paul, wondering where he'd go from here, she got the sense he had something up his sleeve.

"You know," he said to Harmidarrow, "back when you said 'a few people,' you started me worrying that we'd missed something. If you wouldn't mind, I'd like to run a few other things by you— other things we think we've got right about that bombing. NBS doesn't take kindly to its journalists doing sloppy research.''

"Sure," the senator agreed, not looking entirely comfortable. "But I never knew all the details, so don't expect too much."

"Fair enough. Now, our understanding is that nobody had any idea what Colin Birmingham was planning. Nobody with any authority in the group, I mean. I know he did tell a couple of fellows about it the night before..." Paul rapidly flipped through his notebook, then looked at Harmidarrow again. "Tom Walker and Ken Gutteridge. He was drinking with them and got to talking about it. And they're the ones who gave the feds his name."

"Yes," Harmidarrow said slowly. "That's right, although virtually no one was aware it was them. Do you mind my asking how you found out?"

"Sorry, I've got to keep my sources confidential. Otherwise I wouldn't have any. But I gather you were one of the few who was aware?"

The senator nodded. "They came to me the day after the bombing and told me what they knew— wanted my advice, really, on whether to go to the FBI with it or not."

"If they knew who'd killed seven people, shouldn't that have been a no-brainer?" Paul asked.

"Normally, it would have been. But you've got to keep in mind the times and circumstances. Like a lot of people in the movement, Walker and Gutteridge considered the feds enemies. And they didn't like the idea of ratting out someone in the group. On the other hand, they realized that, given the magnitude of the crime, things would be extremely…difficult for them if the feds learned they'd withheld the information.''

"I wonder why they didn't come to you before the bombing,'' April said. "I mean, if they'd told you what Birmingham was up to, you'd have stopped him, wouldn't you?''

"I'd have done everything in my power to. But…''

The senator paused and looked across his desk at her. "You know, that was a very perceptive question. I always wondered why they didn't come to me while there was time to prevent it.''

"Why do you think they didn't?'' Paul asked.

Harmidarrow shook his head. "We've gotten way off track here, haven't we. And my speculations, all these years after the fact, are hardly relevant to anything. I went to see the feds shortly after the bombing—once the dust had started to settle a little—and told them what my thoughts were. And I'm sure they took what I said into consideration.''

April's pulse began to race. The senator had had speculations? Ones he'd talked to the feds about? She'd dearly love to know what they'd been, but she knew he wasn't going to share them.

THE DOOR OF HARMIDARROW'S office suite had barely closed behind Paul and April when she said, "Well?''

He glanced at her expectant expression, then chose

his words carefully, not wanting to build her hopes up too high. "I think we might have gotten a lead."

"You mean the fact that he went to see the feds?"

He nodded, and when she smiled he wrapped his arm around her shoulders. She had a wonderful smile that he didn't see anywhere near as often as he'd like.

"I thought that was something useful," she said. "But I was afraid I was just into wishful thinking."

"I'm sure it's more than that. Whatever Harmidarrow had to say to them, I'll bet we find it interesting."

"You're sure we'll be able to learn what it was?"

"With any luck." As they left the building, he dug out his cell phone and punched in Steve's number.

"Steve Johnston, please," he said to the woman who answered. "Paul Gardiner calling."

"Your special agent contact?" April whispered.

He barely had time to say yes before Steve picked up.

After they exchanged greetings, he said, "I'm just calling to tell you the poker game's switched to my place."

"Oh, okay. Usual time?"

"Uh-huh."

"Fine, see you then."

"Poker game?" April said when he pushed End.

"It's a code asking him to call me back on an outside line. I doubt there's a secure phone in all of Federal Plaza."

Harmidarrow's office wasn't far from the park, and they'd walked along Central Park South and bought pretzels from a street vendor before Steve called back.

"What's up?" he said.

"This is a big one," Paul warned him. "And completely off the record."

April started to look uneasy, so he whispered, "He's okay. We can trust him."

"How big?" Steve asked.

"Remember, a while back, you gave me the names of the guys who ratted out Colin Birmingham?"

"Uh-huh."

"Well, one of them told me they'd lied. That Birmingham wasn't really the bomber."

There was a brief pause before Steve said, "The guy even marginally credible?"

"I think so. And the more following up I've done, the more convinced I am that it wasn't Birmingham. But I need to know about something that'll be in one of the old files."

"What?"

"I'm not exactly sure. Nelson Harmidarrow made a point of talking to you people not long after the bombing, and I've got a feeling he said something that got buried. So…Steve, since I don't really know what I'm looking for, do you think I could actually see the notes from that meeting?"

There was a longer pause this time, then Steve said, "That would be pretty dicey."

He hadn't said no! "Look, I realize it wouldn't be kosher, but I really think I'm onto something major here. And if I can put together enough to be certain Birmingham's innocent, I'll be asking you to get officially involved. Hell, Steve, this is something that could make you look like the best damned agent since Eliot Ness."

"Well...I'll see what I can dig up."

Paul relaxed a little. For a minute, he'd thought he might be asking for too much.

"Come by about seven tonight," Steve added. "The building's pretty well cleared out by then. I'll let security know I'm expecting you."

"Thanks, Mr. Ness."

"Yeah, well, I won't go changing my name just yet."

"Paul?" April said as he put away the phone. "What was that bit about his getting officially involved? My father would have a fit if—"

"Hey, if we get some solid evidence, get to the point of trying to help your parents cut a deal, somebody has to negotiate on behalf of the bureau. And we want someone who won't try anything funny."

She nodded slowly. "I guess it's just that I've spent my whole life viewing the feds as the enemy. It's hard to think of trusting one of them."

"Steve's okay. I've known him for a long time, and he's always been a straight shooter."

"Well...maybe I'll feel better after I've met him. When are we set for?"

"Seven o'clock. Only you're not in on this one."

"But—"

"April, asking to see that file was asking for a serious favor. If Steve lets me look at those notes, he'll really be sticking his neck out for me, so I can't go walking in there with someone he doesn't know from Eve."

"Well..."

He could practically read her thoughts. Even

though she could see his point, she still wanted to be there.

Why? he asked himself. Only because she wanted to see that file firsthand? Or did she still not entirely trust him?

He exhaled slowly, reminding himself she'd been taught never to trust anyone. But, dammit, knowing the way he felt about her, she should feel that she could trust him with her life.

"Look," he said, "I'll come straight from seeing Steve to your place and fill you in."

She still didn't look happy, but all she said was, "Let's just hope there'll be something worth filling me in about."

APRIL BEGAN WATCHING for Paul at seven-thirty, even though she knew he'd be a lot later than that. Unless, of course, the notes from that meeting were so sketchy they'd take no time to read—in which case, there might be nothing useful in them.

Finally, a little after nine, she spotted his Cherokee heading along the street. When he found a place to park and started back toward her building, she stood gazing down at him, wondering if he'd learned anything worthwhile.

He strode rapidly along, looking so darned self-confident that he must have. Then again, he always walked with that purposeful stride.

After she buzzed the front lock for him, she opened her apartment door and headed down the hall, too anxious to wait until he got all the way upstairs.

"Hey, imagine meeting you here," he said when

he turned onto the last landing and discovered her there.

"Just happened to be in the neighborhood."

He pulled her close and kissed her—so hungrily that under different circumstances, she'd have forgotten about everything else.

Under these circumstances, she couldn't. But she did manage to resist asking any questions until they were inside her apartment.

"So?" she said, closing the door.

"So?" he repeated, looking as if he didn't have a clue what she wanted. "Oh, you're curious about my meeting with Steve," he teased.

"Only a tad."

He grinned. "Okay, try this on for size. Harmidarrow told the bureau that he didn't think your father could possibly have planted the bomb."

"What?" she whispered, her knees suddenly weak. "But when I asked if he thought my father might not have been the bomber..."

"He gave you the politically correct answer. That the bureau doesn't make mistakes. But back when it happened he thought they had. And you want to guess who he figured was responsible?"

"Resdoe?"

"No, but you're guessing from the right list. He suggested the feds check into what John Bellavia was up to that day."

"Really?" She sank onto the couch, afraid to read too much into that. But if both her father and Nelson Harmidarrow thought it might have been Bellavia...

"Look," Paul said, sitting down beside her and taking her hands in his. "There's something I'd better tell you right now, something you're not going to be happy about.''

"All right," she said uneasily.

"I had to tell Steve I'd met you, and that you have a way of contacting your parents—that you arranged for me to talk with your father."

"Oh, Paul. That makes me very nervous."

"I know. But I wouldn't have done it if I wasn't sure he'd keep it to himself."

"Sure as in absolutely certain?"

He nodded. "I've trusted him before and things have never gone wrong. And it turned out that when he looked through the notes on Harmidarrow's visit to the bureau, they got him interested enough in the case that he read an overall summary of the investigation—which made him even more interested. And when we got down to the nitty-gritty, and he started telling me things I'd never have learned on my own, I realized it only made sense to level with him. So I filled him in on everything we've done and found out and—"

"Wait a minute," she interrupted anxiously. "Everything? You mean including who's on my father's suspects list and what he told you about them?"

When Paul nodded again, she found it hard to resist saying she thought he'd made a mistake. But what was done was done; there was nothing to be gained by criticizing him after the fact.

Her expression had to be revealing more than she meant it to, because he said, "April, it's okay. Really. That's how things like this work. By pooling information, we both ended up with a better take on the facts."

"I guess," she said, telling herself that maybe his sharing things with this Steve wasn't the worst thing in the world. Not if it meant that, at long last, they were getting down to the real facts.

"What did he think about our suspects?" she asked.

"Well, he couldn't see Harmidarrow having had anything to do with it. As for Resdoe, he was kind of on the spot. I know he doesn't like the guy any more than I do, but he couldn't come right out and say there's even a chance that a federal agent might have been responsible for a bombing."

"But you don't think he was ruling it out?"

"No, I don't think so. Basically, he didn't say much about it at all—except that, as we'd already realized, if Resdoe *wasn't* an FBI agent as far back as 1970, then your father's theory about why he might have been involved doesn't fly."

"But if he was an infiltrator?"

Paul shrugged. "That was something else Steve couldn't say much about. I mean, he could hardly admit that Resdoe might actually have been an agent before the bureau's records say he was. But look, mostly we talked about Harmidarrow's statement to the feds, so do you want me to fill you in on that?"

"Yes. And don't leave out a thing."

"Okay. When he went to see them, he said he thought there was something fishy about Walker and Gutteridge's story. They were claiming your father had said the bombing was entirely his plan and that he was acting completely on his own, but the senator doubted he could have been.

"Harmidarrow figured that either there'd been

more than one person involved or else the bureau was after the wrong man entirely, because your father didn't have the skill to make that bomb. Or to set it to go off on a time delay.''

''But…'' April paused, her thoughts racing.

They were talking about why her father couldn't be guilty, and she didn't want to argue against that. On the other hand, Paul wouldn't have forgotten anything her father had said to him, so she might as well speak up.

''I thought my dad told you the kind of bombs they made were dead simple,'' she said.

''Yeah, he did. And I guess most of them were. But the one that went off at Unique wasn't. And the timing device was really complex—far too complex for someone who hadn't had any experience with sophisticated bombs.''

''And my father hadn't?''

''Not that the feds were able to establish—which strikes me as a real flaw in their case against him.''

She nodded slowly, still not wanting to read too much into what he was saying, but unable to stop thinking that things were starting to sound a lot more promising.

''The FBI didn't release any specific information about the bomb to the press, but—''

''Then how did Harmidarrow know it was one my father couldn't have set?''

''Good question, and Steve couldn't find any explanation in the file. But he had a plausible theory. Immediately after the bombing, the feds spent hours questioning Harmidarrow, because of his leadership status in AWV. Steve figures someone could have let something slip. The senator's a sharp guy, so it wouldn't have taken much to clue him in.''

"No, I guess not. But you know, listening to you, I'm realizing we both seem to have stopped wondering if Harmidarrow could have been involved. Do you think we can completely rule him out?''

"Well, as I said, Steve doesn't think he had anything to do with it. First off, he had an alibi for the afternoon of the bombing. We know that's hardly proof he wasn't involved with the planning, but what would his motivation have been? He's always been known as antiviolence. And if he was involved, surely he wouldn't have gone to the feds and told them they should be digging deeper.''

"No...I guess he wouldn't. He'd have kept quiet.''

"Right. So I've got to think the only reason your father suspected him was because he knew about almost all the protests beforehand.''

"But he didn't necessarily know about every single one of them," she said slowly.

"No. And if the Unique bombing was a one-man show, as Resdoe put it...''

"But he said it was my father's show, so I don't think we should be taking anything he said too seriously.''

"I'm not. Let's get back to your father, though, because his not being a bomb expert is only one reason Harmidarrow thought the feds had things wrong. The other is that he suspected Bellavia.''

She nodded, switching her mind to that track. "Was Bellavia enough of a bomb expert?''

"Harmidarrow figured so.''

"But did he have any real evidence?"

"Not hard evidence."

"Then…" She didn't bother finishing the thought. Paul knew as well as she did that if there was no real proof of anything, they were still stuck with trying to find some. And so far they were batting zero.

"But Harmidarrow told them something pretty interesting," Paul continued. "Not long after the bombing, Bellavia came to him wanting to talk about a hypothetical situation. He said that somebody he knew had committed a murder and the police had charged another person with it."

"Or maybe the hypothetical somebody committed seven murders?"

"Exactly. So there was Harmidarrow, already thinking your father couldn't have been the bomber, and along comes Bellavia asking whether he figures this hypothetical guilty party should fess up."

"And Harmidarrow said he should," she guessed.

"Of course. But if Bellavia was talking about himself and the bombing, he obviously decided not to take the advice."

April slowly shook her head. They'd wanted facts and now they had a whole lot of them. But the more she learned, the more confused she became.

"Something's bothering me," she said at last. "It sounds as if Harmidarrow was Father Confessor. I mean, right after the bombing, Walker and Gutteridge go to him for advice. Then, a couple of days later, Bellavia comes asking for his opinion. Does that strike you as merely coincidental or really strange?"

"I'm not sure. He is the kind of guy who inspires

trust, so maybe people tended to use him as a sounding board. Or maybe…''

''What?''

Paul shrugged. ''This might be totally off the wall, but if Walker and Gutteridge were about to go lying to the bureau, maybe they wanted to test their story on someone first.''

''What do you mean?''

''Well, maybe they were just seeing how believable it was. If Harmidarrow had said he didn't buy it, maybe they wouldn't have tried it on the feds. But he probably wasn't totally convinced it wasn't your father until after Bellavia came to him.''

''And you know, if Walker and Gutteridge *were* just testing their story out, that would explain something else—why they didn't go to Harmidarrow before the bombing, as soon as they supposedly learned what your father was planning.''

April considered all that for a minute, then said, ''How about talking to Walker? What if we said that Harmidarrow told us about them coming to him for advice? Walker's reaction might not tell us anything, but you never know.''

''It sounds like a good idea to me,'' Paul told her. ''Let's try it right now.''

She waited anxiously while he searched through his book for the number and called.

''Tom Walker, please,'' he said after a few moments.

There was a silence, then he said, ''I'm very sorry to hear that. My condolences to the family.

''That was his niece,'' he told her, putting down the phone. ''Walker died yesterday.''

CHAPTER TWELVE

"OH, LORD," APRIL murmured, picturing the shrunken man that Walker had been. Even after what he'd done, she couldn't help feeling sorry for what he'd gone through.

"So that's that," Paul said. "There's no point in bothering to call Gutteridge. Odds are he'd hang up in my ear. But even without being sure... Look, from what we know, I really doubt Harmidarrow was involved."

She nodded slowly. Worried as she was about ruling him out too soon, the likelihood he'd had any part in things did seem remote.

"Okay," Paul continued. "Let's go with the assumption that the senator didn't know anything until after the fact. And even then he wasn't certain who was responsible. But I still think it's pretty darned significant that he suspected Bellavia—particularly that he suspected him strongly enough to tell the feds."

"And how significant did they think it was?"

"Well, they followed up, but it was pretty cursory. They established he didn't have a witness for where he was the day of the bombing, but—"

"And they didn't think that was significant? When

you put it together with the fact he knew about bombs?''

''He was a loner, remember? He probably wouldn't have had a solid alibi for most times. At any rate, they questioned him, but that was about it.''

''They questioned him. Paul…I just don't believe this. Harmidarrow tells them my father couldn't have set that bomb, tells them he thinks Bellavia did, and they only halfheartedly followed up?''

''Well, I think we're looking at a case of serious tunnel vision. The feds had two witnesses willing to testify that Colin Birmingham told them he was going to bomb that factory. Then your father took off, which was a sure sign of guilt in their books.

''And if that wasn't enough, Bellavia was a pretty crazy guy whose family was rolling in money. If the feds had managed to build a case against him, they'd have ended up facing the best defence team all that money could buy.

''So where Steve and I got to, reading between the lines, was that after they'd talked to him, they decided he was a complication they didn't want.''

April shook her head in frustration. ''Right. Why complicate things just to get at the truth?''

Paul pulled her closer to him on the couch, but his nearness only made her feel a tiny bit better. Things seemed downright hopeless again. The bombing had been a lifetime ago, and there were so many pieces of the puzzle they'd never be able to retrieve.

''Hey, we've gotten a lot further than you seem to think,'' Paul said, giving her shoulders a squeeze.

She knew he meant the gesture to be reassuring, but the only thing that was going to make her feel better was a plan that would get them a lot further still.

"So where do we go from here?" she said. "To California? To talk to Bellavia?"

"No. I think visiting him would be a bad idea."

"But he's the only one we haven't talked to. And it's sounding as if he's our man."

"Well, yeah, but if he is, if he's been behind the tapes and all, then he'd know who we were the instant he saw us."

"Just like Gutteridge," April said, recalling the scary, sinking feeling she'd had when he'd recognized her.

"Exactly. And just like Gutteridge, he'd tell us what he wanted to and nothing else. Besides..."

"Besides what?"

Paul shifted position a little, so he could cuddle her even more closely. "April, we're talking about a psychopath who stalks women. On top of that, he might still be obsessed with your mother. And I've seen enough film footage of her to know how much you resemble her. So when we're talking about a guy like that..."

"Yes, I see what you mean," she murmured, barely able to keep from shuddering.

"And even if we've got the obsession bit wrong, if he is the bomber, he's sure not going to want to be found out. So it would be insane for you to get within a thousand miles of him."

"He'd be pretty perturbed if you showed up, too, which means we'd better both stay away from him. But then where *do* we go from here?"

"Well...Steve had a thought."

"What?" she said, still not comfortable with having a fed involved.

"You might not like it."

"There hasn't been much I've liked since the day I got mixed up in this. Present company excepted," she added. "So what's one more thing?"

"Well…okay, here it is. Steve figures the evidence against your father's as flimsy as I do. In fact, he figures that if Walker and Gutteridge did lie, Bellavia easily could be the guilty one."

"Really?"

"Uh-huh. So he'd like to reactivate the case. And he's sure he could convince his boss to let him do it."

"What? Really?" she said again, trying to think through her surprise so she could consider all the possible ramifications of that.

Paul smiled. "Yeah, really. Which means he could go visit Bellavia—he or someone on his team. And they could talk to whoever else they wanted to, look into anything they decide might be useful."

But to have the feds actively working on the case again? Her father might have gone for the idea of an investigative journalist looking into things on the quiet, but the way he felt about the FBI…

There was no point, though, in worrying about how he'd react. Not right now, at least. Instead, she should be figuring out whether there was any risk to this idea. Maybe she was only thinking there had to be a catch because she'd always been taught you could never trust the bureau.

"What about Wayne Resdoe?" she asked. "What if Bellavia wasn't the bomber? What if it was one of their own? You said before that the idea of a fed being involved wasn't something Steve even wanted to think about.''

''I don't think that's exactly what I said. But regardless of that, if it turns out there's evidence pointing to Resdoe, I know Steve won't turn a blind eye to it. Even if it does implicate one of their own.

''And it would get us out, April. We already knew we were playing a dangerous game, but when I told Steve about everything we've done and all the weird stuff that's been happening…''

''He said?'' she prompted, even though she doubted she wanted to hear.

''He said we were lucky to still be alive. And that the best advice he could give us was to get out of town for a few days, until he gets things moving and it's obvious the case is active again. Once it is… Well, we've talked about this before. As soon as the feds are involved, whoever's been giving us grief will realize we've become the least of his worries. Besides, the bureau's a million times more likely to get to the bottom of things than a couple of amateurs and—''

''An investigative journalist isn't exactly an amateur,'' she pointed out, still wondering about a catch.

''No, but I'm not a special agent, either.''

''Well, there were a whole horde of special agents who didn't do very well the first time around.''

That made Paul smile, just for a moment. ''No, but this time Steve would be in charge, not someone who'd decided your father was guilty and wasn't going to look beyond that. And if he strikes pay dirt, we'll still both get what we've been after—proof that your father's innocent and the real identity of the man who killed mine.''

She nodded slowly. She'd never have believed she'd even consider agreeing to anything that involved the bureau. But she couldn't help seeing the merits.

Even before she'd heard what Steve had to say, she'd been afraid that if she and Paul didn't get out soon, they might end up dead. But there hadn't seemed to be any way out—until now. So if turning things over to Steve was a viable way, maybe the only way…

"We have nothing to lose by backing off," Paul pressed. "Hell, I'd even still get my book. Maybe the final chapters would be about how the bureau eventually got the bomber, not about how we did, but who cares?''

"You mean who cares as long as it's a bestseller?'' she said, managing a smile.

He grinned. "Yeah, I still like the thought of a bestseller. So what do you think?''

Doing her best to ignore her lingering reservations, she said, "Well, you know how I feel about the feds. But if Steve really does think my father might be innocent, if he'd really go at things with that mindset…''

"He would."

"Then…then I guess we have to go along with him, don't we.''

"I think it's the only way. But…there's one other thing.''

"Oh?'' she said, his uneasy expression making her

certain there was a catch after all. "Something you've been holding back?"

"Not exactly holding back. Just waiting until you realized it made sense to go along with Steve's plan."

"All right. What is it?"

He hesitated. "Steve would have to meet with your father before he even raises the possibility of reactivating the case."

APRIL WAS STILL AWAKE when the first pale fingers of dawn crept into her bedroom.

Beside her, his body warm and wonderful against hers, Paul had been asleep for hours. But even their lovemaking hadn't left her spent enough to drift off, and the longer she'd lain awake, the more unanswered questions there'd been milling around in her head.

She had the answer to one of the major ones, though. She knew that Steve Johnston's proposition would be dead in the water if she refused to set up a meeting between him and her father. Paul had said there was simply no negotiating about that stipulation.

"If Steve tells his boss he wants to reactivate the case," he'd explained, "he's putting his reputation on the line. He's basically saying he figures the bureau made a mistake. And he's not going to do that without checking out your father first. Without making sure his version of the story isn't full of holes."

"Why can't we just give him my father's version?"

"April, I already did. You know that. But it wasn't

enough. Especially not when the impression Steve got from the files was that Colin Birmingham was part of the lunatic fringe.''

''But he must have realized the files were biased, to put it mildly.''

''Yeah, he did. But he still has to see for himself that your father isn't a crackpot.''

''Even though you know he's not? And I know he's not? Why couldn't we just—''

''Look, you're his daughter. And how much can Steve rely on my impression? I've spoken to your father once. Over the phone. What we're talking about here is credibility. And the only way anyone judges that is face-to-face.''

Stopping her mental replay of the conversation, she began thinking through the situation yet again. Assuming Steve was playing straight, she could see his point. Insisting on meeting her father—to assure himself that Colin Birmingham was sane and rational and quite possibly innocent—wasn't unreasonable.

But from her father's perspective... Lord, in one way she couldn't imagine he'd even consider the idea of meeting a fed face-to-face. Still, if he thought the odds were high that a fresh investigation would determine the real facts, he just might go for it.

The problem was, they had no way of being sure that Steve didn't have more in mind than a simple meeting. What if he saw this as an opportunity to be a hero? A chance to capture the Napalm Bomber after all these years? That possibility was enough to send shivers through her.

Oh, she'd admit she'd been awfully upset with her father yesterday. It had been quite a shock to have him confess he hadn't actually been the peaceful radical her parents had always painted him to be.

Once she'd calmed down, though, she'd pretty well come to terms with that. After all, it wasn't hard to understand why they'd fudged a little on what they'd told her. And there probably weren't any parents on earth who hadn't lied to their children about something or other. Besides, regardless of his views way back when, he was still the father she'd always adored. So if Steve Johnston wasn't playing straight...

Just as she was reminding herself that Paul trusted him implicitly, a whispering fear murmured, *But somewhere along the way, you've completely stopped thinking that maybe you can't trust Paul.*

That was true, of course. Somewhere along the way, she'd decided she could trust him. Now the question was, Could they trust Steve Johnston?

She shifted restlessly, realizing too late that she was disturbing Paul.

"Hey," he said sleepily. "'Morning."

"'Morning." She snuggled even more closely against him and tried not to wonder what she'd ever do without him. There'd been so little permanence in her life that she'd learned not to count on any. But she'd never wanted anything to be permanent as much as she wanted this relationship to be.

He lazily nuzzled the back of her neck, sending a rush of desire through her. And when he began slowly kissing his way down her back, it was enough to drive every other thought from her mind.

PAUL TOOK ANOTHER SIP of coffee and glanced surreptitiously across the dining room table at April.

He knew better than to try pressuring her, so since last night he hadn't uttered a word about Steve's offer. But now that they were showered and dressed and she still hadn't said she'd talk to her father about it, he was having a tough time keeping quiet.

During the night, he'd had a couple of pretty bad dreams about this bizarre situation they'd gotten themselves involved in. And now...

Well, he wasn't sure if it was his sixth sense warning him or simply the way he was putting together the evidence, but he felt certain that whoever had been trying to frighten them had reached the point of giving up on the scare tactics and becoming deadly serious. So he wanted April to set up that meeting as soon as possible.

He had to spend a couple of hours this morning in a story meeting at NBS, and she'd said she could use the time to check in with her clients. But there was nothing else either of them absolutely had to do today. So if she called her father and arranged something, they could get the ball rolling.

Then, once things were in Steve's hands, maybe they could even take his advice and get the hell out of New York for a few days—go someplace where their every move wouldn't be watched.

He glanced over at her again, thinking he might not be quite so concerned if he had only himself to worry about. But if anything awful happened to her... God, he didn't even want to think about that.

Finally, over a second cup of coffee, he ran out of willpower. "Well?" he said as casually as he could.

"How does Steve's idea strike you now that you've had a chance to sleep on it?"

She gave him a weary smile. "It's still making me awfully nervous. But I guess I have to do what I did when you wanted to talk to my father. Get my head around the fact that I can't make a decision like this on his behalf, that I have to tell him where we're at and let him decide where we go from here."

He nodded, trying not to look as relieved as he felt. "You'll tell him everything, though. Not just about Steve's offer, but about the drive-by and that second videotape and the creep we spotted following you yesterday."

When she shook her head, his gut clenched. "You have to," he said as gently as he could.

"No. I don't want him making a decision based on what he thinks is best for me. He's got to do what he feels is right for him and my mother."

"April...can you honestly believe, even for a second, it would be fair not to tell him what's been happening to you? You're his only child. You've got to let him know that if he doesn't take Steve up on his offer, it could mean more trouble for you."

Propping her elbows on the table, she rested her chin in her hands and gazed at him dejectedly—such a picture of unhappiness that he wanted to take her in his arms and tell her he'd keep her safe from harm.

But he couldn't guarantee that. He couldn't guarantee he could keep either of them safe.

He sure as hell intended to try, though. And whatever else he did after his meeting, he'd be stopping by his apartment to pick up his Walther. Normally, he only carried the gun when his research put him in contact with unsavory characters. But regardless of how he came in contact with them, unsavory characters were unsavory characters.

When April remained silent, he said, "Think about what you were saying a minute ago, okay? That you have to tell your father where we're at and let him decide where we go from here. That's not what you'll be doing if you leave out some of the facts."

"But—"

"Look, I understand your point, but if you don't tell him everything, you won't be letting him make his own decision at all. And what if he said no to Steve's idea, then you ended up hurt because of it? Hurt or…worse? He'd never forgive himself, would he?"

"No," she admitted. "But if I tell him everything, he won't have a choice. He'll feel he has to meet with Steve."

Thank heavens, Paul said silently. "And when he does, it'll go just fine," he said aloud, reaching across the table and taking her hand in his. "I promise it will."

APRIL HUNG UP the pay phone's receiver and took a deep breath.

Her father had been working away from the office today, and all afternoon long, while she'd been unable to reach him, she'd worried about whether calling him was the right thing to do. And now that she'd talked to him, updated him on everything and told him what Steve Johnston was proposing, she was so frightened things were going to go wrong that she almost wished she hadn't phoned him.

Forcing herself to turn and face Paul, she said, "All right. He'll see Steve tonight if we can set it up that soon."

"We'll set it up. I'll call him now. And this is the right thing to do," he added, apparently reading her mind.

"If it's not, I'll never forgive you—or myself," she said. And she wasn't kidding.

"Where do you want Steve to meet us?" he asked, ignoring her threat.

"There's a coffee shop at the corner of Amsterdam and Seventy-third. That's not much of a walk."

He took his phone from his pocket, punched in the number, then spoke briefly with Steve.

"He said he's on his way," Paul told her as he put the phone away and they began walking.

"You didn't say a word about why we wanted to see him."

"He'll guess. And haven't you noticed by now? I don't trust phones any more than you do. It'll be better to discuss the details in person. But what are they? Where are we meeting your father?"

"He didn't name a place. He said he'd call my cell number in an hour or so to see if we're on for tonight. And if we get going before he phones, we should just start driving north on Highway 87. He also said to make damned sure nobody's following us. That's going to be the hard part, isn't it," she added anxiously.

Paul nodded. "We'd better do the rental thing again, just in case somebody's bugged my car."

She glanced at her watch, wondering if they should get a car before they met Steve.

"Not a good idea," Paul said, obviously aware of what she was thinking. "We don't want to let the rental out of our sight after we've got it. If someone *is* watching us, it would take them about half a second to stick a transponder under the bumper."

They walked the rest of the way in silence, April's stomach churning harder with each step she took. *This is my court and my rules,* she told herself as Paul opened the door to the coffee shop. And so far, at least, Steve Johnston didn't know enough to be of any real danger to her father.

But none of that was keeping her from feeling like a little girl pretending to be an adult.

"He beat us here," Paul said as the door closed behind them. "That's him in the booth near the back."

She sized him up as they started in his direction, trying to ignore the fact that she'd begun shaking inside.   The agent was somewhere in his mid-to-late thirties, with short brown hair and wire rimmed glasses perched on a prominent nose.

As he rose to greet them, she added average height and weight to her mental description and told herself that he was hardly a threatening figure.

Once he'd asked her a few questions, though, he'd probably be in a position to charge her with obstructing justice or something. Not that he would. Not as long as Paul was right about him. But she still found the idea that he'd have that power pretty darned intimidating.

When Paul introduced them, she smiled and shook Steve's hand, certain her cool, calm and collected act wasn't fooling him in the slightest. He already had coffee, and a waitress immediately appeared to fill two more mugs.

"You've spoken with your father?" Steve asked once the woman retreated.

April nodded. "He's agreed to meet you. But it has to be entirely on his terms."

"That's fine. I know Paul's explained that I only want to hear his thoughts on the bombing."

Unless you've got a trick up your sleeve, she said silently.

"And what are his terms?"

"There aren't many. He chooses the place. You ride with Paul and me to get there. There were a few others—like no phone, no weapon, no wire—but since Paul trusts you, I don't even have to mention those."

She intentionally had, though, and while she had, she'd carefully watched his face for any reaction. There'd been nothing.

He reached into his jacket pocket and took out a phone. "We can leave this and my gun in the trunk of my car. I'm parked nearby. As for the wire..." He glanced at Paul. "I'll understand if you want to check for one."

"April?" Paul said.

When she didn't immediately reply, Steve slid out of the booth. "Come on. The washroom's just back here."

Paul shot her a glance that said this wasn't necessary, but she looked away. There was no way she was going to compromise her father's safety.

CHAPTER THIRTEEN

By the time Paul, Steve and April were heading north on Highway 87, she'd pretty well convinced herself they weren't being followed.

She'd turned around a hundred times to check without seeing anything suspicious. And not only had Paul taken a circuitous route out of the city, he'd also done another impersonation of Michael Andretti driving flat out in the Indy 500. Now, even though he was still routinely looking into the rearview mirror, he seemed confident that no one was on their tail.

Of course, way back on day one of their little adventure, he'd been confident he'd lost the green Taurus.

That recollection was almost enough to make her turn around again. Resisting the urge, she glanced over at him, thinking they'd been through an awful lot since that first day. She'd had enough excitement to do her for the next twenty or thirty years, if not the rest of her life. All she wanted in the foreseeable future was peace and quiet. And Paul, she silently added.

But did he feel anywhere near as strongly about her as she did about him? That was a scary question, and every time she reminded herself he might not, she cringed inside. Just as she was telling herself there was nothing she could do but wait and see, the cellular in her lap began to ring.

She jumped at the sound, even though she'd been expecting the call.

Paul looked over at her. Steve leaned forward from the back seat into the space between the rental's bucket seats.

Grabbing the phone, she answered it.

"It's me, Mouse," her father said.

When she nodded to Paul, Steve leaned forward another inch or so.

"Is everything going okay?"

"Yes. We're on our way and there's been no sign of anyone following us."

"And you checked this Steve out carefully? He's not carrying or wired?"

"No. Paul made certain he was okay."

There was a pause, and she knew her father was wishing he'd had some way of making certain *Paul* was okay. But all he finally said was, "Good. Where are you?"

"On Highway 87."

"How far north?"

She repeated the question out loud.

"About half way between Newburgh and Kingston," Paul told her.

"You heard that?" she asked into the phone.

"Uh-huh. When you reach Kingston, take Highway 28 west, then 42 north, then 23 west."

"28 west out of Kingston, then 42 north, then 23 west," she repeated. Out of the corner of her eye, she could see Steve jotting down the instructions.

"I'll call again in a while and give you the rest of the directions. And Mouse?"

"Yes?"

"If by any chance things start to go wrong when we get together, take cover the instant you realize it. Don't wait around to see what's happening. Not for even a second."

She couldn't answer because her throat was suddenly tight with tears, so she simply clicked off and put the phone back into her lap.

"Where to after we hit 23 west?" Steve wanted to know.

"He's going to call back," she managed to say. Then she stared out into the rapidly gathering twilight, hoping neither man asked her another question before she got her emotions back under control.

Once they'd reached Highway 23 west and her father still hadn't called back, she began thinking of that old cliché about tension thick enough to cut with a knife.

When the phone finally rang again, all three of them started.

DARKNESS HAD FALLEN before Paul reached the turn-off Colin Birmingham had told them to take, and he might have missed the small sign indicating the road to Lake Elizabeth if Steve hadn't said, "There! Just ahead!"

He hit the brakes and half swerved onto the gravel side road.

They were in the midst of the Catskill Mountains, and mere yards after they left Highway 23 behind the forest closed in on them, trees overhanging the road and blocking out what little light there was from the quarter moon.

The car's headlights cast a stream of pale yellow before them, but the surrounding night was pitch black. He felt as if he were driving in an unlit tunnel.

"Watch out for deer," Steve said. "They've got to be everywhere around here."

Paul eased his foot off the gas until they were barely crawling, then glanced at April. "How far did your father say we go?"

"About two miles in from the highway."

She'd barely spoken the words before the road came to an abrupt end. A huge boulder kept them from going any further. Behind it was a stand of trees. Through them, barely visible, was a clearing with a lake beyond it.

"This looks like what he described," she said.

Paul cut the ignition and started to get out of the car, then stopped and reached over to take his Walther out of the glove compartment.

"Expecting to need that?" Steve asked.

"Phobia about wild animals," he said.

Both Steve and April had to figure that was a lie, but neither of them called him on it. If they had, he'd probably have told them the truth, even though it would have made April anxious as hell to know that his sixth sense had warned him not to leave it behind. Once he'd climbed out of the car, he tucked the gun against the small of his back and they walked forward through the trees.

The clearing beyond, lit by the moonlight, stretched about fifty feet to the shore of the lake. Directly ahead, with three rowboats tied to it, was the dock where Colin Birmingham had told them to wait for him.

Off to the right stood a weathered wooden shack— a laughable sign over the door reading Lake Elizabeth General Store. A faded, hand-lettered notice in the window announced it sold bait, beer, soda and sandwiches. It was in darkness, and except for the reedy hooting of an owl, there was no hint of life anywhere.

They walked the twenty or so feet to the far end of the dock, as Birmingham had instructed, then stood gazing out over the lake and listening to the quiet lapping of the water.

"Think we're in for a long wait?" Steve asked April.

She shrugged. "He said he'd join us as soon as he felt it was safe."

In other words, they all knew, as soon as he felt confident they hadn't been followed.

When minutes stretched into a quarter of an hour, Paul paced the length of the dock and back.

"He said to wait at the end," Steve reminded him. "And you don't want to do anything to spook someone in a situation like this."

"Yeah, okay," he muttered.

April had given up on standing and was sitting with her legs dangling over the edge of the dock, so he sat down beside her. Steve continued to stand where he was, keeping a close eye on the clearing.

As the wait grew longer and longer, April could feel her nerves being stretched to their limit. Why was her father taking so much time?

Because he's afraid this is a trap, she silently answered her own question. And what if it was?

She glanced up at Steve, suddenly dreadfully afraid. What if he did somehow double-cross them?

Then she heard a creaking sound and looked in the direction it had come from.

"The shack," Paul whispered.

Her gaze flew to it. The door of the ramshackle structure was slowly swinging open.

She scrambled up from the dock with Paul, her eyes never leaving the door. When it was about halfway open, a dim light went on inside the shack.

"Okay, I'm in here," her father called. "Come on over. We'll talk inside."

She wasn't sure whether knowing he was right there made her more relieved or more frightened, but whichever it was, her heart was beating a mile a minute.

Paul reached for her hand and they started forward. They'd taken about three steps when all hell broke loose.

The clearing suddenly lit up like Times Square. Then a voice boomed through the night.

"Colin Birmingham! This is Special Agent Wayne Resdoe of the FBI! We have you surrounded! Give yourself up!"

Terror hit April like a hard-breaking wave. For an instant she stood frozen in place. Then she started forward—only to have Paul stop her in her tracks, holding her hand so tightly that when she tried to pull free she couldn't.

"Let me go!"

"Not on your life."

She stood there trapped, staring at him—the pounding in her ears and her fear for her father almost paralyzing.

Then a single question broke through the fear and lodged in her heart. What part did Paul have in this?

"You promised me things would go just fine," she whispered fiercely.

"April, I don't know what the hell's happening! I swear!"

She didn't know whether she should believe that or not, but Resdoe was yelling again, so she turned and looked toward shore.

"Birmingham!" he hollered. "Come out with your hands up."

"Stay here," Steve snapped, starting down the dock.

When he did, Resdoe stepped out into the beams of light that were crisscrossing the clearing and yelled, "Stop right where you are, Johnston."

"Like hell!"

"Stop or we'll blow that shack to smithereens."

Another wave of terror hit April.

Steve took one more step forward, then stopped.

"Okay, Birmingham!" Resdoe shouted. "Last call. Come out of there."

"Just a minute," Paul said, his words ringing evenly across the water. "Just a damned minute."

Steve turned.

Resdoe looked over at them. "What the hell do you think you're doing? Do you know what you can get for pulling a weapon on a federal agent?"

Only then did April realize Paul was pointing his gun at Resdoe.

"He'd love to charge you," Steve said quietly, heading back toward them. "Don't play Rambo with him."

Looking over his shoulder at Resdoe, he called, "He didn't pull the gun on you. He's just returning it to me. He was hanging on to it for me. One of Birmingham's conditions was that I wouldn't be armed."

Steve stopped in front of them and held out his hand for the gun.

"Did you cross us?" Paul demanded.

"No. I don't know how the hell he found out. But he must have a dozen armed men out there, so give me that before it's too late."

Paul looked at Steve for a long moment. Then he handed him the gun.

As the agent turned toward the clearing once more, Resdoe shouted, "You've got to the count of three, Birmingham. Then we open fire. One."

"No!" April whispered, trying to pull free of Paul again.

He wrapped his arms around her.

"Two."

"Let me go!"

"Three."

Paul dragged her down onto the dock; the clearing turned into a shooting gallery.

Shots were exploding from everywhere and April was screaming, a single hysterical thought in her mind. They were killing her father!

The firing stopped as suddenly as it had erupted. In the ensuing silence, she tried to move but couldn't.

Paul was still lying over her, pressing her against

the dock. But even if he hadn't been, the horror of what had happened was so numbing she was virtually frozen in place. She could hear herself crying, could feel the raw pain that filled her entire body, but she couldn't move.

"Oh, God, April," Paul was whispering against her hair.

Seconds passed. Or maybe minutes. And he was still murmuring, "Oh, God, I'm sorry."

She didn't want him holding her. Didn't want him anywhere near her. But when she tried to tell him to let her go, the words came out as unintelligible garble mixed with sobs.

And then, as if through a fog, she heard Steve saying, "April, listen to me. Your father's all right. They didn't shoot him."

She almost couldn't believe that, but she swallowed hard and tried to stop crying.

"How could they have missed?" Paul demanded, sitting up and pulling her with him.

"He wasn't in the shack. He had it rigged so the door would open and the light would come on, but he wasn't in there."

"I heard him," she whispered.

Steve shook his head. "You heard a tape of his voice."

"Then where...?"

"I don't know. Probably watching from somewhere in the woods. Resdoe's got his men searching," he added, gesturing across the water.

April looked toward the shore. Her vision was blurred from crying, but she could see that the clearing was in darkness again. The woods, though, were alive with the beams of powerful flashlights.

"So many of them," she murmured, her eyes filling with fresh tears. "They're bound to find him."

She'd barely finished speaking when, from what seemed like a long distance away, came the faint sound of someone starting a motor. It was followed by the rhythmic droning of a boat moving through the water of Lake Elizabeth.

Scarcely breathing, she listened to the sound grow gradually less audible. Finally, it faded into the night.

There was no guarantee it was her father in that boat, but she knew in her heart it was.

Fingering her locket, she wondered if it kept more than the wearer safe from harm.

WAYNE RESDOE'S MEN were still searching the woods, but Resdoe, Steve, Paul and April were standing in the moonlit clearing, halfway between the water's edge and the shack.

Or, more accurately, Paul thought, what was left of the shack. It was so full of bullet holes he was surprised it hadn't collapsed into a pile of sawdust.

The special agents were snarling at each other, both sounding as if they'd love to tear the other apart, and as Steve shot another question at Resdoe, Paul turned his attention back to them. He didn't know whether Steve had double-crossed April and him or not, but if he had, he and Resdoe were putting on one hell of a good performance.

Instead of answering Steve's question, Resdoe was waving in their direction and snapping, "Get them out of here! I'm not discussing bureau business in front of civilians."

"Oh?" Steve snapped back. "Well, you weren't so damned concerned that they were civilians when they were standing on the dock! When you started shooting the hell out of the night!"

"Get out of here. Now," Resdoe ordered, looking over at Paul and April.

"We'll head back to the car, Steve," Paul said, reaching for April's hand.

When she jerked it away, he simply gestured her to follow him, swearing to himself as he did. The last thing he wanted was her thinking he might have had something to do with this.

But even though he'd give the world to straighten things out right this minute, there was something even more important. If they could stay within listening range, without Steve and Resdoe noticing, they might learn for sure which side Steve was on.

As they reached the shack, a quick backward glance told him the two men were still eyeing each other blackly—and probably not noticing diddly.

"What the hell did you think you were doing?" Steve was demanding.

Quickly, Paul motioned April behind the shack. She gave him a glare that was worthy of Steve and Resdoe combined, but she scurried after him and moved up tight against the wall.

From that vantage point, they could hear Resdoe talking sarcastically about what an intelligent question Steve had just asked.

"What the hell do you think I was doing?" he replied. "I was trying to nail the Napalm Bomber.

Which was what you should have been doing. But since that's not what you had in mind, I—''

"How the hell do you know what I had in mind? You're suddenly clairvoyant?''

"Oh, give me a break, Johnston. You sign out some of the Unique bombing files. Then Gardiner comes skulking into your office after hours, when I know he's poking around about that case because he's already talked to me about it, and—''

"Let's just cut to the chase. How did you track us here?''

"Are you really an agent? I'm starting to think you got your badge out of a cereal box.''

"Oh, that line's hilarious, Resdoe. When did you start using it? Back when Hoover was a boy?''

"Very funny. But you obviously need a refresher in Surveillance 101, so here it is. Since Gardiner paid you that visit, I've had somebody keeping an eye on you. And when I discovered you were taking off with him and the daughter, I called in some backup and gave the car jockey a twenty to slap a transponder on that rental before you brought it from the lot.''

"Then you just followed us from way back out of sight,'' Steve muttered.

"Hey, give the agent with the cereal badge a gold star.''

"Listen to me, Resdoe,'' Steve said menacingly. "If you ever mess with one of my cases again, I'll—''

"Your case? That's a laugh. You've been interested in it for what? A couple of days? I was involved with it way back in the beginning.''

"Like hell. You weren't with the bureau in 1970 any more than I was."

"Oh? Well, that shows how much you know. It was the bureau that had me join AWV—months before the Unique bombing. And I was instrumental in the investigation. It was me who learned that Birmingham was the bomber. And I'd have nailed his ass to the wall, way back then, if some idiot hadn't warned him to run."

Paul looked at April. She studiously refused to look back, but he knew she hadn't missed that. The Network had been right and the official information wrong. Resdoe had been spying for the feds when he was a member of AWV. And that meant Colin Birmingham's theory about why he might have been behind the bombing could be bang on.

"If you handled things as well back then as you did tonight," Steve was saying, "you'd never have managed to nail a dead raccoon's ass to the wall."

"Why, you—"

"You blew it tonight, Resdoe! Nobody's been able to get to Birmingham in almost thirty years, but I was going to meet one-on-one with him. Until you blew it."

"What the hell good would meeting with him have done? You don't meet with a killer, you arrest him. Or are you going to try telling me that's what you had in mind? That you were suckering your buddy and the daughter?"

"No. I was going to talk to Birmingham because I don't think he was the bomber. I think the investigating agents settled on the wrong man. And if you were part of that team, then you'll be one of the guys who ends up with egg on his face, won't you. Is that why you're here—because you wanted to kill Birmingham before I could get the case reactivated?''

''Don't be absurd!''

''Absurd? Hey, if you'd killed him, you'd have finally gotten your man, right? Then it would have been case closed—forever. And the fact he probably wasn't the real bomber wouldn't have mattered, would it. Not to you.''

''You should be writing fiction,'' Resdoe snapped. ''That's worthy of a Ludlum plot.''

''Yeah? Well, let's just see how it plays out.''

''It's not going to play out, because I'm going to the top with this, and by the time I've made my case, I—''

''You do what you please, Resdoe. But if I were you, I wouldn't be too damn fast about drawing the big boys' attention to how badly you just screwed up. Regardless of what you do, though, I'm getting this case reactivated. And you know what's funny? Before tonight, I wasn't sure I was going to. It depended on what Birmingham had to say.

''But your showing up makes me figure you know you were wrong, that he is innocent. So I'm going to do what I can to prove that. And when I get proof he isn't guilty I'm going to rub your nose in it.''

CHAPTER FOURTEEN

ONCE THE CONFRONTATION between Resdoe and Steve had completely disintegrated into childish threats, April and Paul sneaked back to their car undetected.

By this point, she was ninety-nine percent convinced that neither Paul nor Steve had had the slightest clue Resdoe was going to show up. Even so, she wished there was some way of getting home that didn't involve riding with them. But considering that her only other option would be to catch a ride with Resdoe or some of his men, she was stuck with Paul and Steve.

"I'll sit in the back on the way home," she said, opening the rear door. "Steve can sit up front with you."

"April..."

When Paul rested his hand on her arm, she shrugged it off.

"Hey, come on," he said. "You heard everything as well as I did. You can't possibly think Steve was in cahoots with Resdoe. And how the hell was he supposed to know Resdoe was keeping an eye on what he was doing?"

"He should have known. He's a special agent, and they're supposed to be suspicious. And careful. And they're not supposed to get people like my father killed!''

"He didn't get your father killed. He—"

"Well, he would have if my father hadn't been too smart for the whole bunch of them. Dammit, Paul, I've hardly trusted anyone in my entire life, but I trusted you. And because of you, against my better judgment, I arranged this meeting. And look how it almost ended up!''

Paul raised his hands, palms facing her. "What can I say?''

"Don't say a thing. Steve's going to get the case reactivated so we're out of it. Right?''

"Right," he agreed slowly. "But...April, I think we should talk about this a little.''

She shook her head. The way she was feeling, it would be better not to say another word.

Luckily, before Paul could press her, Steve appeared through the trees.

"Look, I can't tell you how sorry I am," he said by way of greeting. "I just hope you believe I had nothing at all to do with what happened.''

"We didn't come straight back to the car," Paul told him. "We hung in and listened to you and Resdoe go at it. So, yeah, we pretty much know what's what.''

"That's a relief." He reached into his jacket pocket, produced Paul's gun and handed it to him. Then he looked at April. "I guess the only thing we've got to be grateful for is that your father got away safely.''

"You're sure he did?''

"Yeah, Resdoe's men were trailing back to the

clearing when I left. They hadn't seen any sign of him.''

But now the feds knew who she really was, and... And suddenly she felt less sure that Steve hadn't had anything to do with all this.

''Steve?'' she said, eyeing him closely. ''How did Resdoe know I'm Colin Birmingham's daughter?''

When he looked uncertain, she said, ''He referred to me as 'the daughter' back there. But when Paul and I went to see him, we gave him the impression that I was Paul's girlfriend. So how did he know the truth?''

Steve glanced at Paul, making her even more anxious. Exactly who'd been up to what?

''I don't know,'' Steve said at last. ''I didn't tell anyone.''

She looked at Paul, checking his expression. He seemed worried.

''You think your office could be bugged?'' he asked Steve. ''That Resdoe was listening in when I was there? When I told Steve about you,'' he added to her.

Steve swore quietly. ''Bugging another agent's office? That would be a lot, even for him.''

''Can you sweep it and see?''

''Damn right I can. There's detection equipment in the building, so if you drop me off there, I'll do it tonight—before anybody has a chance to debug it.''

April slowly looked from one man to the other, still wondering exactly who was zooming whom. Was Resdoe the only double-dealer? Or was Steve far less innocent than he was making out?

And then, of course, there was Paul. The man she'd fallen in love with. The man who'd convinced her to set up a meeting between her father and a fed.

If it turned out that she'd been wrong to trust him, she'd want to die.

When she looked at him once more, he was watching her. Trying to read her thoughts?

If he was, good luck to him. Because, right now, she was so confused that she didn't have a single unconvoluted thought in her head.

AFTER THEY'D DROPPED Steve off at Federal Plaza, Paul tried again to get April to talk about what had happened.

But as desperately as she wanted to believe he'd had nothing more to do with things going wrong than she had, she knew she'd be wise not to share her thoughts until after she talked to her father. She had a horrible feeling, though, she wasn't going to be able to contact him.

He'd realize the feds would suspect he was living somewhere not too far from Lake Elizabeth. And right now, her parents would be making another of their night moves. So unless she caught them before they took off...

Exhaling slowly, she remembered, once again, the trauma of those sudden uprootings. And now she'd subjected them to yet another. She was still brooding about that when Paul turned down West Seventy-fifth. He found a parking space just along from her building, then wordlessly walked her to it.

"Can I come up?" he asked while she was unlocking the front door.

She closed her eyes, wanting the comfort of his arms so much that she could almost feel them around her.

Tonight had been a major mistake, though. Almost a deadly one. And until she was certain he really hadn't played any part in it, she couldn't let herself be influenced by the way he made her feel when they were alone together.

"I'm stressed to the max," she said without turning from the door. "I'd be terrible company."

"April, I just want to be with you. Stressed or not." He rested his hand on her arm and the warmth of his touch almost undid her.

"No." She forced the word out. "Look," she added, turning toward him, "what happened tonight means that my parents are going to take off. And until I hear from them, until I know they're safe... Well, I just need to be alone."

For a minute, she thought he was going to argue. Instead, he finally said, "Okay. Don't sit waiting for the phone to ring, though. Try to get some sleep."

She nodded, although she knew that she wouldn't get much.

"I'll call you in the morning and... Look, promise me you won't go off anywhere on your own, okay? Promise you'll stay right here until after we've talked."

Nodding again, she pushed the door open and escaped before she could change her mind about his coming in with her.

The moment she was inside her apartment, she dug out her cellular and punched in her parents' number. Tonight, there was no point worrying about it showing up on her phone bill. By the time it did, they'd be long gone from their cottage on Ludlow Pond.

The number rang, and rang, and rang. She tried it again, hoping against hope that she'd punched it in wrong. But of course she hadn't.

They were already gone, and she had no way of reaching them. Until they contacted her she couldn't be certain they were safe, that Resdoe hadn't arranged for roadblocks to trap them, that she hadn't delivered them into the hands of the enemy.

Heading for the bathroom, she stripped off her clothes and had a hot shower. Then, feeling utterly miserable, she crawled into bed and had a good therapeutic cry.

WHEN THE DOOR of April's building had closed behind her, Paul went back to the Jeep and simply sat for a while, feeling as if the whole world had come crashing down around him.

Less than twenty-four hours ago, they'd been making love. Less than twenty-four hours ago, he'd been thinking they might be able to take Steve's advice and get out of the city for a few days.

Now they wouldn't be going anywhere. Hell, for all he knew, she wouldn't even want to see him again.

But what did he expect? She'd trusted him, and her father had almost gotten killed because of it. He was still worrying about how much damage that had done to their relationship long after the lights on the third floor went out.

Finally, he reached for his cell phone and tried

Steve's office number—on the remote chance the agent would still be there.

Surprisingly, he answered.

"Just wondering if you found anything of interest," Paul said, carefully keeping his words vague.

"Not a thing. But you wouldn't feel like coming by for an hour or so, would you?"

"You mean now?" Glancing at his watch, he saw it was past 2:00 a.m.

"If you've got nothing better to do."

"I'll be there as soon as I can."

"Good. I'll tell Security I'm expecting you."

He made it from West Seventy-fifth down to Federal Plaza in barely ten minutes—a darned good time even considering the light traffic—and Security escorted him up to Steve's office without any hassle.

The agent's desk was overflowing with file folders. Some were in stacks. Others were lying open, their contents spilling every which way.

"What's up?" he asked, sinking into a visitor's chair as Steve closed the door.

"That mess on my desk is the entire Unique bombing case. If it was on computer, finding specific bits of information would be a breeze, but these old records are a bitch."

When Paul merely nodded, Steve said, "It's safe to talk. I swept every inch of this place, and if Resdoe did have a bug in here, he took it out again."

"You think he'd have done that?"

"No. I think that if he'd gone to the effort of getting one in place, he'd have left it there. If he was that damned interested in what I was up to, he'd have wanted to learn everything he could."

"So you don't figure there ever was any bug?"

"Right."

"Then how the hell did he find out that April is Colin Birmingham's daughter?"

"I don't know. But like I said before, I didn't say a word to anyone."

"Then how the hell..." Paul let the words trail off. There was no point in repeating a question that neither of them had the answer to.

"When I phoned," he said, changing the subject, "I didn't really expect you'd still be here."

"Yeah, well, I've been poring over these files. Regardless of what the records say, Resdoe must have been an agent at the time of the bombing. I can't believe he'd have told me he was involved with the case if he wasn't—although he's so full of it, anything's possible.

"But assuming he *was* involved, I'd like to see something in writing that tells me what his role was. That way I can get an idea of whether there's any argument he could use to try to keep the case from being reactivated."

"You think there might be one?"

"I don't know, but I don't want any surprises. And if it *was* him who decided Birmingham was the bomber, if he did screw up and accuse the wrong man, he wouldn't want anyone learning that. So he'd either come up with some reason the case should remain inactive, or he'd ask that he be put in charge of any new investigation."

"Would the big boys go for that?"

"If he was part of the original team, they might. And if he was, what I need is something that shows he screwed up. That he jumped to conclusions when he shouldn't have.''

"Or that he was behind the bombing?" Paul asked quietly.

Steve looked at him but didn't say a word.

"I heard what you said to him at the lake, remember? That maybe he'd come there intending to kill Birmingham? I assumed you were thinking he'd have to have a pretty strong reason for trying to murder someone in cold blood that way. A reason like figuring that if the alleged Napalm Bomber was dead, it would be case closed—before you had a chance to get it reactivated and learn who was really guilty.''

"Well," Steve said slowly, "as I said before, when it comes to him, anything's possible.''

His glance flickered to the files, making Paul suspect he was dying to get back to them. And that, if he had to, he'd spend the entire night going through them.

"Want to hear an interesting detail about the case?" he said.

"Sure."

"Well, as Colin Birmingham told you, Walker, Gutteridge and Resdoe all had alibis for the time period when the bomb was planted.''

Paul nodded.

"But I guess, if that's all he said, he didn't know that the three of them alibied one another.''

"What?"

"Uh-huh. They went to see the Jason Robards remake of the *St. Valentine's Day Massacre*. They had ticket stubs to prove it, and they claimed they sat through it twice. The film runs a hundred minutes.

When you double that and add in previews and intermission, there was no way any of them could have planted the bomb.''

"If they all really did sit through the film twice.''

"Yeah. Interesting 'if,' isn't it.''

Swearing to himself, Paul wondered whether Walker and Gutteridge should be added to their list of suspects—regardless of whether Colin Birmingham figured they were unlikely ones or not.

"Birmingham doesn't think Walker and Gutteridge had anything to do with the bombing,'' he said. "Nothing except pointing the finger at him, that is.''

"He's probably right. From what I can tell, neither of them knew a damned thing about bombs.''

"Which means that neither of them would have sneaked out of the movie and headed for the factory. But what about Resdoe?''

"Well…'' Steve paused, shaking his head. "We've got to keep in mind that even if Birmingham wasn't the bomber, Resdoe's still not the most obvious suspect. John Bellavia wins that one hands down. So it's a lot more likely that Resdoe simply screwed up.''

"You really think he'd try to kill Birmingham just so nobody would learn he accused the wrong man?''

"I don't know,'' Steve said wearily. "But… Hell, I'm so tired I'm starting to repeat myself, but if he did screw up, I need something to show that. And I need it fast.''

He glanced at the mess on his desk again, then looked at Paul once more.

"Are you telling me you'd like a hand?''

The moment Steve nodded, Paul's fingers began itching to get at those files.

"It's hardly normal protocol," Steve said, handing him one of them. "But this is hardly a normal situation. And after what happened tonight, it's obvious that Resdoe has no intention of playing by any rules."

"Okay, so what am I looking for?"

"That's the sixty million dollar question. But if you come across any reports by an agent whose name is a color, give them special attention. An infiltrator would have filed reports under a code name, and during the Vietnam era the bureau was big on using colors as codes. So if there's an Agent Brown or Black or whatever…"

They pored over the contents of the files until Paul's vision began blurring. He was about to suggest they take a break and grab some coffee when he opened a fresh folder and discovered a report by an Agent Green.

It quickly became apparent that Green had infiltrated AWV in 1969, posing as a recent university dropout. But there was nothing—in the initial paragraphs, at least—to indicate that Green was, in reality, Wayne Resdoe.

Paul skimmed another few lines, then his eyes locked on the next section of the report. "Listen to this," he said, excitedly beginning to read aloud.

"'My conclusion is that AWV member Colin Birmingham is solely responsible for the bombing. This is based not only on the testimony of Tom Walker and Ken Gutteridge, but also on the fact that Nelson Harmidarrow, a prominent leader within AWV, believes Birmingham is guilty.

"'Harmidarrow has actively questioned other group members about Birmingham's activities, asking, specifically, if they had any personal knowledge of his whereabouts during the hours before the incident or any prior knowledge of his intention to bomb the Unique factory.

"'It is my feeling that Harmidarrow's belief in Birmingham's guilt should alleviate the bureau's concerns that Walker and Gutteridge may have given false information.'"

Paul stopped reading and looked at Steve.

"I don't believe it," the agent said. "The bureau suspected those two were lying? Yet we still went ahead and charged Birmingham?"

"Because Harmidarrow was asking questions about him," Paul said, having trouble making that sink in. "But to state in a report that 'Nelson Harmidarrow believed Birmingham was guilty...Hell, that's just not true. And the whole tone of this implies he was asking questions to find supporting evidence of Birmingham's guilt. But from what he told April and me, that wouldn't have been what he was up to at all. He'd have been looking for evidence that Birmingham was innocent."

"You're right. Something isn't adding up." Steve began searching through the files. "The statement Harmidarrow came in and gave us made it perfectly clear that he doubted Birmingham was guilty."

Eventually finding the file he was looking for,

Steve opened it. "Here it is. Nobody who read this could have had any doubt that..."

"What?" Paul asked when Steve stopped speaking and sat staring at the file.

"What if nobody read this?"

"Meaning?" Paul said, feeling his adrenaline beginning to pump.

"Meaning that I had no reason to mention this to you before, but it took me a hell of a long time to locate this particular file. In fact, I'd started thinking Harmidarrow had lied to you, that he hadn't come in and told us about suspecting John Bellavia at all, because there was nothing about it with the rest of the info on the Unique case."

"Then where was it?"

"Well, the bureau kept records on all the leaders of protest groups. And whoever took Harmidarrow's statement filed it with the other information on him, not with the Unique bombing material."

"But why?"

Steve shrugged. "When I finally found it, I figured that was pretty peculiar. Then I got interested in what he'd had to say and stopped wondering why it hadn't been with the Unique stuff. But now...

"And you know what else? It was tucked way in the back of the records on Harmidarrow, instead of being filed chronologically—as if somebody had intentionally made it as difficult as possible to find."

He flipped over a few pages, then swore under his breath. "I think I've got it," he said. "The agent who took Harmidarrow's statement was a guy named Charlie Barnes. He's retired now. He's about Resdoe's age or a few years older. But the thing is.

Barnes was as much of a jerk as Resdoe, and they were good buddies—as far as I know, from early on.

"So if Resdoe was Agent Green, and he was aiming to be a hero by identifying the Napalm Bomber... And then Harmidarrow walks in and gives Barnes some information that doesn't exactly help make the case Resdoe's building against Birmingham..."

"Then maybe that information was suppressed?"

"Yeah. Maybe it was."

Paul's heart had begun beating double time. "And is that the sort of thing your boss would consider a good argument for reactivating the case? With someone other than Agent Green in charge?"

Steve merely grinned.

APRIL CAME AWAKE with a start. For an instant she thought the sunlight streaming into the bedroom had woken her, then she realized it had been a phone ringing. But which one?

She held her breath, waiting to hear. Her parents would risk phoning her cellular, because tracing calls to cell phones was a slow process. But nowadays, on regular phone lines, a calling number was locked in instantaneously. And if the feds had her line tapped, they'd get an exact fix on where the call was coming from.

Her hopes were dashed with the next ring. It was her apartment's line.

Quickly getting out of bed, she headed for her office extension, and answered it.

"It's me," Paul said.

Hearing his voice did funny things to her insides.

She'd been so awful to him last night that she was almost surprised he was still speaking to her. Almost surprised and very relieved.

When she said "Good morning," the words came out a touch mumbled, making her suspect she sounded as if she'd spent the entire night tossing and turning, which was precisely what she'd done.

She'd drifted in and out of sleep, growing more and more certain that Paul hadn't had anything to do with what had happened at Lake Elizabeth.

Then, toward dawn, she'd had a horrible dream about him walking down a long tunnel, away from her, without a single backward glance. She'd wakened from the dream terrified it was prophetic.

"I woke you, didn't I," he said.

"That's all right. I had to get up to answer the phone, anyway," she added, remembering the old line in time to make him chuckle.

Tense as she was, the fact that she'd amused him made her feel better.

"I'm usually up long before this," she added. "And...and I'm glad to hear from you."

"I'm glad you're glad."

That made her feel better yet.

"You're going to be even more glad," he added, "when you hear what I've got to tell you. Our friend's going to talk to his boss this morning, and he's certain things will be a go."

"The phone," she murmured in warning before he could say anything more.

"I know. I'm coming over to tell you the details. But I've got a stop to make on the way, so I'll be an hour or so. See you then."

"See you then," she repeated.

After hanging up, she took her cellular into the bathroom with her while she showered, just in case her parents chose those few minutes to call. They didn't. But they'd contact her soon, she told herself while she got dressed. They were just fine and they'd call as soon as they could.

Making a concerted effort not to worry about them, she forced herself back into her office and phoned a couple of clients, then worked on her computer until Paul finally buzzed from the front steps.

After she let him in, she headed to the staircase, cellular in hand, and met him on the second-floor landing. He was carrying a carton that was bulky enough to prevent her from kissing him.

"What have you got?" she asked as they started for her apartment.

"A surprise."

"For me?"

"Uh-huh."

"A surprise *plus* details about what Steve's up to? You've really gone all out."

When he laughed, she felt a happy little tingling around her heart.

"Well, there aren't really many details," he admitted. "I was just afraid you might not let me come over if I didn't say I had something to tell you."

"You were afraid for nothing," she told him.

"Good." He gave her a smile so warm it made her blood sizzle. "At any rate, I ended up down at Steve's office last night, and we went through the files on the bombing."

"We? You mean he actually let you look at them?"

"Yeah, but don't ever breathe a word about it."

"No, of course not. I interrupted, though. You went through them and...?"

"And we came across something that practically guarantees the case will be reactivated."

They'd reached her apartment, and once they were inside, Paul put down his carton and gave her such a passionate kiss that she knew the walking-away-without-a-backward-glance dream hadn't been even marginally prophetic.

"So?" he said, finally releasing her. "Aren't you curious about the surprise?"

"Not that I'd let on. When I was little, my mother always used to tell me that curiosity killed the cat."

"Funny you should mention cats." He bent down and opened the carton, revealing a big fluffy orange one. It blinked up at her with bright green eyes, then hopped gracefully out of the box and stood surveying the living room.

"You know what his name is?" Paul said.

She knew, but her throat was too tight to speak. "It's Marmalade, isn't it," she managed to say at last.

"Well, I thought it probably would be. I stopped by an animal rescue place on my way over, and he seemed perfect. The people said he was really affectionate. And they were sure he'd love to sleep at the foot of your bed."

"Oh, Paul," she murmured, "he is perfect."

"Hear that, cat?" he asked it.

Kneeling down, she said, "Hey, Marmalade."

Without the slightest hesitation, he moved closer and pressed his head against her leg.

"Looks as if he likes you," Paul said. "Which makes two of us," he added quietly.

She gave the top of Marmalade's head a quick rub, then stood up and wrapped her arms tightly around Paul.

"April...are we okay?" he murmured against her hair. "Last night, I thought..."

"I was really upset last night."

"And now?"

"Still upset, but not with you. And I'll be all right once I've heard from my folks."

"Maybe that's them now," he said as her phone began to ring.

She shook her head, reluctantly taking her arms from around him and heading over to the living room extension.

When she answered, a woman said, "April Kelly?"

"Yes. Speaking."

"Ah. Well, you don't know me, but I'm a friend of your father's."

She closed her eyes, relief flooding her. It was someone from the Network. Her parents had decided to get a message to her this way.

"Are my parents all right?" she asked, her heart freezing when the woman didn't answer immediately.

"As far as I know, they're fine," she said at last. "I haven't been able to reach them this morning, though, so we decided I'd better call you. Your father asked us to check out a man who'd approached you about them," she continued. "A Paul Gardiner."

"Yes, I'm aware he did." Now that her memory had been jogged, she recalled her father saying he was going to do that when she'd first told him about Paul.

"He asked about it a while back," she added when the woman didn't go on.

"Yes...well...these things do take time."

"Of course. But he checked out all right?" As she asked the question, she glanced across the room to where Paul was crouched down playing with Marmalade.

He looked over and gave her another of his warm smiles. Thinking she'd never want to live a day without seeing them, she smiled back.

Then the woman said, "No, I'm afraid he didn't. That's why we decided we'd better get the information to you, rather than waiting until we could reach your father. You see, Paul Gardiner is a federal agent."

CHAPTER FIFTEEN

ONE INSTANT APRIL was smiling at Paul, the next she was looking at him as if he were evil incarnate.

"He checked out all right?" she'd said. Seeing the way her face grew pale and tense after that was enough to tell him that the question had been about him and the answer had been no.

When she swung around so her back was to him, still listening to whoever was on the phone, he pushed himself up from the floor. What the hell was she being told?

Just from the way she was standing, and the stiff way she was holding her head, he could tell she was getting more upset by the second. It made him feel as if someone were twisting a knife in his gut.

"Well...thank you," she finally murmured.

She slowly lowered the receiver but remained facing away from him.

His heart pounding, he waited, knowing she was trying to gather her composure.

Finally, she turned toward him, radiating tension.

"That was someone in the Network," she said, her voice catching on a couple of the words. "Calling to tell me you're a fed."

As desperately as he wanted to cross the room and

take her in his arms, he didn't move. He simply said, "It's not true."

"And if it was? Would you admit it?"

"No, I guess I wouldn't. But it's a lie. Did he say where the information came from?"

"She. It was a woman."

"What woman?"

"I don't know. She didn't tell me her name."

"Oh, come on, then. She must just have been some crank who—"

"No. They don't always say who they are. And a crank wouldn't have known that my father contacted the Network about you. But to answer your question, she didn't tell me where the information came from. She'd only been told to call and…and let me know that's what they'd found out."

She was watching him appraisingly, so he tried to look calm. He was sweating bullets, though. What if she didn't believe him?

"April, listen to me. If there was any way of proving I'm not a fed, I'd have done it long ago. We both know there isn't, though. I can only tell you I'm not. But that's the truth. Their information is wrong, and I'd say the only way they could have gotten it is if someone learned they were nosing around about me and intentionally fed it to them."

"Who?" she demanded. "And why?"

He shook his head, utterly frustrated. They had enough unanswered questions to fill a book.

"Maybe it was Wayne Resdoe," he said. "Or maybe someone we don't even know about. As for the why, someone obviously wanted you to think I was with the bureau so you'd have nothing more to do with me. We already knew there's at least one person out there who doesn't want us doing what we've been doing. And probably doesn't want your father cooperating with me again, either.

"Look, I know there are a whole lot of gaps here, and I don't have any more solid answers than you do. But I've never lied to you, and I'd never do anything to harm you. Never. Because I'm in love with you."

He swallowed hard then, not at all certain this was the right time to have told her. And she wasn't giving him any reaction, either. She was eyeing him with that completely expressionless look she was so good at.

"April, can you really believe what some woman whose name you don't even know has to say over what I'm telling you?"

"I don't want to," she murmured, tears beginning to trickle down her cheeks. "But I'm so afraid of making another mistake like last night. Of what will happen if I do."

"Trust me," he said quietly. "Make a leap of faith and trust me. I won't let you down. I swear that on my father's grave."

While she stood staring at the floor, he began praying she'd believe him.

They weren't out of the woods yet as far as danger was concerned. They wouldn't be until Steve got the case reactivated and the bomber was aware that he had. Until then, Paul didn't want to let April out of his sight—not only because of the danger, but because saying that he was in love with her was the understatement of his life. He'd fallen so hard that he just knew there had to be a future for them.

But if she couldn't bring herself to believe him now, after all they'd been through together, it would tell him something he didn't want to know.

She finally looked up, her eyes luminous with tears and her cheeks damp with them. Meeting his gaze, she whispered, "Say it again?"

"What? That it's safe to trust me?"

"No. That you love me."

He took a single, tentative step toward her. "I love you, April. I'm so crazy in love with you that I can hardly think straight."

"Oh, Paul," she murmured. "Oh, Paul, I love you, too."

A second later he was gathering her into his arms and kissing her, tasting the salt of her tears and the sweetness of her lips and thinking that he'd never let her out of his arms again.

Then Marmalade meowed loudly, making him realize he was going to have to release her—at least briefly.

"Hey," he said, kissing his way from her lips to her throat. "I picked up a litter box and cat food and stuff, but I couldn't carry it and the cat, too. You wait here and make sure he doesn't do anything he shouldn't. I'll go back down and get everything from the Jeep." Reluctantly, he headed for the door. "I'll be right back," he said, opening it. "Don't go anywhere while I'm gone."

April stood listening until the sound of his footsteps faded to nothingness. Then, after putting a bowl of water on the kitchen floor for Marmalade, she wandered over to the couch, where he was making himself comfortable, and sank down beside him.

As frightened as she was to trust anyone under the circumstances, she was going to make that leap of faith. She felt such raw pain at the thought of a life without Paul in it that she had to give him the benefit of the doubt.

It wasn't just a case of her emotions overruling her brain, though. After all, someone *could* have fed the Network false information. That wouldn't be half as unbelievable as some of the other things that had happened—like someone sending those tapes or staging a drive-by with blank bullets.

Besides, as her father always said, "There comes a time when you have to fish or cut bait." And the time had come when she either had to let herself completely believe in Paul or not believe in him at all.

She only hoped, with her entire heart, that she was making the right decision.

"I am," she whispered. "Right Marmalade?" She stroked the cat's furry body. "Paul's on our side and the Network people got taken in, didn't they."

He gazed at her for a minute but didn't offer an opinion. Then the front door buzzer sounded, making her jump.

That startled Marmalade, so she gave him a reassuring pat. "Sorry, little guy. I just didn't expect Paul to be back so soon. He must have had a space right across the street."

Hurrying to the door, she released the downstairs lock, then headed along the hall to meet him again.

This time, though, the man coming rapidly up the stairs was a stranger.

Stopping dead, she quickly appraised him. He was middle-aged, with longish but carefully styled graying hair, and was dressed in an expensive suit that had to have been tailor made.

He didn't look like trouble. Most likely he'd come by to see one of her neighbors and had buzzed her apartment by mistake. Or maybe he'd tried her because her neighbors were both at work and he'd brought something that was too large for the mail slot.

But if he had a delivery for one of them, why was he coming up to her floor carrying nothing?

Her New Yorker wariness on full alert, she took a backward step.

"April?" he said, climbing the next stair more slowly. "April Kelly?"

"Yes."

Before she had time to ask who he was, he spoke again.

"I'm sorry. You look as if I startled you. But you did buzz me in."

"Yes. I was expecting someone else, though," she explained, uneasily fingering her grandmother's locket.

"That's very pretty," he said.

"Thank you."

He looked at it for a second too long, then met her gaze again.

"I won't take much of your time, but if I could just have a minute or two..."

He'd reached the top of the stairs; she took another

couple of backward steps and said, "We haven't met, have we?"

"No. And my name won't mean anything to you, but let me give you my card so you'll at least know I'm legit."

He pulled out a wallet, took a business card from it and handed it to her.

When she looked at it, his name did mean something to her. And her blood froze in her veins.

CLUTCHING THE PET store bags in his right hand and gripping the covered litter box under his left arm, Paul was reduced to trying to buzz April's apartment with his knee.

That didn't work, so he put the box on the top step and buzzed again. When there was no response, he told himself she must be in the bathroom or somewhere. He waited a minute and tried again. Still nothing.

On the principle of "better safe than sorry," he put the bags down beside the litter box and buzzed the other two apartments in turn. If anyone was home in either of them, they weren't interested in knowing who was at the door.

His anxiety growing, he dug out his phone and punched in the apartment's number. By the time it had rung four times, a vision of April lying dead was forming in his mind and he was seriously thinking about calling 911.

Then she answered. Her hello sounded a little nervous.

"Is anything wrong?" he demanded. "I buzzed twice and you didn't answer."

"Oh. Sorry. I was out in the hall. Someone dropped by unexpectedly, and I was talking to him by the stairs before he came into the apartment."

His heart had begun slamming against his ribs. Someone was up there with her. And her voice was just enough off its normal tone to tell him she was afraid of whoever it was.

"You managed everything from the Jeep in one trip?" she said.

"Can you tell me who's there or is he listening?"

"Uh-huh."

"But we're playing things cool?"

"Absolutely. Just a second and I'll go buzz you in."

He rested his hand against his pocket, felt the reassuring weight of his gun and was thankful he'd decided to start carrying it. He didn't know what the hell was happening, but if he had to, he'd kill to protect her.

When the lock buzzed, he grabbed the handle and practically yanked the door off its hinges. Whoever was up there had heard April say he'd been getting things from the car, so he took the time to pick up the cat stuff before he headed for the stairs. Then he climbed them as quickly as he could, the damned litter box banging against the railing with each step.

The door of her apartment was slightly ajar, so he walked right in.

She was sitting on the couch with a man he'd never seen before. Marmalade was lying on one of the overstuffed chairs grooming himself, apparently unconcerned about the company.

Paul doubted that meant anything. He didn't think

cats had the same instincts for assessing strangers that dogs did.

"Paul," April said, shooting him an anxious smile, "this is an old friend of my parents'. An artist. From California."

Oh, God. He picked up on who it was before she said the name.

"John Bellavia, this is…well, you know who Paul Gardiner is," she said as Paul put everything down.

And just how, he wondered uneasily, did John Bellavia know who he was? And what else did the guy know?

As he started across the room in their direction, April said, "Mr. Bellavia was—"

"John," he corrected her gently.

She nodded. "John was just telling me that he's been wanting to get in touch with my parents for some time, and… But why don't you begin the story again?" she suggested to Bellavia. "I know Paul would be interested in hearing it from the start."

Bellavia smiled warmly. "Sure."

Paul told himself to take it easy. Bellavia might not have all his oars in the water a hundred percent of the time, but for the moment, at least, they were being treated to the Dr. Jekyll side of his personality.

"You both must have spent a lot of time lately wondering what on earth has been going on," Bellavia said.

"And you know something about it?" Paul sank into the chair Marmalade wasn't occupying, trying to look casual and get a better read on the situation at the same time. April had obviously gone with the pretense that she'd never heard of John Bellavia, so the only thing to do was play along and see where they went from here.

Leaning forward on the couch, Bellavia said, "I'd better start by explaining that, some time ago, I became involved in a program that promotes... I guess mental well-being is the best way of putting it. It's one of the 'steps' programs that are based on the A.A. approach."

Paul nodded. "I work on 'Today's World,' and we did a segment on some of them."

"Oh? I usually watch the show, but I must have missed that one. In any event, one of the steps in this program involves contacting someone we've injured in the past and doing what we can to make amends. That doesn't necessarily mean physically injured, you understand, just someone we've caused difficulty for. Not surprisingly, we're supposed to contact whoever we did the worst thing to."

Paul nodded.

"And as much as I hate to admit it," Bellavia continued, "I'm responsible for the fact that April's parents have been forced to live in hiding for so many years."

"You're responsible?" Paul's glance flickered to April. She shot him a look that said, *You ain't heard nothing yet.*

"Yes. You see, Colin Birmingham isn't the Napalm Bomber. But even though I knew who actually was, I never told the authorities."

For a moment, the apartment was stone silent. Then April said, "That's how far John got with his story before you came in."

"And the actual bomber is...?" Paul asked.

Bellavia smiled once more. "You like to get straight to the point."

"Yeah, I guess it's a spillover from my job."

"Well, if you don't mind, I'll leave the bomber's identity a mystery for the moment, because I really should fill you in on a few other things. That's something else my program encourages—explaining your rationale when your actions have impacted others."

"Explain away," April said, managing a much more natural-looking smile than she had before.

Addressing Paul, he said, "Well, as Jillian mentioned... Or I guess you prefer April?" He looked questioningly at her.

"It's what I'm used to now."

"Fine. April it is, then. As she mentioned," he explained to Paul, "I'd been wanting to get in touch with her parents for some time. I'd even hired a private eye to find them, but he drew a blank. Then I saw your ad in the *Times* and realized that if I could find you, it would give me a way of finding Colin and Mary. From the ad, of course, I assumed you were their son."

Paul nodded. What he and April had hypothesized had been right on the money. Someone—John Bellavia, as it turned out—had seen that ad and started his own investigation.

"This time," Bellavia went on, "I hired an entire team of detectives. They immediately learned that you'd placed the ad, Paul, and that you weren't actually April's brother. They had you under surveillance when you met her, and then—"

"So it was them who taped us," Paul said. "Would you mind telling us why?"

Interrupting wasn't always the best idea when people were telling a story, but since Bellavia was so clearly eager to give them details, they might as well try to get all of them.

The man shrugged. "Mostly because I was curious to see what Mary's daughter...what Colin and Mary's daughter looked like as an adult."

For a split second, April's nervousness showed, then she was back to simply looking interested in Bellavia's story.

"At any rate, they followed you from the airport and established where April lived. From then on, you were both under surveillance. Of course, that's over and done with now. There'll be no more need for it. Once I've finished explaining everything, you'll see that we'll be best off working together to do whatever else should be done." He smiled yet again, looking very pleased with himself.

April glanced uncertainly at Paul, then back to Bellavia. "If I was under surveillance right from the start, why didn't you learn where my parents were living? I went to see them the day after that meeting at the airport."

"Yes, well, unfortunately my people slipped up that first time you rented a car. It hadn't occurred to them you'd be so adept at foiling an attempt to follow you. Once they discovered you were, they didn't make any more mistakes."

"So you know that I went to see..."

He chuckled. "You're testing me, aren't you. Well, yes, I do know you went to see Walker and Gutteridge. You didn't lose my people that time. And even if you had, we had a backup system by then."

"A backup system," she repeated.

"Uh-huh. There's a tiny but powerful transponder in your locket. They had its signal to follow when you weren't in sight."

April pressed her hand to the locket.

"You're wondering how we managed that, aren't you?"

"Yes."

"Well, we did it the night after you visited your parents. The night Paul had his phone conversation with your father."

"You knew about that?"

"Oh, knowing about that was child's play. But my people were rather proud of the trick with the locket."

When she reached up and took it from around her neck, Bellavia extended his hand. "They glued it shut so you wouldn't discover the transponder. So, please, let me look after having it removed without doing any damage."

She shook her head. "No. Thank you, but I'll take care of it. Just tell me why you'd… I mean, I might easily have gone somewhere without wearing it."

"We were counting on your not doing that. You see, when you met Paul on the street that evening, my people were using long-range microphones to pick up your conversation. So when you told him your mother had just given you the locket, and that you intended to wear it all the time…"

"But how did you get a bug into it?" Paul asked.

"Came in through the bathroom window, to quote the Beatles."

"What?" April whispered.

Bellavia nodded. "They hooked a little rope ladder onto the roof in the middle of the night. It was only a short climb down, and you were fast asleep while they did the job."

"Oh, Lord," she murmured. "Someone was right in my bedroom?"

"They didn't harm you."

"Even so..."

Paul could tell she found that part of the story unsettling, but he couldn't cut Bellavia off. They had to learn as much as they could from him.

"Are you going to explain everything else?" he asked. "The video of someone supposedly planting a bomb in my car? And the drive-by? And why you sent the tape of April and me—and that threatening note—to Gutteridge?"

"Ah, well, not all of those things were my doing."

"No?"

Bellavia shook his head. "I did send Gutteridge a copy of the tape. You see, I believe that people who lie deserve to be punished for it. And since Gutteridge lied about April's father being the bomber...

"Well, it was a long time after the fact, of course, but I liked the idea of letting him know you two were after the truth. I'm sure it's given him some sleepless nights."

"Did you do something to punish Tom Walker, too?"

"No. I'd kept track of both Walker and Gutteridge over the years, and I knew Walker was dying. I figured that was punishment enough.

"But getting back to where we were, I was only responsible for one of the things you mentioned—

sending Gutteridge the tape. You've got Special Agent Resdoe to thank for the drive-by and the car-bomb video. Oh, and for that fellow you spotted following you the other day, as well. My surveillance people got a big kick out of watching you chase him, Paul."

"Lord," April murmured, "it sounds as if we had half the city following us."

"Oh, no," Bellavia said. "Only my people and Resdoe's."

"But you were saying that Resdoe was behind most of the weird stuff?" Paul said, not wanting to lose track of that thread.

"Uh-huh. And what he was doing worried me. But as long as he stuck to just trying to scare you off, I let it go."

"Why was he trying to scare us off?" April asked.

"Because he didn't want you to learn the real story about the bombing."

Paul waited in anticipation for Bellavia's next words. Were they actually going to get the real story now? Handed to them on a platter like this? And would it reveal that Resdoe had been the bomber? But even if that was what Bellavia told them, how would they know whether it was the truth?

When he finally went on, instead of what Paul was hoping to hear, the man said, "Before we get to the bombing, I want to explain about a few more things. As I said, I wasn't too worried while Resdoe's moves were harmless. But last night, April, there's no doubt he was trying to get your father killed."

"You know all about last night, too," Paul said.

"Of course. My people observed the whole thing. That's why I'm here. You two could have ended up dead, so we have to put a stop to Resdoe right now. I've caused Mary...Mary and Colin, enough grief. I can't stand by doing nothing when their daughter's life is at risk."

"You really think it is?" April said, looking worried.

"Well, if Resdoe had to choose between him and you... But let me back up for a minute and tell you how he learned you might cause him grief. When I sent Gutteridge the tape and note, they got him concerned enough that he alerted Resdoe."

"How do you know?" Paul asked.

Bellavia gave him a look that said he must be a little simple. "My people weren't only keeping an eye on you two. I was curious about how Gutteridge would react, and he phoned Resdoe half an hour after he got the package."

"That gives us the answer to something we were wondering about," April said.

Paul looked at her.

"When Resdoe called me 'the daughter' last night, that's how he knew who I really was. The note John sent with the tape said I was Colin Birmingham's daughter."

"So he knew all along, knew when we went to see him in his office but didn't let on."

April nodded, then turned back to Bellavia. "Sorry I interrupted. What happened after Gutteridge got the tape and called Resdoe?"

"Well, a few days later, after you'd been to visit him, Gutteridge got on the phone to Resdoe again.

That had to have been when Resdoe decided he'd better scare off the both of you. And with the Toronto airport getting fogged in, he had time to trace your tracks and find out you'd rented a car.

"So he set up the drive-by for when you returned it. And as I said, he had that car-bomb tape made. I guess he assumed you'd figure whoever was responsible for the tape Gutteridge had gotten must be responsible for the second one, too."

"That's exactly what we did figure," Paul said.

"Uh-huh. Resdoe's no dummy. And I'm sure he also assumed the bomb tape and the drive-by would be more than enough to make you back off.

"You see, you were getting too close to the truth for comfort, and he sure didn't want you to learn he was the one behind the bombing."

CHAPTER SIXTEEN

SO RESDOE HAD BEEN BEHIND the bombing. Or was that only what Bellavia wanted them to believe? One glance at April told Paul she was feeling the same uncertainty he was.

John Bellavia sounded so matter-of-fact that it would be easy to believe everything he'd said. But most psychopaths were consummate liars. And there was no forgetting that, regardless of what he was telling them, Steve had him pegged as the most likely suspect.

"Are you positive Resdoe was behind it?" Paul said at last.

"Of course. I've always known. Months before the bombing, I got suspicious that he was an FBI infiltrator, so… But did you know he was with the bureau back then?"

Paul nodded.

"Ah. Well, as I said, I suspected it at the time. So I bugged his apartment and found out for sure. I've always been good with electronics and things like that."

Things like that, Paul knew from the fed's records, included bombs.

"Why would an FBI agent plan a bombing?" April asked.

Looking at Bellavia, Paul wondered if he'd give them the same line of reasoning Colin Birmingham had.

"So he could be a hero with the bureau," the man explained. "You see, first he set up an incident that was guaranteed to get an incredible amount of press coverage. Then he was the one to learn who was responsible for it—supposedly, that is."

"Because it wasn't my father at all," April said.

"No, of course not. But as long as no one ever discovered that Resdoe had actually planned the bombing, the fact that he solved the case, so to speak, looked good on his career record."

Paul nodded. That was pretty much how Birmingham had figured it, all right.

"So Wayne Resdoe's our bomber," April murmured.

Bellavia shook his head impatiently. "No, I said Resdoe was behind it. Tom Walker actually planted the bomb."

"But...Tom Walker didn't know anything about bombs," Paul said.

"Says who?"

"That's what we were led to believe." They'd already learned, though, that all the bureau's files weren't entirely accurate.

"Well, it's not true," Bellavia said, "because I saw him plant that bomb."

"You saw him?" April repeated. "You were in the factory?"

"Well, no. I should have said I practically saw him. To be perfectly accurate, I followed him to the factory and saw him sneak inside."

"Why were you following him?" Paul asked.

"Because I knew what the plan was, and I wanted to see if he'd really go through with it."

"You knew what the plan was because once you'd planted the bug in Resdoe's apartment, you just left it there," Paul said.

"Right."

"And exactly what was the plan?" April asked.

Bellavia shrugged. "Just that Walker would plant the bomb, then he and Gutteridge would claim your father was responsible. And Walker, Gutteridge and Resdoe would alibi one another.

"They all went to a movie together the day of the bombing. But Walker came back out a few minutes after they'd gone in, went to the factory and planted the bomb. Then he returned to the theater so the three of them could leave together. After that, they went to a bar and acted rowdy so people would remember their being there."

"And Walker and Gutteridge were willing to get involved in a bombing because...?" April asked.

"Because Resdoe paid them enough to make it worth their while. The agents who infiltrated the protest groups had access to what were known as 'discretionary funds.'"

There was a long silence, then April said, "John?"

"Yes?"

"Why didn't you ever tell the feds this?"

Paul could almost see Bellavia's confident manner disintegrating.

"It's difficult for me to admit," he said, staring at his shoes. "But... Whew, the program people told me this step was a tough one, but it's even worse than I expected. I..."

He paused again, then looked at April. "Okay, here goes. Back when we were all members of AWV, I was in love with your mother. But she left me for your father and married him. I...I had some pretty serious emotional problems when I was a young man, which meant my judgment wasn't always what it should have been. So when I learned that Resdoe's plan involved blaming the bombing on your father, I thought...

"Look, I know how awful it sounds, and it was. My head just wasn't screwed on right back then. But at the time, I figured it was in my own selfish best interest not to say anything. And since I hadn't told the feds what I knew in the beginning, I couldn't see how it would help to say anything years later, after I'd realized what a truly despicable thing I'd done. I mean, why would they have believed me? They'd have just written me off as some loony looking for attention."

"Then what's happening now," Paul asked, "when even more years have gone by? Are you intending to tell the feds what you've told us?"

He nodded. "I think they might believe me now. I think if I tell them that hearing Tom Walker died is what jolted me into finally coming forth... You figure they might buy that?" he asked, looking as if he needed assurance.

"Well," April said slowly, "it doesn't sound totally unbelievable."

"Yes, but I'm worried that if I do tell them the truth and explain that I'm facing up to what I did because of the program I'm in… Well, some people don't think much of those programs, do they. Especially not when they originate in California. So I'm worried that even now the feds might think I'm a loony. And that I just invented all this stuff about knowing the truth to satisfy the people in the program—to impress them that I was taking this major step to make amends.

"But what do you two think? I mean, if I tell the feds my story, Resdoe's going to say I'm crazy and claim he had nothing to do with it. Do you think there's any chance they'd believe me over him?"

Paul swore under his breath. He'd been so damned intent on listening for holes in what Bellavia had to say, trying to decide whether it could possibly be true, that he hadn't thought about the obvious.

Even if Bellavia's story was legit, the feds would never believe a guy who regularly checked into private "clinics" over one of their own. Not unless there was something that solidly backed up what he was saying.

ONLY MINUTES AFTER John Bellavia left April's apartment, Paul called Steve Johnston. Less than an hour later, the special agent met the two of them on top of the Great Hill in Central Park.

April had suggested the location because she'd had it up to her eyebrows with being followed and watched and listened in on. And that couldn't happen here.

Since it took more than a little effort to get to, they had the area practically to themselves. It was open enough that they'd notice if anyone was trying to spy on them, and spacious enough that even long-range microphones wouldn't be able to catch their conversation.

Wanting to concentrate on Steve's reactions, she pretty much let Paul tell him the story. While he listened, she could see him go from surprised to incredulous in very short order.

"I don't believe this," he said once he had the basics. "I don't believe he showed up like that or what you've got in mind. I thought you were both happy to leave this up to me from here on in."

"We were," Paul said. "But that was before Bellavia gave us his version of things."

"His version's probably a lie. In fact, I'd lay heavy odds on it."

"But it might be the truth. And when you consider that, the idea makes sense."

"Oh? You want to explain how? Because the prospect of you and April traipsing up to Canada with a psychopath—one who could well be the Napalm Bomber—doesn't make even an ounce of sense to me."

April cringed inside. She'd known Steve wouldn't like their plan. In a lot of ways, she didn't, either.

Still, she and Paul had thought the idea through carefully, and unless Steve saw a serious problem that they'd missed, they had to make the trip.

"Okay, here's how we've added things up," Paul was saying. "Assuming Bellavia's story is true—"

"Big assumption," Steve muttered. "Especially when he's claiming *Walker* planted the bomb, and dead men can't defend themselves."

"Yeah, well, even so, the obvious thing to do is

confront Gutteridge with the story. Because if he realizes the truth's out in the open, it might make him decide the time's finally come to admit he and Walker lied.''

"Look, Paul, if anybody goes to confront Gutteridge, it should be me. If he did lie, a fed arriving on his doorstep would be a lot more likely to scare him into confessing. Besides which, I've got the authority to discuss what sort of deal we could cut him.''

''But you'd have a problem, wouldn't you,'' Paul said. "I mean, Canada's not exactly within the bureau's jurisdiction.''

''No, but that doesn't mean I can't go there and officially talk to someone. It just means there's red tape involved—which, unfortunately, takes time.''

''How much time?'' April asked.

''It depends. I'd have to clear questioning him with the RCMP, but they're usually pretty cooperative. The only real problem would be if I got to… Exactly where did you say he's living?''

''A place called Port Credit. On the outskirts of Toronto.''

''Yeah, well, the real problem would be if I got to Port Credit and Gutteridge simply refused to discuss things with me.''

''I'll bet he would,'' Paul said.

''Then I'd have to charge him here and start extradition proceedings.''

''And how long would it take to get him into the States?'' Paul asked. ''Months?''

''Probably.''

''Which is why it makes sense for April and Bellavia and me to go and talk to him unofficially.''

Steve slowly shook his head, then said, "Paul, was this trip Bellavia's idea?"

"You're asking if he's trying to sucker us into something?"

"Yeah. Exactly."

April glanced at Paul. That was one of their main concerns.

"I don't think he's got anything up his sleeve," Paul said after a moment. "I think he simply realizes that if he came to the bureau with his story, nobody'd buy his word over Resdoe's."

"But he knows you're filling me in?"

"Uh-huh. I told him we would, and he's okay with it, which is one more reason we're inclined to believe he's telling the truth. At any rate, once we started talking about the fact the bureau would need more than just his word against Resdoe's, he decided the best thing he could do was go and confront Gutteridge."

"The best thing *he* could do. So it wasn't him who suggested that you two go with him?"

"No. April and I figured he wouldn't get anywhere on his own. But if we're along, if Gutteridge sees that we believe the story, he'll have to assume the feds might, too."

Steve was silent for a moment, then looked at April. "So you'll get to Port Credit and say what to him?"

She shrugged. "Bellavia will confront him with the truth and we'll be there as witnesses."

"And then?"

"And then I guess we'll have to play it by ear," she admitted. She didn't like that part. The last time she'd played something by ear with Gutteridge, she'd quickly come to regret it.

Steve stared down at the grass, kicking at something she couldn't see, then looked back up. "As I said before, I'd lay heavy odds he's lying."

"And as I said before," Paul told him, "he might not be. We know he's actually involved in this 'steps' program. My buddy mentioned it in his E-mail. So maybe that really is what's brought him out of the woodwork after all these years."

"Yeah," Steve said. "Or maybe he's come out of the woodwork because he's still obsessed with April's mother, and this is all some nutty plan to get to her. Or if he is the bomber, maybe he's planning on snuffing the two of you because he figures you've gotten too close to the truth. Maybe you'll go up to Canada with him and no one will ever hear from you again."

"Oh, come on," Paul said. "We're talking about a guy who's loaded. He's got so much money he hired his own little army of private detectives after he saw my want ad. So much that he's arranged for a private plane to fly us to Toronto."

"What?"

"Yeah, it leaves at six. But the point I was making is why would he even think about taking us to Canada to kill us? With all his money, if he wanted us dead, why wouldn't he just hire a contract killer or two?"

"Because he's a psychopath?" Steve suggested. "Because his mind doesn't work the same way ours do? Because he's figured out some bizarre scenario that has the three of you going to visit Gutteridge and everybody ending up dead except him?''

While Steve was speaking, Paul moved closer to April and wrapped his arm around her waist.

She exhaled slowly, amazed that his mere touch could reassure her.

''Steve,'' he said, ''Bellavia knows we're telling you all this, remember? He's hardly going to have us disappear or turn up dead in Canada when you know we went there with him. And the bottom line is that if Bellavia's version is the true one, we need Gutteridge to back it up.''

''And you figure there's even a chance he might? Paul, he knows there's no evidence. Even if Resdoe did pay Walker to plant that bomb, and paid them both to say Birmingham did it, there's nothing to even suggest that's how things happened—nothing except what a psychopath's saying almost thirty years after the fact.''

''There's Walker's statement.''

''Not enough. All he basically said was that Birmingham wasn't the bomber. And now that he's dead and can't be questioned, the statement's virtually worthless.

''As for Bellavia, we're talking about a guy with a lengthy history of emotional problems. And claiming that he's decided to speak up after all this time because some self-help group convinced him it was a good idea... That's downright laughable. Nobody would take him seriously and Gutteridge will realize it.''

''Then maybe we can figure out a way to bluff him.''

"Actually, we played around with that idea with Bellavia," April put in, wanting to see what Steve thought of it.

"What sort of bluff?" he demanded.

"Well...maybe say that Tom Walker gave Paul more than he actually did? Gave him some solid proof along with names?"

"Will you two listen to yourselves?" Steve said. "This is real life, not a TV show. Now, can we go back to what we decided last night? That you'll let me handle things from here?"

When Paul glanced at April, she shook her head. Things had changed since last night.

"Look," he said to Steve. "Bellavia's going to see Gutteridge whether we go along with him or not. And if he goes on his own, who knows what he'd say? If he blew it, if he said something that made Gutteridge decide to take off, by the time you cut through your red tape, he'd be catching the rays on a beach in South America."

"He'd only run if he was actually involved in the bombing."

"Maybe...maybe not. That's what everybody believed about April's father. But...Steve, April and I just can't let Bellavia confront Gutteridge alone. Not when Gutteridge might be the key to proving her father's innocence."

"I'VE GOT TO SAY THIS one more time," Steve told them after they'd walked down the Great Hill and out onto Central Park West. "I think you're making a big mistake."

"I know you do," Paul said.

April said nothing, but Steve's outspoken disapproval of their plan was awfully disconcerting.

He pushed his glasses further up onto his nose, then gestured across the street. "I'm parked down that way. So...I guess if you're determined to go, good luck. And get in touch afterward, huh? No matter how late it is, give me a call."

Paul nodded.

For a moment Steve looked as if he was about to say something more, but he finally just shrugged and headed off.

Paul reached for April's hand and they silently walked to where they'd left the Cherokee. As they were climbing into it, she said, "Steve's so certain we're doing the wrong thing it's got me shaking in my boots."

"You aren't wearing boots," he pointed out.

When she looked at him and he smiled, she tried to smile back. But she knew she wasn't managing very well. Not only was she terrified they might be making a major mistake, she was worried sick because she still hadn't heard from her parents.

Then, not ten seconds after Paul pulled out of their space, her cellular rang. Her fingers trembling, she answered the phone.

"Mouse, it's me," her father said.

Hearing his voice brought tears of relief to her eyes.

"It's your parents?" Paul whispered.

He gave a thumbs-up at her nod.

"Where are you?" her father asked. "Is it safe to talk?"

"Yes, your timing's perfect. We're in Paul's car."

The words were barely out when she thought about how many people had been spying on them. "Don't tell me where you are, though," she added quickly. "Just in case. But are you and Mom okay?"

"Fine. But I'd be full of holes if I'd been in that damn shack last night. What went wrong? Did Paul's contact double-cross him?"

"No."

"You're sure?"

"Yes, Resdoe just knew a lot more than we realized."

"So where do things stand now? What's happening?"

She hesitated, knowing he'd like their plan even less than Steve did.

"Mouse? Fill me in. Keeping me up to date was part of the deal, remember?"

Covering the speaker with her hand, she whispered to Paul, "He wants me to fill him in. How much should I tell him?"

"Tell him everything. He might think of something we haven't."

She took a deep breath, then said, "We had a surprise visit from John Bellavia."

"You're joking."

"Dad, trust me, I'm not in a joking mood."

Her father muttered something she didn't catch, then said, "He didn't...scare you or anything, did he?"

"No, he was a perfect gentleman."

"And what did he want?"

She recounted the details as quickly as she could. Sure enough, when she got to the part about Bellavia chartering a plane so they could go and see Gutteridge, her father practically exploded.

"That isn't something you should even consider doing!"

"Well, we're a little beyond considering it. See, here's our thinking." She rushed on, barely pausing to take a breath so that he wouldn't interrupt.

"It isn't worth it, Mouse," he said when she'd finished. "It just isn't worth the risk."

"It'll be our last shot, Dad. We're going to do this, and then… Well, whatever comes of it, we'll back off and leave the rest up to Steve."

"If you're in any shape to back off. Mouse, I don't want you going there."

"I know," she murmured. "But I have to."

CHAPTER SEVENTEEN

JOHN BELLAVIA HAD SAID he'd rather charter a plane than use a commercial airline because it would be far more time efficient. He'd even joked about their making it to Port Credit and home again before April's new cat got lonely.

But when Paul discovered they were taking off from a small flying club on Long Island, he suspected the man's real agenda was avoiding an airport security check. He'd bet the farm Bellavia was carrying—and so was he.

He had no idea whether Gutteridge might react violently when they confronted him. Or whether Bellavia had something different in mind than what he'd told them. In either event, his Walther could turn out to be worth its weight in gold. And even though Canada's gun laws made it illegal to bring a handgun into the country, it was worth taking the chance that customs wouldn't check three respectable-looking people very closely.

As it turned out, customs didn't figure into things.

The pilot set down somewhere outside the Toronto area—in a field that had nothing but a dirt runway and a small hangar. Obviously, he'd filed a false flight plan so there'd be no record of their entering or leaving Canada. Assuming they did leave.

Trying to ignore that thought, Paul reached for April's hand as the Cessna taxied toward the hangar. But one worrisome possibility after another was flashing through his mind.

There was a lot about this trip he found unsettling, and the plane had barely taken off before he'd begun wishing April wasn't along. He knew, though, that even if he'd tried to convince her to stay behind, there was no way she would have.

"Okay, let's get this show on the road," Bellavia said, unsnapping his seat belt as the plane came to a stop.

"I'm not sure how long we'll be," he added to the pilot.

"That's okay. I'll be here whenever you get back."

The three of them climbed down from the plane into the diminished sunlight of the evening, then headed over to a nondescript Chevy parked beside the hangar.

Bellavia opened the driver's door, reached up under the visor and located a key. "Why don't you drive," he said, handing it to Paul and walking around to the passenger's side.

He politely ushered April into the front, closed her door and got into the back. "I have directions," he said, producing them as Paul started the engine. "Turn left when you get to the road."

Once they reached the main highway, they reviewed the bluff they were going to try on Gutteridge. After that, none of them said much. By the time they pulled into the lot of the Port's View Motel, the tension in the car was palpable.

As Paul cut the engine, April gazed out at the motel's office, thinking this was the last place on earth she'd ever have imagined coming back to. Then Bellavia opened his door and Paul reached over and gave her hand a warm squeeze.

It started her praying that nothing awful would happen. She loved him so much that just the thought of losing him chilled her heart.

"Time to rock and roll," he murmured.

Through the office's big front window, she could see Gutteridge behind the desk. Before they reached the door, he glanced out and spotted them.

He looked taken aback, but not as surprised as she'd expected he would.

"Well, well," he said when they walked in. "Mr. Gardiner and Ms. Birmingham. And you've brought a friend along."

"You don't recognize me," Bellavia said.

"Should I?"

He shrugged. "I'm John Bellavia."

Gutteridge simply stared at him.

"Is there someplace we can talk?" he asked. "Privately?"

"Joey?" Gutteridge called into the back.

The young man April recalled from her first visit appeared.

"I'll be out for a while," Gutteridge told him. Without another word, he led the way to his apartment and gestured them toward the couch.

Bellavia sat down on one end of it, April on the other.

"Been sitting too long," Paul said, casually leaning against the door.

Gutteridge remained standing, as well. He nervously drummed his fingers on the top of the television for a few seconds, then said, "So? What's this about?"

"I assume you heard that Tom Walker's dead?" Bellavia said.

"Yeah, I heard."

"Well, Paul received something after he died."

April glanced anxiously across the room. Paul looked totally relaxed, but she knew he couldn't be.

"It's a statement Tom left with his lawyer," Bellavia continued. "With instructions it be given to Paul after Tom's death. It details the true circumstances surrounding the Unique bombing."

"Really," Gutteridge said.

A disquieting feeling that something was wrong slithered up April's spine.

Last time around, Gutteridge hadn't struck her as much of an actor. So if Bellavia's version of things was true, he should seem a lot more concerned than he did.

"In his statement," Paul said, "Walker names names. He admits that he planted the bomb and says Wayne Resdoe planned the whole thing."

"I've heard enough."

April looked toward the sound of the voice and her blood ran cold. Wayne Resdoe was standing in the bedroom doorway, pointing a gun in the direction of the couch.

Then Gutteridge reached behind the television, produced another gun and aimed it at Paul. The chill in April's heart turned to ice.

"You dirty double-crossing scum," Bellavia snarled.

April glanced at him, her heart racing. He was glaring at Gutteridge.

"You're the one who was trying the double-cross," Gutteridge snapped. "We've all stuck to our deal through the years. Until today. Until you phoned me with your little scheme.

"But did you really figure I'd trust a lunatic like you? That I'd believe you were really going to hand me two million bucks so I could take off? That I wouldn't realize if you'd decided to get Resdoe, you'd try to get me, too?"

"You called him after I phoned you!" Bellavia practically screamed.

"Damn right I did! My only part in that bombing was lying about Birmingham. And if you thought I'd help you kill a fed to keep from facing the music for that, you're even crazier than you used to be."

When Paul cleared his throat, April looked at him, terrified they were both going to die.

"I don't know exactly what's going on here," Paul said more evenly than she'd have believed possible. "But whatever Bellavia had in mind, we knew nothing about it. We had no idea he'd phoned you," he added, focusing on Gutteridge. "And this is the first we've heard about any plan to kill anyone."

"That's because he was planning to kill you, too," Resdoe snapped.

"That's not true!" Bellavia shouted. "I'd never harm Mary's daughter! I was only trying to make amends!"

"By killing me?" Resdoe shot back.

"Why not? You killed those people in the bombing."

"I did? You planted the bomb, John boy. I only told you when and where."

Tears began to sting April's eyes. They'd *all* been part of the bombing. And now that Resdoe had admitted he'd been behind it, there was no way he'd let either her or Paul walk away alive.

"Okay, on your feet," Resdoe said, gesturing toward a glass door that led to a tiny patio. "We're going out the back. There's a van parked just along to the right. April's going to drive and I'll be in the front with her. Ken will be in the back seat and you two in the middle," he added, glancing from Bellavia to Paul. Then he motioned to Gutteridge. "You go first. Make sure the coast's clear."

Gutteridge stepped outside, glanced around, then nodded that everything was okay.

"You two follow him," Resdoe ordered Paul and Bellavia. "April and I will be right behind you." He grabbed her arm and stuck his gun into her ribs.

She swallowed hard, trying to hold back her tears, and walked out into the twilight with him.

Gutteridge opened the van's sliding door and was just about to get in when a man shouted, "Resdoe!"

He turned toward the sound; April wrenched herself free. She lost her balance and stumbled, but before he could grab her again, Paul was diving toward them.

He tackled Resdoe. A gunshot exploded and a scream split the air.

Terrified that Paul was hurt, April focused on

them. Resdoe was clutching his arm, and Paul was pointing a gun at him.

"You two freeze!"

That voice again. That voice she knew so well.

Her gaze found him—standing in the shadows beside the motel with a gun trained on Bellavia and Gutteridge.

"Drop your guns or I'll drop you," he said menacingly.

Gutteridge tossed his down. Bellavia hesitated, then followed suit.

The only ones left holding guns were the good guys—Paul and her father.

IT WAS LATE BY THE TIME the Cessna delivered Paul and April back to the Long Island flying club and they'd walked to the Cherokee.

But Steve had said to call no matter what the time, Paul reminded himself. Besides which, they were dying to find out exactly what he'd done.

All they knew was that when the police had arrived at the Port's View, the officer in charge had suggested April and Paul fade into the night and get back to their plane before anyone "officially" noticed them.

Steve must have had something to do with that, because he was the only one they'd told about the plane—aside from April's father.

As for him, he'd disappeared before the police had even arrived. But brief as his surprise appearance had been, it had been most welcome. If he hadn't shown up...

Paul told himself not to even think about that. Still,

he was awfully thankful they'd decided to tell Colin their plans in detail. And very glad he'd been too worried about what might happen to stay away.

Climbing into the Jeep, Paul took out his cellular and punched in Steve's number.

The agent answered on the second ring, but before there was time to ask a single question, he suggested they meet in the coffee shop at Amsterdam and Seventy-third.

He was waiting when they got there, and greeted them with a self-satisfied smile.

A waitress appeared with coffee the minute they slid into the booth across from him. As she walked away, he said, "So? You figure you got to the bottom of who did what?"

"I think so," Paul said. "Resdoe admitted that he was behind the bombing."

Steve nodded. "I figured that must be it when I heard he was one of the ones they arrested."

"You heard?" April said.

"Yeah, I know someone fairly high up in the Ontario Provincial Police, and I phoned him after you told me you were going with Bellavia. Then he called me back after the excitement was over."

"So you already know everything," Paul said.

"No, I don't know much at all. Our friends refused to talk to the police without lawyers present. But once I heard that Resdoe was there, I figured a few things out.

"I'm still finding it tough to believe, though—that seven innocent people ended up dead just because he wanted to get himself noticed by the big boys."

When April covered Paul's hand with hers, he

looked at her and slowly exhaled. The fact they'd actually learned who was responsible for his father's death hadn't entirely sunk in yet.

"What happens to our friends now?" he asked, looking over at Steve once more.

"We'll get them back into the bureau's jurisdiction as soon as we can. When it comes to Resdoe and Bellavia, we shouldn't have much trouble. They both entered Canada illegally when they didn't clear customs. Getting our hands on Gutteridge will be trickier, but we'll work it out. That's enough of that, though. Let's hear the rest of your story. What happened before the cops arrived?"

After they'd told him, Steve shook his head. "So even though Bellavia's guilty as sin, he figured he could lay the entire blame on Resdoe."

Paul nodded. "And he might have managed it if he'd been able to convince Gutteridge to go along with his version of things."

"But instead, Gutteridge called Resdoe and told him what Bellavia was up to. I wonder what tipped that scale? Two million bucks is a lot of money."

"Gutteridge didn't believe Bellavia would have given it to him, though. I think, bottom line, he figured Bellavia intended to kill all of us. So maybe he wanted Resdoe there for protection as much as anything else."

"We're lucky Bellavia *didn't* kill us," April said quietly. "We shouldn't have trusted him any further than Gutteridge did."

"Hey, things turned out fine," Paul said. "But next time, we'll listen to Steve."

"Next time?" She gave him a wan smile. "I don't want any next time. Not ever."

"No, you're right. I don't, either." He held her gaze for a moment, trying not to think how totally devastated he'd have been if anything had happened to her.

Turning back to Steve, he said, "And what are the details from your side? You called whoever you know in the provincial police and said...?"

"Don't ask. Just be glad you're not in some Ontario jail facing an attempted murder charge for shooting Resdoe." Steve drained his coffee, then slid over to the edge of the booth.

"You're really not going to tell us anything?"

He shook his head. "I've already bent too many rules on this case. Oh, but if you're talking to your parents, April, you can mention it shouldn't take long to get the charges against them dropped."

"All the charges?" she asked anxiously.

"I think that's a fairly safe bet. I'll phone you as soon as everything's arranged, and we can all get together. And this time," he added, pushing himself out of the booth, "Resdoe won't be crashing the party."

When Steve started to walk away, April said, "Steve?"

He stopped and looked back.

"Thanks," she murmured.

WHEN THE PHONE STARTED ringing, April snuggled even more closely to Paul and tried to ignore it. It was Saturday—the first Saturday they'd had together without any worries that someone was out to get them—and they'd promised themselves a lazy, do-nothing day.

After listening to a couple more rings, she gave up and forced her feet to the floor.

Marmalade, who, it had turned out, did like to sleep at the foot of the bed, gave her a throaty whine of annoyance at being disturbed, then jumped down and stalked off.

Tugging on her robe, April headed into her office and picked up.

"April, it's Steve Johnston."

"Well, hi," she said, her heart skipping a beat.

Despite what he'd said the other night, she hadn't let herself fully believe that every single charge against her parents would be dropped. If he was calling to tell her they had been, she'd be breaking out the champagne for breakfast.

"I tried to get hold of Paul," he said, "but all I got was his machine."

She felt her face growing warm and told herself that was a ridiculous reaction. She was a grown woman and very much in love. There was no reason to blush about the fact that she and Paul hadn't been spending a minute more apart than they absolutely had to.

"He's here," she said. "Would you like me to get him?"

When Steve hesitated, she couldn't help imagining him smiling to himself.

"No, I can talk to you as easily as him," he said at last. "I just decided that after all you'd been through, I'd bend another rule and tell you how the case is going. The details will make the news soon, but as long as you keep quiet until then..."

"Of course."

"Well, it could hardly be looking better. One of the things Bellavia told you that wasn't a lie is that he had Resdoe's apartment bugged way back before the bombing. When we searched his house, we discovered thousands of old audiotapes—one of which has a conversation between Resdoe, Gutteridge and Walker, talking about laying the blame on your father."

She couldn't breathe for a moment, and her last lingering fears about the final outcome of all this began fading away.

"Did you learn why they lied?" she asked. "Was it only for the money?"

"Uh-huh. As far as we can tell."

That made her feel like crying. Her parents had spent all those years as fugitives from the law because a couple of men had wanted some easy money.

"And what about John Bellavia?" she asked. "He already had a ton of money, so why did he get involved? It had to do with my mother, didn't it?"

"No, surprisingly enough it didn't. Not that Bellavia's admitting, anyway. One of the bureau's psychologists has spent a lot of time talking to him. And according to her, your father was suspecting him for the wrong reason. It turns out he had an older brother who'd been killed in Vietnam. They'd been very close, and losing him apparently exacerbated Bellavia's mental problems.

"At any rate, Resdoe convinced him that planting the bomb would be some sort of restitution for the brother's death. As for everything he's been doing recently," Steve continued, "he's too skillful at mixing truths with lies for us to be certain of his motivation. But the psychologist's convinced he really had taken that steps program seriously. And that he was convinced his planting the bomb made him responsible for your parents having to go underground."

"Even though it was Resdoe's idea to blame my father?"

"Yeah, the way he saw things, if he hadn't agreed to plant the bomb... Well, in any case, when he saw Paul's want ad, he took it as a sign that the time was right for making amends. But he didn't want to admit that he was really the Napalm Bomber, so he came up with his scheme to pin the entire blame on Resdoe."

"Wow," April murmured. "If this was fiction, people would say it was just too unbelievable."

"Well, you know what they say about truth being stranger than fiction."

"But why didn't Resdoe ever go beyond scare tactics with Paul and me? If he was so worried we'd learn the truth, why didn't he..." She couldn't make herself add the words "kill us."

"I guess he thought it would be too risky," Steve said. "Other people knew you were looking into the bombing, so if you'd turned up dead, it would have drawn attention to the case. And odds were your deaths would have been linked to what you were doing—and ultimately to him."

"Yes...I guess that makes sense."

"Anything else?"

"Only something about my parents. Is it safe to tell them that everything will be fine?"

"Go ahead. I'm just waiting for a couple of signatures and it'll be official."

Closing her eyes, she offered up a tiny prayer of gratitude. "I can't thank you enough, Steve."

"Hey, you and Paul did so much of the work, I should be thanking you. Anyway, I'll get back to you once those signatures are dry. Say hi to Paul for me."

"I will. Bye." She hung up, then slowly wandered back to the bedroom.

Paul was sprawled across both halves of the bed, dead to the world, the sheet drawn up only to his waist.

She watched him for a minute, her gaze drifting over the rugged lines of his face, softer in sleep than when he was awake, then across his broad shoulders and down the lean muscles of his chest.

She loved him so much that just looking at him started a tug of longing within her. She wanted to crawl back into bed and cuddle up beside him again. Wanted to wake him up with kisses and make hot, passionate love.

But first, she took her cellular into the living room, called the motel where her parents were staying and told them the good news. There was only one phone in their room, but they both listened in on it.

When she'd finished relating everything Steve had said, she could hear the emotion in their voices. It brought happy tears to her eyes.

"I never really thought this day would come," her mother murmured.

"I did," her father said. "When Mouse sets her

mind to something, the result's a foregone conclusion.''

''I think you have to give Paul and Steve at least a little of the credit,'' April said, laughing.

''Speaking of Paul, will we be meeting him?'' her mother asked.

There were, April knew, a hundred different questions in those few words.

''I've already met him,'' her father said.

''Oh, Colin, I don't consider what happened in the parking lot of Gutteridge's motel meeting him.''

''Yes, you'll be meeting him,'' April told them. ''I know he'll want to be there when you get together with Steve.''

''Ah,'' her mother said. ''And after that?''

''After that... I guess we'll have to wait and see.''

Her mother didn't press further, and when they'd said their goodbyes, April went back to the bedroom once more—via the kitchen, this time.

Paul was awake now. He glanced at the tray she was carrying, then smiled such a sexy smile it practically melted her on the spot.

''That's not a mirage, is it?'' he said, eyeing the champagne and orange juice.

''Uh-uh.'' She put down the tray and handed him the bottle to uncork.

He didn't take his gaze off her while he removed the foil.

''You want to guess what we're celebrating?'' she said as he untwisted the wire.

''That it's Saturday? That we're alone together? That we're in love?''

His last guess made her smile. "All of those, but something else, too."

When she slipped off her robe and slid naked into bed beside him, he said, "This is getting better by the second."

He gave her shoulder a lingering kiss, then popped the cork.

"I love a man who can open champagne without spilling any," she teased, reaching for the partially filled flutes of juice, then watching him top them up.

"To us," he said, touching his glass to hers.

"To us," she murmured, almost afraid to say the word. She'd never been part of an "us" before. Not this kind of us. And it was so wonderful it was scary.

"Okay." He looked at her over the rim of his glass. "What's the something else we're celebrating?"

"Steve called while you were still asleep."

She proceeded to tell him about that conversation, then moved on to the one with her parents.

"That's just great," he said when she'd finished. "They must be floating on air. And I'm glad we've got some more pieces of the puzzle filled in."

"Me, too." She put down her glass, wanting to ask about a couple of things before being in bed with him drove them completely out of her mind.

When April set her glass on the bedside table, Paul put his down, too. Before he got to kissing her, though, she said, "I guess there are some questions we'll never know the answers to, aren't there. Like why Walker didn't just come right out and tell you that Resdoe and Bellavia were the guilty ones."

"He was probably afraid of what they might do.

Even a dying man would worry about something horrible happening to him, so getting me interested enough to start digging must have been as much as he felt was safe."

"I guess that could be it."

"That's probably what I'll hypothesize in my book."

"Your bestseller," she teased, snuggling a little more closely against him and curling a few chest hairs around her finger.

It almost did him in, making him even hotter and harder than he already was.

"And then there was that woman who called and told me you were a fed."

"Resdoe must have been behind that."

She nodded slowly. It focused his attention on that slender, sexy neck of hers. He was just leaning closer to nuzzle it when she said, "And what about—"

"Hey," he interrupted, stilling her hand with his. She'd started to trail her fingers down his chest and there was only so much a man could take. "Do I get to ask a question in here someplace?"

She gave him a to-die-for smile. "Ask away."

He took a deep breath, then said, "Getting back to the being-in-love part of this conversation, I've been thinking about that a lot lately, and..."

Pausing, he gathered his courage. "And...I think we should get married."

"Oh, Paul," she whispered.

He gazed into the dark depth of her eyes, willing her to say she thought that was a wonderful idea.

When she didn't, his heart began pounding in his

ears. "So?" he finally said. "What do you think? Will you marry me?"

"Oh, Paul, I think that's the best question I've heard in my entire life."

Deciding that must mean yes, he eased her down in the bed with a slow, deep kiss. Then his heart went wild as she proceeded to make him absolutely *certain* she'd meant yes.

HARLEQUIN SUPERROMANCE®

9 MONTHS LATER

HIS BROTHER'S BABY (#796)
by Connie Bennett

The two brothers were as unalike as brothers could be.
Now the one Meg Linley loved with all her heart is dead,
and the other wants custody of her unborn child. And what
Nick Ballenger wants, Nick Ballenger gets...*usually*.

Available in July 1998
wherever Harlequin books are sold.

HARLEQUIN®
*M*akes any time special ™

Heat up your summer this July with

Summer Lovers

This July, bestselling authors Barbara Delinsky,
Elizabeth Lowell and Anne Stuart present three
couples with pasts that threaten their future happiness.
Can they play with fire without being burned?

FIRST, BEST AND ONLY
by Barbara Delinsky

GRANITE MAN
by Elizabeth Lowell

CHAIN OF LOVE
by Anne Stuart

Available wherever Harlequin and Silhouette books
are sold.

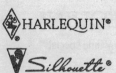

HARLEQUIN®

Silhouette®

Presents
Extravaganza

25 YEARS!

It's our birthday
and we're celebrating....

Twenty-five years of romance fiction
featuring men of the world and captivating women—
Seduction and passion guaranteed!

Not only are we promising you three months of terrific
books, authors and romance, but as an added **bonus**
with the retail purchase of two Presents® titles,
you can receive a special one-of-a-kind keepsake.
It's our gift to you!

Look in the back pages of any Harlequin Presents® title,
from May to July 1998, for more details.

Available wherever Harlequin books are sold.

HARLEQUIN®

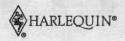

HARLEQUIN®

Not The Same Old Story!

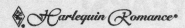 HARLEQUIN PRESENTS®

Exciting, glamorous romance stories that take readers around the world.

 *Harlequin Romance*®

Sparkling, fresh and tender love stories that bring you pure romance.

HARLEQUIN® *Temptation.*
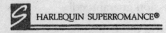

Bold and adventurous—Temptation is strong women, bad boys, great sex!

 HARLEQUIN SUPERROMANCE®

Provocative and realistic stories that celebrate life and love.

HARLEQUIN® AMERICAN ROMANCE®

Contemporary fairy tales—where anything is possible and where dreams come true.

HARLEQUIN® INTRIGUE®

Heart-stopping, suspenseful adventures that combine the best of romance and mystery.

Love & Laughter™
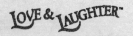

Humorous and romantic stories that capture the lighter side of love.

MEN at WORK

All work and no play?
Not these men!

July 1998
MACKENZIE'S LADY by Dallas Schulze

Undercover agent Mackenzie Donahue's
lazy smile and deep blue eyes were his best
weapons. But after rescuing—and kissing!—
damsel in distress Holly Reynolds, how could
he betray her by spying on her brother?

August 1998
MISS LIZ'S PASSION by Sherryl Woods

Todd Lewis could put up a building with ease,
but quailed at the sight of a classroom! Still,
Liz Gentry, his son's teacher, was no battle-ax,
and soon Todd started planning some
extracurricular activities of his own....

September 1998
A CLASSIC ENCOUNTER
by Emilie Richards

Doctor Chris Matthews was intelligent, sexy
and *very* good with his hands—which made
him all the more dangerous to single mom
Lizette St. Hilaire. So how long could she
resist Chris's special brand of TLC?

Available at your favorite retail outlet!

MEN AT WORK™

Look us up on-line at: http://www.romance.net   PMAW2

S HARLEQUIN SUPERROMANCE®

COMING NEXT MONTH